A Secret

No More

To Mary

From Christine's

Daughter

Linda

L. Buckley

GW00492724

A Secret No More

Cover design and typesetting by Let's Get Booked
www.letsgetbooked.com

Chapter 1

Christine was born in the UK in May of 1939, at a time when the world was about to embark on a bloody and deadly world war. Her memories of the war were vague but the bomb shelters were unforgettable. Her most vivid memory of wartime was of a shopping trip with her parents, Albert and Florence. Her mother stood at the shop counter paying for her groceries and Christine and her dad were both waiting outside for her. Suddenly the harrowing sound of sirens blared through the streets. The noise and panic from the people around them scared Christine.

"It's OK love," her dad said whilst swiping her into his arms as his eyes scanned the sky above them. "I have you, you are safe." He then called his wife to follow him.

Her mother held the shopping bags and they made their way to the nearest air raid shelter situated in the grounds of the local college. As they entered the shelter, Christine clung to her dad afraid to let go. She was just five years old so she didn't understand what was happening. Her dad placed her down on the floor where they all huddled together.

"What is happening daddy? I want to go home," she cried.

"I know you do love. So do I but we have to stay here for a little while and then we can go home. I promise."Albert smiled at Christine but her mother never spoke a word. She just sat quietly with her head resting on Albert's shoulder. Suddenly the shelter became silent as people huddled in fear whilst the sky filled with the chilling sound of war planes flying overhead. Eventually the skies fell silent and after about half an hour the familiar sound of sirens were heard once more which signalled to everyone that it was safe to leave the shelters and return to their homes.

"Oh, thank goodness. Grab the child Albert and let's go home." Florence grabbed the shopping bags and made her way to the doors of the shelter.

Albert looked at Christine with a big smile on his face. "C'mon you, let's get you home. I told you we would be fine, didn't I?"

They made their way home safely and as they walked into their house, Christine ran into the kitchen to see if Patch was OK. Patch was her pet dog. She could see him cowering under the kitchen table. He came running out to greet her and wagged his tail furiously which he did every time she walked into the room. "Let's play Patch," Christine said. They both ran out to the back garden together and Christine threw stones for Patch to run after. She had no siblings so Patch was the only company she had.

Patch was a wartime dog. Her dad, Albert, was on the high street one day and saw his friend, Jack, standing in a queue outside the vet's office. He was holding a young dog in his arms and told Albert he had to bring him to the vet to be destroyed. Because of food rationing, he and his wife just could not afford to feed their pet any longer. Albert took one look at Patch in Jack's arms and offered to take the dog and give him a good life. He arrived home and made his way into the kitchen where Christine was sitting playing with her wooden blocks. His wife, Florence, was standing washing clothes in the kitchen sink.

"Look what I found on my way home," announced Albert. He held Patch in his outstretched arms for Christine to see.

"Doggy!" yelled Christine. She had a huge smile on her face whilst running to the dog to give it a big cuddle.

Albert told Christine the dog's name was Patch because he had a big white patch of fur around his eye.

Florence glanced over her shoulder. "And how do you expect us to feed the animal? You can give it food from your plate because I am not sharing my food rations with a dog." She scowled at the dog before turning back to finish what she had been doing.

Patch became Christine's best friend. Not once did he bite her no matter how much she pulled out of him. They formed an inseparable profound bond and were always there to comfort eachother in their times of most need.

On the 8th May 1945 Sir Winston Churchill, the UK Prime minister made a special radio broadcast to the nation declaring Victory in Europe against the Germans. There were many street parties across the whole of the UK to celebrate VE day.

* **

Christine's parents were like chalk and cheese. Albert,

her dad, was a kind and loving man who always made time for Christine. However, Florence was not very maternal at all. Any time Christine tried to spend time with her she would say she was 'Far too busy'. Her mother's sister, Ivy, was the same. She would call to visit Florence every week on a Saturday and she never had a good word to say to Christine. On one occasion, Christine heard her mother and aunt discussing the dwindling population of the UK.

"Florence, I was reading an article in the paper the other day. It was all about how women were told just before the war to have many children. They knew the war was coming and wanted to ensure the country would be well populated."

"Oh my goodness," exclaimed Florence. "One child is more than enough for me. I have done my duty for Queen and country."

When Christine heard this, she thought that must have been the reason her mother had her. It wasn't because she wanted children but because the Queen had ordered her to and Christine firmly believed that even her mother would not be brave enough to say 'no' to the Queen.

Her Aunt Ivy would hold big parties in her house every Christmas. She gave presents to every person who came but when Christine went to her looking for her gift the reply was always the same.

"Oh, Christine, I am sorry. Your present seems to have been lost. Here, have this instead." Ivy would then hand her an old used decoration from the Christmas tree. Infact, Aunt Ivy never bought her a gift on any occasion.

Apart from her Aunt Ivy's parties Christine loved Christmas because everyone seemed to be happy and in good spirits. Even her mother. She loved Christmas carols and would sing her heart out at the church Christmas carol services every year. She never knew why but she always felt Christmas was the most magical time of year.

Chapter 2

Christine never forgot the Christmas of 1947. Her dad was bringing her to visit his brother Fred, and Fred's wife, Daisy. It was a frosty morning and her dad was hesitant about leaving the house. However, he could not disappoint Christine so they wrapped up warmly and set off together. When they arrived, Daisy had a roaring fire lit and rushed them both into the house to get warm. Whilst her dad was busy talking to her aunt and uncle, Christine looked under the Christmas tree and could see what she thought were her presents waiting for her to unwrap.

Daisy noticed Christine staring at the gifts under the tree and nudged Fred with her elbow."What do you think Fred? Should we wait till after we have eaten or will we give them to her now?"Daisy smiled at Christine whilst waiting for Fred's reply.

Fred placed his hand on Daisy's shoulder and smiled."OK Daisy, I think we can give them to her now," he replied with a wink.

"Oh OK then."With that, Daisy stretched out her hand towards Christine. "Come with me my lovely these presents are all for you. We hope you like them. Would you like to open them now?" she asked.

"Oh yes please Aunty!" Christine clapped her hands together in excitement as she knelt down beside the tree and began opening the smallest gift. It was a packet of her Uncle Fred's favourite sweets, which she secretly loved as well. The second gift was a beautiful woolly hat and gloves that her aunt had handmade especially for her. Finally, she was opening the biggest gift of them all. It was wrapped in gold-coloured paper with a big red bow on top. As she gently tore the paper, her eyes opened wide with excitement. "Oh I love it, I love it. Is this really for me to keep?"

It was a doll. Her very first doll and it was beautiful. She wore a lovely baby pink dress and bonnet with matching pink booties and a cream and pink cardigan. The eyes were a deep sea-blue colour that closed when it was lying down and opened when picked up.

Just as she had finished opening her gifts her Uncle Fred stood up and went into the kitchen. He returned holding a large closed box which he placed on the floor in front of Christine. "We almost forgot this. Take a look. It's all yours!"

Christine immediately ran to the box and could not believe her eyes. "Oh, Uncle Fred did you make this just for me?"She was so happy. "Thank you, thank so much!" She flung her arms around them both unable to contain her excitement and cried happy tears. Her uncle had made a cradle for the doll to lie in. Daisy had knitted a small blanket to match the doll's clothes and had stuffed and sewn a pillowcase to make a mattress. It was the best surprise ever. She ran over to her aunt and uncle and gave them both another hug and kiss. Her dad was so happy to see her excitement and thanked Fred and Daisy for their kindness.

She sat playing with her doll and could not wait to bring it home. Daisy had prepared a lovely lunch and they all sat around the kitchen table eating laughing and talking about everything and anything. There was always a lovely calm cheerful atmosphere in their house and Christine loved spending time there. After lunch, Albert and Christine left to go home. They gathered up all of Christine's presents and loaded them into the car.

"Thank you so much for my presents," Christine said.

Her aunt Daisy smiled at her and gave her a hug. "You are very welcome. I could even teach you to knit, and then you can make more clothes for your doll.

Would you like that?"

"Oh yes, yes please Aunty I would love that."

***

When they arrived home, Christine showed her mother all of her presents but Florence did not seem too interested and told her to bring them up to her room. Her dad carried the doll's cradle up the stairs for her and then went back downstairs. Christine sat on her bed holding her new doll and inspecting the clothes that her aunt had made. After a few minutes she heard Patch scratching at her bedroom door.

"Come in Patch." She beckoned him to sit on her bed and made some space for him. "Look, look what I have. Aunt Daisy and Uncle Fred gave these to me. I am so lucky. She is going to teach me to knit as well so I can make my doll some new clothes. If you are a good boy, I might be able to knit you a jumper as well.

Would you like that?" she said. Patch barked as if to say, "Yes, please." He then leapt down from the bed and ran out of the room.

After jumping off the bed herself she looked at the cradle her Uncle Fred had made for her. She could just imagine her aunt sitting by the fire knitting the blanket and stuffing the pillowcase. She noticed a carving of an anchor on the end of the cradle. Running her fingers over it made her think of her Uncle Fred. He used to be a sailor and seeing the carving reminded her of all the stories he told her about his time at sea.

Of course, Florence did not really like Uncle Fred because he was not afraid to stand up to her and she was not used to that. She would often make excuses not to go to Fred's house, which Christine did not mind because she was so much more relaxed when her mother was not with her.

She lay in bed that night feeling content with her day and so much love for her aunt and Uncle Fred. They were so different compared to her mother's

14

family. They would never ignore her or make her feel like an inconvenience. They were a very special part of her life.

***

Her aunt Daisy kept true to her word, she did teach Christine to knit. It was a skill she never forgot.

Chapter 3

In 1953, life was changing for the better across Britain. Rationing was slowly ending. New fashion trends to encourage women to look their best were all the rage. This excited Christine. Her mother did not share her excitement and made it known that she disliked seeing unmarried girls with makeup on their faces. Of course, her mother's attitude made Christine want makeup even more. She did not care what her mother thought. She was going to save the little pocket money she got and buy her own makeup. What's more she was going to wear it every chance she got.

***

One afternoon on her way home from school, Christine saw one of her neighbours, Alice Brown. Alice was stepping out of a car parked outside her house. As she closed the car door, she stopped and looked at Christine with tears streaming from her eyes. Christine tried not to stare but she couldn't help but notice that Alice was crying. Mrs Brown had appeared and was rushing Alice into the house. It had been some time since Christine had seen Alice and she had often wondered where her friend and neighbour had gone. As she walked along her garden path, she wondered what could have been the matter. She hoped nobody was sick. Alice's father was a very hard-working man and suffered from terrible back pain so she hoped he was OK. Looking at her house as she walked she could see her mother and aunt peeking through the window from behind the net curtains. They could not have been

17

more obvious.

She walked through the front door and as she wiped her feet on the doormat, she heard her mother and aunt shuffling back to the kitchen as fast as they could. They were acting like two naughty schoolchildren trying not to be caught eavesdropping.

"What's going on with the Browns?" Christine shouted from the hallway and paused to hear the reply.

"Nothing is going on. Mind your own business," replied her mother as if she herself was not in the slightest bit interested.

Huh, she has a nerve to say that to me. She and Aunt Ivy were the very ones poking their noses out the window to see what was going on in the Browns. Christine decided to go straight to her bedroom but first she stood listening with her ear to the kitchen door and could just about hear her aunt and mother discussing Alice.

"So Florence, what were you saying about the girl nextdoor before we were interrupted?"Asked Ivy.

"I was telling you the Brown girl had to go away. It was all very hush-hush. But she's home now," Florence replied. Aunt Ivy was her usual judgmental self. "Oh really? That can only mean one thing. The shameful girl. Her poor parents must be so disappointed in her."

Christine was annoyed. She couldn't understand why her mother and aunt seemed to get so much pleasure out of other people's troubles. After all, who made either of them the Judge and Jury? Over the next few weeks, Christine gathered from all the talk on the street that Alice had been working as a house cleaner to a local wealthy family when she fell pregnant. Her parents told her she could not keep the baby. Rumor had it the baby's father was Alice's employer. Christine had heard he paid the Browns a pretty penny to make the problem go away. Mr and Mrs Brown told Alice she had to leave her baby behind in the orphanage where she gave birth.

Soon after Alice came home from the orphanage, the Browns bought a brand-new television. They didn't rent it they owned it outright which must have cost them a lot of money. Although the picture was in black and white, it was such a novelty that it seemed the whole street gathered in the Brown's house to see the broadcast of the newly crowned Queen of England leaving Westminster Abbey. Christine sat in awe of the new queen's beauty as the commentator described the colours of her gown cape and crown in enormous detail.

Everyone was celebrating at the Browns' house. Christine could not help but notice that Alice seemed sad.

"Hi Alice, are you OK? You look a little distracted. Is there anything I can get you?"

Alice looked at Christine and wiped her eye as if to stop a tear from falling. "I am sorry but I am fine, honestly, I just wish—"

"Alice, Alice," Mrs. Brown called her daughter and beckoned her to come over to her.

Alice looked at Christine and smiled."I have to go,

sorry. Maybe we can catch up another time?"

"Yes, I would like that," replied Christine. She stood there watching as Mrs Brown appeared to be having stern words with her daughter. As Alice turned away from her mother she made eye contact with Christine, she smiled and then left the room and wasn't seen again for the rest of the day.

***

The following Monday Christine was about to walk through the school gates when she noticed a woman staring at her from the other side of the road. Before Christine could walk across the road to talk to the woman the sound of crying from the school grounds stole her attention. She looked around and saw a girl who was obviously upset huddled against the wall in the school grounds. As she approached the girl, she recognised her as Mary, one of her school bullies. Christine wondered what could possibly have made her cry. For a moment, she felt she would have been fully justified if she continued walking and ignored her.

21

However, that was not in her nature. Christine wanted to be a nurse and a nurse would walk right over and offer to help someone in so much distress. She glanced back across the road but the woman had gone.

Christine walked up to Mary slowly. "Whatever is the matter with you Mary?"

"Leave me alone you wouldn't understand. I suppose you think it's funny seeing me cry like this," Mary muttered as she turned away trying to hide her face.

Christine put her hand on the girl's shoulder. "No Mary, I take no pleasure in seeing anyone cry. Surely things cannot be that bad," she said as she turned to walk away.

"I have to stop going to school. My mother needs me to help her at home with the babies. She's here talking to the teacher now," Mary whispered through her tears. "I love school. I have always wanted to be a teacher but that can never happen now." Mary looked up at Christine her eyes red and swollen with tears. "My father says I must help mother and then they will find me a husband." She sobbed whilst wiping her eyes with the back of her hands. "I don't want to get married."

"I am so sorry to hear that. Maybe the teacher will change your mother's mind so you can stay at school after all," Christine said softly whilst reaching into her bag for a clean handkerchief to give to Mary. Even though Mary had not been nice to her in the past, she did not like to see anyone cry. Mary was inconsolable. "Let me tell you something. I want to be a nurse and nothing is going to stop me. My father always tells me I can do anything I want and that nothing is impossible." Christine was trying to offer comfort to Mary. "So even if you do have to leave school surely there is another way for you to become a teacher. There's always a way. You must believe that." Christine did not know what else to say so she turned to walk into the school building.

Upon entering the school, she passed Mary's mother in the doorway. Taking a glance back, she saw the woman take her daughter by the hand and walk out of the school gates. *I am so glad my mother didn't have more children or I would no doubt have had to look after them all. Why do adults have children if they cannot look after them?* So many girls in her school had to leave early to help their parents at home. Most children she knew only stayed in school long enough to learn how to read and write. Christine was truly grateful for her education. Even if school was a difficult place for her, she valued every second of her time there.

Mary did not return to school after that day. Word had it that two years later she was married to a widower who lived in the country, so at just seventeen years old, she became a wife and a stepmother to four children.

***

Christine made her way to her classroom and as soon as she entered the room, she was met with taunts from her classmates. "Good morning four ears," they jeered from the back of the classroom. The teacher was not present so the pupils took advantage of that time to make fun of her because she wore hearing aids. In those days, hearing aids were not discrete. Christine's hearing aid looked like a brick clipped to her jumper with a long piece of wire in each ear. Eventually the teacher arrived and class began but Christine was distracted as she thought of Mary. She hoped she was OK.

During break-time, Christine was in the schoolyard when the music teacher Mrs Reed was calling her. *Oh no, what have I done now?* Christine thought as she walked over to her.

"Christine I would like to have a chat with you. Follow me, please." They both sat on the schoolyard bench. "I am trying to put together a school choir and was wondering if you would like to join?" Mrs Reed asked.

Christine was not expecting this at all. "Me?" she asked. "Are you sure you mean me? I am not sure I can do that because I have a hearing problem. My ears do not work as well as other peoples."

"Christine, I have heard you sing and I am positive that I want you in the school choir. Moreover, it's your voice I want not your ears. You have a beautiful voice and it would be a real shame not to let everyone hear it. Just have a think and let me know as soon as possible."With that, Mrs Reed stood up and made her way towards the school building.

Christine was shocked. Nobody had ever picked her for anything before so she immediately ran after Mrs Reed. "Please, Teacher," she called out. Mrs Reed turned to look at her. "I don't need to think about it. If you think I am good enough then I would love to join the choir."

"Of course you are good enough. Don't ever let anyone tell you any different. I am glad to have you onboard and will talk to you next week about the details."Mrs Reed then told her to go back to class as the break was over.

Christine noticed two of her classmates were listening to what Mrs Reed had said to her. Huh, I bet they thought I was in trouble. *I doubt they expected to hear me being asked to join the choir. That will teach them to ear wig into other people's conversations.*

As she walked past the two girls, she held her head high with a big smile on her face. Nothing her bullies would say could take that smile away from her.

Chapter 4

It was a Saturday morning and the sun was shining brightly in the summer sky. Christine awoke to the sound of birdsong emanating from her garden. As her eyes opened, she saw Patch standing at her bedroom door wagging his tail. "C'mon Patch my furry friend. Jump up here beside me," she said whilst making a space beside her on the bed. "So what will I do today? It's the weekend so I can't waste a second." Suddenly she realised it was Saturday which meant her choices for the day were one of two. "Oh no Patch, it's Saturday. You know what that means don't you?"Patch was lying on the bed resting his head on her tummy with his eyes wide open and staring at her as she spoke. "Yep, it means I can either sit in the house listening to Aunt Ivy and her endless gossiping to mother or I can take myself out for the day and avoid her for a change!" Patch looked up at her tilting his head to one side. "Oh don't look at me like that Patch you know I simply can't be around them with their pointless chatter. I am always the one to make them their cups of tea and don't get me started on the constant nasty remarks that Aunt Ivy always directs at me." She hushed Patch out of the room so she could get ready for the day ahead. Once dressed, she ran down the stairs and into the kitchen where her mother was sweeping the floor.

Upon hearing Christine walk in to the kitchen, Florence momentarily stopped what she was doing."Christine, your Aunt Ivy is calling today so you need to get your breakfast and then I need you to do a few jobs for me around the house."

"Alright Mother but then I am going out. I don't want to be stuck inside any longer than I need to be. Not on a glorious day like this," Christine replied whilst getting herself a bowl out of the cupboard for her porridge.

By 12 O'clock her chores were completed, and she began to get ready for her afternoon ahead. She had packed a lunch, which she placed in a bag along with a book that she was reading and made her way to the front door. Her aunt was just pulling up outside in her car as Christine skipped down the garden path. Phew, that was great timing. "Hello Aunt Ivy, sorry I can't stop. Mother is in the house waiting for you. The front door is open." Christine waved at her aunt as she passed her by. As usual, her aunt did not speak to her but that was OK. She was used to her aunt's rudeness at this point.

Across the road from her house was a large green area with a long pathway that led to a wooden gate. The other side of the gate was a shortcut to the public park. The weather was glorious so she found a spot in the park to just sit and eat her lunch whilst reading her book. Once she was sitting comfortably, she leaned her head backwards, took a deep breath and relaxed in her thoughts whilst breathing in the many beautiful fragrances expelled by the flowers growing around her. After a few minutes she opened her book and began reading.

However, no sooner had she opened her book when she heard the sound of a voice calling out to her. Looking around she saw her neighbour Alice Brown running towards her.

"Christine, you dropped this."A ribbon draped from her fingers. "It fell out of your pocket whilst you were walking," said Alice who was slightly out of breath.

"Thank you, Alice. I forgot I had my ribbons in my pocket."Christine could see Alice had been running so she asked her if she would like to join her. Alice smiled and sat herself on the grass next to Christine. The girls sat in silence, both obviously lost in their own thoughts. Alice took a sandwich and bite into it."So how are you, Christine? I don't see you much. I hope you are well."

"I am good Alice and how are you, after... you know ... after."Christine stopped mid-sentence realising she should not be asking such things. After all Alice's business was not hers to discuss. Her face was red with embarrassment." I am so sorry Alice I hope you don't think badly of me but I heard about your news you know...about your baby and I was just wondering how you are feeling. Please tell me to mind my own business. I should never have mentioned anything. I am so sorry."

A startled look crossed Alice's face. However, after a few moments her expression softened. "No, it's OK. At least you're asking me to my face and not talking horribly about me to someone else behind my back unlike so many other people I could mention. You can ask me anything. You are the only person who has ever asked me how I am feeling. Usually, it's all about my parents and how they are coping with the 'mess and shame' of it all. It's as if they're the ones who had to have their baby taken from them as if they're the ones who have been to hell and back." At this point Alice took a deep breath and sighed. "But to answer your question, I suppose I am OK. It has been a very difficult year. I have seen and experienced things that have hurt me badly," Alice said before taking another bite of her sandwich.

Christine took a drink of her orange juice. "Alice, can I ask you another question, a personal one?"

After swallowing her bread Alice nodded her head with a smile. "Of course you can. I like your honesty so go ahead ask me anything."

Christine cleared her throat. "OK, well, is it true that your last employer is your baby's father?"

"I'm not allowed to talk about that. If I told you I'd be in big trouble. However, I can tell you that nobody else is the father," Alice replied with a cheeky wink.

Placing her hand on Alice's shoulder Christine tried

to offer her friend some comfort. "Oh you poor thing. That must have been awful for you. How did it all come about?"

At first there was silence. Alice then wiped crumbs from her mouth and sighed."Do you want to know everything? If I tell you then you cannot tell another soul do you promise?"She waited until Christine finally nodded and promised she would tell no one. Alice lay back on the grass staring at the sun filled clear blue sky above her."OK well last year I was given a job as a domestic house cleaner to the good Dr Green. His brother is my father's employer. It was he who mentioned the job to my father. He thought my mother might like it but she was already working so my parents decided I should take it instead."Alice turned onto her side to face Christine as she spoke. "At first, I loved it. It was a job in a big house with a huge garden. There were always people coming and going. The other staff members were so friendly and helpful. The doctor was very nice to me. He always made me feel so good about my work and he told me I was the best house cleaner they had ever had. I felt so proud and grownup."

Christine had heard of Dr Green. Her Aunt Ivy went to him a number of times. In fact, Dr Green was well known and respected in the area. "And what about his wife? What was she like?" Christine asked.

Alice smiled. "Oh Mrs Green was lovely but she was hardly ever at home. She was always out meeting the ladies or playing tennis. She had the most amazing wardrobe filled with clothes ordered specially from France. Very posh indeed."

The girls continued eating their last sandwich and Christine packed her lunchbox back into her bag. "So if everything was so perfect, how did it all end so badly? Where did it all go wrong for you?"

Alice wiped crumbs from her lap and sighed heavily. "Well Dr Green would ask me to clean his office every Wednesday. He was very particular about his office and said only I was allowed to enter it. This made me feel so good, you know, as if he really trusted me. How foolish was I?" Alice said throwing her hands in the air."He would regularly come in to the room whilst I was cleaning. He would stand there watching me in silence. On one occasion I asked him why he was staring at me and he told me he just loved the way I moved." Alice closed her eyes as if she were recalling his words in her head. "Sometimes he would ask me to take a break with him. He would ask me to sit beside him on the sofa and place his hand on my knee or he would brush his hand across my cheek telling me I had perfect skin."Alice stroked her cheek with the back of her hand. "Oh he knew exactly how to make me feel good about myself. He was quite the expert."Alice stopped talking. She could see Christine was listening to her every word."Sorry Christine, I don't want to bother you with all this. Tell me to stop if you don't want to hear any more of my ramblings."

"Oh no, please continue. If it helps you to talk then I am here for you."Christine said.

"OK, well, only if you're sure Christine. I remember on one occasion I was climbing up the stepladder so I could reach the curtain rail. It needed a good dusting. My foot twisted on the third rung. I slipped off and hurt my ankle." Alice rubbed her ankle. "He made me lie on the sofa and insisted that I let him check me over. He pulled my dress up to my waist and rubbed his hand all the way from the very top of my leg right the way down to my ankle. He told me I was very grownup for my years. He kept telling me I had the *legs of a lady* and I thought he was just being nice. He was a doctor and we're supposed to trust doctors, aren't we?" Alice exclaimed as if she was questioning herself. "It was when he asked me to clean his art studio in the loft that's when things really got awful for me." Alice bowed her head in silence.

Christine was shocked at what she was hearing and could see Alice was upset so she told her she did not have to say another word if she didn't want to.

Alice lifted her head to speak "No not at all, it

actually feels good to finally tell someone what happened to me. It's good to talk to someone who does not judge or look down on me," Alice said with a sigh.

Christine asked Alice about the art studio. "What was that like Alice, I have never seen an art studio before?"

"Dr Green is a bit of an artist in his spare time. He loves to paint. When he's in the loft it means he's well hidden from the rest of the household. The loft has a huge window with an amazing view of the lake and the land surrounding the house. It really was a lovely sight."

"That sounds lovely," Christine said as she tried to imagine the view. "Did he bother you in there as well Alice?"

"Yes, it was truly awful. He asked me to clean the loft one day when his wife was away visiting family. I did what I was asked and as usual, he came into the room and just stood there in silence staring at me. Then, after a while, he told me to take a break and sit with him. He brushed his fingers through my hair and told me how he loved women with long hair. He was sitting so close to me I could almost hear him breathing in my ear. He then asked me if I would let him paint me."

"Oh really? What did you say?" Asked Christine

"I didn't know what to say. He was my employer and for some reason it didn't feel right to say no. He showed me one of his paintings. It was a portrait of a young girl wearing a lovely long Emerald green gown draped around her loosely and hanging off her shoulder. She was lying on the sofa and it was a beautiful painting. She was beautiful," Alice said as she recalled the portrait in her mind's eye. "I asked who the girl was and Dr Green told me she was the only other person he ever allowed to clean his office and studio. He told me she moved to America and so that is why he needed me to take her place. He stroked my cheek and told me I would be a far better subject to paint." Alice became silent again.

"So did he actually paint you Alice?" Christine asked

to break the awkward silence.

Alice looked at her and smiled. "Like I said he made it hard to say no. He told me he often spoke to his brother about me. He knew my father worked for his brother and he talked about how his brother always loved hearing about me. I felt safe so I agreed to let him paint me and he said he would do it the next day."

"Wow. I'd be far too shy. Did he give the portrait to you?" Christine asked.

Alice shook her head. "The next day he called me up to the loft where he locked the door because he said he did not like any interruptions whilst painting. He handed me a hairbrush and asked me to brush my hair and let it hang down over my shoulders. He directed me to change into the same beautiful green gown that was worn by the last house cleaner. He turned his back and promised me he wouldn't look. I felt uncomfortable but did it anyway." Alice laughed as if she were ridiculing herself for being so trusting. "When I was ready, he sat me on the sofa and fixed the gown loosely around my shoulders. He told me to clasp it together with my hands so it barely covered my chest. He stood behind his easel and he began to paint me. He worked in silence and every so often he would stop and ask me to change position or smile etc."

At this point Alice went silent. She had a tear in her eye and tried to wipe it away with her sleeve. "He then put down his paintbrush and walked toward me and asking me to lie back on the sofa. He placed his hands on my shoulders and gently pushed me backwards. My leg caught the gown. I could feel the material falling away from my body. He wouldn't let me fix it and without any warning he pulled the gown wide open. I became distressed and begged him to let me close it. I told him I had changed my mind and wanted to get dressed. He just looked at me in silence whilst pressing his finger to his lips as if to tell me to stop talking and not make any noise. I could feel his eyes scanning my entire body as he stroked my neck with his other hand. I was so upset. It just didn't feel right. Then I felt his hand on my legs rubbing me up and down just as he did when I hurt my ankle but this time, he didn't stop at that and he hurt me. He hurt me so very badly."Alice stopped talking, she was overwhelmed with emotion and tears fell as she reached into her pocket for a handkerchief to dry her eyes.

Christine was stunned hardly able to talk not knowing what to say. She could clearly see how upset Alice was so she just put her arm around her and told her she was OK. She told her friend that what happened to her wasn't her fault and Dr Green was not a good man.

Alice turned to look at Christine. "You're so kind. I hope I've not upset you too much."

"No not at all don't worry about me, like I said, it was not your fault," Christine replied.

"You know nobody has ever told me it was not my fault. Nobody has ever blamed him. Even the nuns who worked in the orphanage told me I was a 'sinner.' They had a prayer room with a sign on the door that read

'*Sinners'* prayer room'," Alice reminisced. "I along with all the other sinners had to spend two hours a day on our knees in silence praying for forgiveness before breakfast. It was torture in there. Why did I need forgiveness? To this day I still don't know what I did that was so wrong."Alice tried to describe the orphanage but she couldn't find the words to do it Justice."As for Dr Green, he told me it was my fault for being so grown up and smiling at him all the time. He hurt me every day for nearly three weeks and told me never to say anything or he would tell his brother to sack my father. My parents needed the money so I said nothing." Alice bowed her head.

Christine asked what he said when he discovered she was pregnant. Alice told her he demanded she left his house and made it clear he wanted nothing to do with her.

"He called me awful names. He made my life hell and told my parents if I didn't keep quiet then he would make sure they would lose everything, my dad's job and even our house. He then offered my parents what he called 'A decent sum of money' to get rid of the problem, so of course that meant I couldn't keep my beautiful baby boy. His money bought the new television that my parents insisted on showing of to the street by inviting everyone to watch the televised Queen's coronation. That was why I was so upset that day. Everyone saying how fancy it was. If only they all knew the sacrifice I had to make for their enjoyment. My baby is worth far more to me than any stupid television." Alice went quiet.

Christine packed her book in her bag. To their right there was a large open grassy space full of daisies. "Alice, let's make a daisy chain. It will take your mind away from your troubles," suggested Christine. "I love daisies. Come on Alice, it will be fun."So as the sun began to fade, the two girls sat amongst the vast bed of daisies making daisy chains. As the sun disappeared, Alice smiled and thanked Christine for listening to her. At that point the girls stood up and made their way home wearing their daisy chains around their necks. The girls giggled wondering what people would think of them covered in flowers. Christine didn't care because they both had fun making them and that was what mattered.

Christine went in to her house and entered the kitchen where her mother was busy at the sink. Her mother turned to look at her. She scoffed at the sight of the daisy chains wrapped around her neck. "And where have you been all day?" her mother asked.

"I have had a lovely afternoon Mother. I met Alice and we have had a great chat. She is such a lovely girl."

"Oh really. You have lots to learn child. Now clean yourself up and take those weeds off your neck. I'm about to put the dinner on."

As Christine turned to leave the kitchen, her dad walked in smiling. "Oh you look lovely. I love daisies too. Her dad said with a wink"

Christine giggled as she took off one of her daisy chains and placed it around her father's neck. She then left to go upstairs where she put her book away and washed her hands before dinner.

That evening Christine was tired after a long day in the sun so she went to bed early. She said a special prayer for Alice. *Please God, keep Alice safe and let her be happy. Please look after her baby boy and may he find a special home with a mother and father who will love him and give him a good life. Amen.*

She climbed into her bed and pulled her blankets around her to keep warm. The earlier conversation with Alice played through her mind. No matter how difficult her life was she felt grateful that her mother did not leave her in an orphanage or that nobody forced her mother to give her away. She did not know how she would cope with that.

Chapter 5

Four months had passed since Christine had sat with Alice on that warm summer's day. Life seemed to move so fast but she never complained. Mrs Reed her music teacher encouraged her to join a children's deaf club. The club was run by a charity that worked with children with hearing difficulties. They taught children sign language and lip-reading techniques. This was a club where Christine felt like she belonged. For once she was no different to any other child in the room and she loved it. She followed her teacher's advice and joined the church choir. Christine loved nothing more than to sing her heart out at the top of her voice knowing that for once she was no different to anyone else in the room. Being a member of the church choir also meant she could take part in the Christmas carol service.

With just four weeks to go before the Christmas carol service Christine was attending the usual weekly rehearsal when the choir leader, Mrs Fleming, approached her and asked if she could speak to her. *Oh no, I knew it. I'm being taken out of the choir*, she thought to herself as she glanced around to see if anyone was looking at her.

"Christine, I have a bit of a problem. Sarah has had to step out of the choir for family reasons," Mrs Fleming said.

"Oh really? How can I help?" asked Christine.

"Well, I was wondering, since you have such a beautiful voice would you take her place and sing the solo? It would be such a help to me."

Christine could not believe what she was hearing and was lost for words. "Me? Really? Oh, Mrs Fleming, it would be an honour. I won't let you down, I promise."

"Oh I know you won't let me down. I wouldn't have asked you if I thought you couldn't do it," Mrs Fleming said whilst placing her hand on Christine's shoulder.

I must be good. I must be really good, Christine thought as she clapped her hands with excitement.

She was even more excited when she learned that she would be singing her favourite Christmas song, Silent Night. She practiced day and night. The first dress rehearsal was just two weeks away. She went to bed singing and woke up singing. Her mother always asked her to sing a little quieter, whilst her dad encouraged her to sing even louder.

***

On the night before dress rehearsals, Christine chose her finest clothes and laid them out ready for the morning. She even washed her hair using her mother's expensive shampoo without her knowing. She placed her lipstick on her bedside locker and her black-painted shoes at the foot of her bed. She then climbed into bed and tried to get some sleep. It was just a rehearsal but she took it all very seriously. The next morning, she bounced down the stairs with a massive smile on her face. She ran into the kitchen but was upset to see her dad had already left for work and did not stay to wish her well. Her mother was sitting at the table reading the paper.

"Right," her mother announced. "I have to go out now. You'll have to make your own breakfast." She took the last mouthful of tea from her cup and then prepared to leave for the day.

Christine's smile soon disappeared. "But I thought you were coming to see me in the rehearsal?"

"Oh don't be silly child it's just a rehearsal. We'll be there on the night but for today I have far more important things to be doing with my time," her mother said as she picked up her coat and hat and walked out of the house.

Christine watched her mother leave. She was stunned. *Huh, she left me without so much as a 'goodbye' or 'good luck'.* She decided not to let this spoil her day and had some toast before running up to her bedroom to get ready for the rehearsals. Once dressed, Christine brushed her hair and put it up in two ponytails with ribbons and nice fancy hairclips. She then put on her shoes whilst singing her Christmas song at the top of her voice. With her lipstick applied, she went into the kitchen and said goodbye to her beloved dog. "Wish me luck Patch," she shouted to her furry friend who looked at her with his tail wagging. She smiled at him before closing the kitchen door and making her way out of the house.

Wrapped up warm in her winter coat against the frosty morning she headed to the church hall, which was locked when she arrived so she stood there patiently waiting for the vicar to turn up. It felt like forever but when he arrived, he told her she looked lovely and he couldn't wait to hear her singing because she always sang so well in church. This was her first compliment and she thought it must be true because he was a 'man of God' so he couldn't possibly tell a lie.

Soon everyone had arrived and the entire choir and their parents filled the hall. Christine felt a pang of jealousy because the other children had their parents with them. She tried not to let it upset her too much because she knew her parents would be there at the real thing.

It wasn't long before the choir took their place on stage eagerly waiting for the rehearsal to begin. The curtains were slowly drawn open and silence fell across the hall. Whilst standing on stage scanning the audience Christine's gaze rested on a woman standing at the back of the hall. Her tummy tightened at the realisation that she seemed familiar to her somehow. Lately, wherever she went she had seen this woman standing close by. *Who is this woman and why does she always seem to be watching me?* Just as that thought entered her head, it was interrupted by the sound of the choirmaster tapping the top of his music stand signalling the choir to prepare to sing the first carol.

The choir was to sing the first two carols and then Christine was to step forward and take her place at the microphone. She sang beautifully and everyone clapped as she curtsied before returning to her place with everyone else. Christine beamed with pride.

Her mind once again turned to the strange woman standing at the back of the hall. She had a big smile on her face and stood there with both hands clutched to her chest just like a proud mother watching her child. Christine thought it was a bit odd but she would take praise no matter where it came from, even from a stranger. Praise was sadly lacking in her home so it felt great to know people loved her singing.

After rehearsals, the choir went into the back room where they hugged and congratulated eachother on their efforts. Christine was excited after her performance and couldn't wait until the real carol service so she could sing in front of an even bigger audience.

The choir soon made their way to the main hall and back to their families.Christine put on her coat and then took out her gloves and scarf. As she put them on, she stood in a daze, looking around at all the mothers hugging their children and praising them. *How lucky they are.* She nearly jumped with fright when she felt a tap on her shoulder. She turned around expecting to see the vicar with a big smile on his face and high praise for her performance. Instead, she saw the woman from the back of the hall standing there staring at her. *Oh my god, it's her. What do I say?* What do I do? The woman was dressed in a long blue coat and a matching blue hat with a lovely purple flower attached to the side. Christine didn't recognise her and wasn't sure what she should say. The woman seemed shy at first and stood in an awkward silence just staring at her. Christine felt very uncomfortable. She had to do something, say something.

"I'm sorry. Can I help you?" She asked the lady.

The woman smiled and beckoned her to sit with her. Christine was unsure what to do, her dad always told her not to talk to strangers but she was in a room filled with people she knew so it felt like a safe place.

"This may come as a surprise to you, but I know you. I know who you are," the woman said whilst gently taking hold of Christine's hand. "I just wanted to speak to you."

Christine thought this was very strange. "I am sorry. I don't know you but I'm sure I've seen you in the area. Are you sure you've not mixed me up with somebody else? Maybe if you give me a name, I can find them for you."

The woman spoke quietly trying not to let the people around them hear their conversation. "No, I know you don't know me and yes you have seen me lately. I hope I haven't scared you. That wasn't my intention."

Christine shuffled her feet on the floor and looked around to see if anyone was watching her. She didn't know what to do or say next. "I'm sorry, but I'm confused. I really don't understand what you're saying to me. Who are you?"

The woman leaned in closer to Christine. "Oh please don't worry about that right now. I assure you I do know you. You were abandoned as a baby. You were found in a garden just across the road from a hospital. Then you were adopted by your parents."The words fell out of her mouth at a hundred miles an hour without stopping to take a breath.

Suddenly, Christine felt like she was watching the television with the sound turned down. She could see the woman talking. Her mouth was moving but there was no sound. Everyone around her seemed to be moving in slow motion. She was in shock and became visibly upset as her whole body trembled.

The woman stopped talking and her expression softened. She could tell that Christine had no idea what she was talking about. "Oh, my child I am so sorry. Did you not know you were adopted? Has nobody ever told you? I promise you I do not mean you any harm. Please forgive me, "she said in an effort to ease the situation.

Christine sat in her chair in shock unable to believe what she had just been told. She pulled her hand away from the woman's grasp. "No. You must have me mixed up with someone else. What you're saying isn't true. Why would you say that to me and who are you anyway?"She clasped her gloved hands together but it did not stop her from shaking. Looking around the hall again, she noticed people were staring at her. *Oh my goodness, did everyone hear. Does everyone know what this awful woman has just said to me?* The room spun around her. She couldn't hold in her tears any longer. After what seemed like forever, Christine stood up and ran out of the church hall with the vicar calling for her to come back. She couldn't look back. She could barely see through her tears. When out of sight of the church hall she stopped to catch her breath. *What did that woman mean? Why would she say such a thing to me? It can't be true. She must have me confused with someone else.* Christine questioned everything as she stood there quietly sobbing trying to comprehend what had just happened. She walked the rest of the way home in a daze, her eyes swollen with tears and her body shaking as she approached the road to her house.

***

She walked up her garden path with her head bowed. As she reached to put the key into the lock, she felt an icy shiver vibrating through her entire body. She had no idea how she was going to tell her mother but she knew she had to know the truth. She needed her mother to tell her it was all lies. When Christine walked into the house, she went straight into the kitchen where her mother was busy ironing her father's work shirts.

"My goodness child, was your singing that bad? Whatever has you in such a state?"

Christine pulled a chair from under the kitchen

table and sat down. She could hardly breathe as she blurted out what the woman in the church hall had told her. Her mother sat at the kitchen table unable to keep still. Fidgeting with her hair and rubbing her face, she seemed to struggle to make eye contact with Christine.

"Please, Mother, tell me it's not true. Tell me it's all lies. Please just tell me she is a crazy woman."Her mother would not even look at her.

"Please say something. Why aren't you talking to me about this?" Christine slammed the kitchen table with both hands. Here she was pouring her heart out feeling hurt and scared yet her mother was saying nothing to try to comfort her.

It seemed to Christine in that moment that her mother's silence was the loudest and most painful thing in the room.

Eventually her mother raised her head. Her face was white as snow. "OK, you want to know the truth. I will tell you the truth. Yes, yes, we adopted you. I didn't give birth to you but you were not abandoned. That was all lies."

Her mother's words were like punches to her chest. "But why did you not tell me? Why Mother? Why did I have to find out like this and who was that woman?"

"Oh stop your nonsense child. What does it matter? You know now don't you? Now I have to go out. Your dinner is in the oven and you can see yourself to bed."Her mother pulled herself together. She began straightening her jumper and practically ran out of the house forgetting her coat in her haste.

Christine was astonished and heartbroken at her mother's attitude. She ran up to her bedroom and lay on her bed sobbing into her pillow unable to console herself. She couldn't understand how something as big as this could have been kept a secret from her. Why did she have to find out from a stranger? This was devastating and she didn't know how she was ever going to get over it.

A familiar scratching could be heard at the bedroom door. She looked up and saw Patch nudging the door open with his nose. He was making his way towards her. Usually, Patch would lick her face but this time he just jumped on the bed, cuddled into her and laid his head on her chest. It was as if he knew exactly what she needed at that moment.

"Oh Patch, they've really done it this time. My heart is breaking and I don't know why this is happening."She sobbed as she rubbed her dog's head. Patch looked at her. He pricked his ears up in the air and tilted his head to the side as if he was listening and understood every word she was saying. Her head was full of questions. *Why was I adopted? Why was I not wanted? Why is this happening to me?* She even wondered if her life would have been better if she hadn't been adopted. It was now clear to her why she lived her life feeling like an outsider in her own home. Even her aunt and cousins were not her family. This was something she was rather relieved about when considering her current situation.

Christine blamed her mother for everything that felt

wrong in her life. Why would she agree to adopt me? I wish she had left me alone so that someone kinder and more caring could have adopted me instead. However, she felt bad for thinking this way because that would have meant she would never have had her dad in her life and she loved him. She stayed in her room for the rest of the day praying the world would disappear.

As nighttime fell around her, she looked out the window at the starry sky before closing her curtains. The world was quiet. She jumped into her bed, pulled her blanket around her shoulders and with the faintest tear in her eye, Christine prayed she would wake in the morning to discover that this day had been one big bad dream.

Chapter 6

The next morning Christine awoke to the sound of raised voices coming from the kitchen. She got out of her bed and opened the curtains. The winter sun was trying to shine above the glistening frost on the ground. As she turned to hop back in to her bed, she heard raised voices coming from downstairs. Her parents were having an argument. Christine tip toed to her bedroom door and opened it slightly. She quietly sat on the top step trying to listen to her parents.

"Well, I am telling you what I told you when you decided we should adopt her. I do not want trouble brought to my door. I told you back then that it was all going to be more trouble than it's worth but you would not listen, would you?" Her mother was yelling.

Her dad sounded frustrated with Florence. "Oh really? You were perfectly happy when we were being paid to foster her. Oh but when the money stopped you changed your tune then. She is a child for God's sake. Our daughter and no matter what you say I know you care about her. Why can you not just admit that at least?"Her dad said.

"And what good would that do? In my day whenever I was upset I was told to stop fussing and get on with it. No, Christine will be fine once she has had time to get used to it. She knows now so that is that, there is nothing more to be said or done."Her mother's stern words were followed by stark silence.

Dad will surely talk to me about this. He won't be so cruel. Just as that thought entered her head, she heard both her parents leave the house slamming the doors behind them. She made her way back into her bedroom and hopped back into her bed. It was Sunday morning she had no school so she did not have to get up just yet. She couldn't even bring herself to get up for church. *How can I possibly go to church? The vicar must be so upset with my outburst yesterday. I bet everyone is talking about it. I bet everyone there heard what that woman said to me. I just can't face them. Not today. I will say a few prayers in my room instead. I'm sure God will understand.* She pulled her blankets up over her head to block out the world.

*****

The house was silent and as she lay in the bed under the blankets, her tummy soon grumbled with hunger. She had not eaten since before the rehearsal the previous day so she went downstairs to the kitchen and prepared some breakfast for herself. She looked at Patch fast asleep in his usual spot. *I would be lost without you, my furry friend.* Picking up her toast, she sat down on the floor beside her pal. Patch raised his head at the smell of her food so she shared her breakfast with him. Christine listened to the clock ticking in the bare silence of the kitchen as her thoughts drifted back to the events of the last twenty-four hours.

The kitchen window was open and she could hear noise coming from the back alley behind the house.

"Alice, don't forget your bag," a loud voice shouted from her neighbour's back garden gate. She thought of her friend, Alice Brown.

"What do you think Patch, hey, do you think my birth mother was similar to Alice? A young girl forced to give me up for adoption." Patch licked her hand as she spoke. Christine giggled to herself. "Oh Patch if only you could speak, you would know how to make me feel better wouldn't you boy."She thought about all the nasty, horrible names that she heard people call Alice and her baby. *Was my birth mother also devastated and heartbroken just like Alice was when she had to say goodbye to her baby boy? Would people say the same about me if they knew the truth about my adoption? And what about Alice's baby? Was a kind loving home found for him or is he still in the orphanage?* Christine wondered if she was taken to one of those orphanages. She tried to remember but couldn't understand why she had no memories of that time in her life. She knew she was just a baby at the time but she thought she would surely have some memory of that time. Her earliest memory was of her sitting in a pram looking around at a strange building. However, she had no idea where she was or even who was caring for her at that time. She wondered what her birth mother looked like. Was she pretty? Was she young? Was she rich? Did she look like her? Did her birth mother have a good singing voice? All these questions kept flooding into her mind. It was like a whirlwind of what, Why and Who? She wondered if she would ever find the answers to those questions. Would she ever discover the truth about who she was or where she came from? She thought about her birth dad. *Who was he? Why did he not want me? Did he even know about me or did he force my birth mother to give me away?* It felt strange that somewhere in the world there could be someone thinking of her. There could be someone out there who was missing her. A whole family somewhere in the world that could love her and she love them back.

Oh, my child I am so sorry. Please forgive me. The woman's words kept going through her head. She wondered if this woman could've been her birth mother trying to reach out to her. She wondered how the woman could have known who she was and what she would say to her if she was to see her again. Once she had finished her breakfast, she took herself back upstairs to her bedroom. She cleaned her room to try to take her mind off things but it was pointless.

After a short while, she heard somebody downstairs opening the front door. She could not avoid her parents forever and she had so many questions that she needed answers to. She went downstairs where her mother was unpacking a bag in the kitchen. "Mother, can I talk to you?"

Her mother turned and looked at her. "OK but make it quick because Ivy will be calling soon. She couldn't make it yesterday."

Christine stood at the kitchen table. "Mother, when you adopted me what was my name?" Christine waited patiently for an answer.

"Oh not this nonsense again. Look, your name was and always will be Christine. That is the name the courts gave you and I didn't bother changing it. It's no big mystery."

"You didn't bother?"Christine clutched the back of the kitchen table chair and could feel her grip tightening as anger built up inside of her.

"Oh stop it Christine. Stop overreacting. Look, you're adopted. Your father and I took you in and gave you a roof over your head. Now, instead of feeling sorry for yourself why don't you help me unload the rest of this shopping and then go and play?"Florence was very abrupt. However, Christine knew she had no maternal instincts whatsoever and if she were to be brutally honest, she guessed that her mother never wanted children to begin with.

Christine had to get some fresh air she felt like she was suffocating under the weight of her emotions. She passed her Aunt Ivy as she walked out her front door and down the garden path. Her aunt said hello but she was in no mood for pleasantries so she ignored her and kept walking. As she walked, she heard the hustle and bustle of life going on around her. It felt strange that everyone else's life carried on as normal when her world was collapsing around her.

As she crossed through the park, she saw mothers pushing their prams. There were children playing with their siblings, laughing, joking, and having fun. She sat watching them and wondering what was wrong with her. Was she really such a bad person that her own birth mother did not want her? Maybe all those bullies were right. Maybe she was just a stupid girl who would amount to nothing. When she thought she could not possibly cry any more she felt the familiar sting of tears stream down her face again. She wiped her eyes and glanced around her only to see a lady looking in her direction so she got up from the bench and started walking. She could not face questions from strangers.

She eventually got home and walked into the house where she could hear her mother and Aunt Ivy talking. She walked into the kitchen and there was silence, the kind of silence where you know you were being talked about.

Christine looked at her mother and shook her head in disappointment. It was obvious her mother had told her aunt about what had happened. My life is just one big joke to them. She felt like she must have been the last to know and wondered who else knew. How many more people were secretly talking about her behind her back?

Her mother broke her silence. "Christine, the Brown girl was looking for you while you were out. I told her you were out and would be busy for the rest of the day."

Christine stopped in her tracks as she was about to leave the kitchen. Bemused by what her mother was telling her. "Why would you say that to her?" Asked Christine whilst turning to look at her mother.

Her mother threw her a scathing look. "Because you're not to have anything to do with her. She's troubled and a bad influence on you. You've been spending far too much time with that girl"

Christine threw her hands in the air in despair. "Oh really, Mother, am I not allowed friends now?"

"Don't talk to your mother like that," Aunt Ivy butted in.

Christine threw an indignant glance at her aunt not caring if she was being rude. *Who does she think she is telling me what to do and who is she to me anymore.*

"Uncle Fred and Aunt Daisy always tell me I should never ignore a friend when they are troubled. Are you both saying they're wrong?"Her eye contact switched between her mother and her aunt.

Again, her Aunt Ivy interrupted, unable to mind her own business. "They're not your parents."

Christine moved closer to Ivy and made eye contact with her aunt. "Oh really, and who exactly are my—"

"Enough," Florence shouted as she stood up from her chair.

Christine knew she would've been in big trouble if she had finished what she was about to say, so she took a deep breath and tried to calm herself down. "Well, I'm going to see Uncle Fred and Aunt Daisy tomorrow after school so shall I tell them you both send them your love?"

***

Christine had deaf club later that day. She was not in the mood for it but she had to go. She walked into the club and sat at a table waiting for the club leader to come in. Everyone else sat around chatting and signing to eachother but Christine just could not join in. She sat silently with her thoughts. She sat through an hour-long lesson on sign language and lip reading and honestly thought it would never end. When the time was up the club leader gave everyone some sheets to work on.

Just as Christine was about to leave the room the leader asked if she could have a word with her. "Christine, are you OK? I couldn't help but notice you seemed a little distracted."

"I'm fine thank you. I just have a bit of a headache that's all but I'll be fine, I promise."

"OK, if you're sure. I'll see you next week then."The group leader smiled and they both said their goodbyes.

As Christine walked home, she felt like such a fraud. So I'm a liar now am I? Why couldn't I tell her the truth? After all, I've done nothing wrong. Her stomach churned from the stress.

She made her way home and noticed her dad had come home from work. Her dinner was about to be dished up and they all sat around the table in silence. Christine had lost her appetite but her mother told her to eat up and stop moping. Once she had finished her food, she went in to the sitting room and sat on the armchair beside the fireplace looking at the flames dance around the grate. Her dad finally came in and sat on the sofa. Christine knew she would have to talk to him some time.

"Dad, can I talk to you please?"

"Of course you can. What's up with my girl?"He asked softly.

Christine stood up and sat beside her dad on the sofa. She looked him in the eye and told him what the woman in the church hall had told her. As she was talking, she could feel her mother's eyes staring at her like razor-sharp daggers being thrown at her from the doorway to the sittingroom. "Why did you keep my adoption from me Dad? Why didn't you tell me the truth?"

Albert placed his hand on hers. "Oh, love I am so sorry that you—"

As if out of nowhere her mother suddenly spoke up.

"Albert, don't pander to the girl. I've told you I dealt with this already and that's an end to it."She then turned her attention to Christine. "As for you, I will say this only once. I do not ever want to hear you talk about this nonsense again. Not to your father not to me and not to anyone. Do you hear me?" Standing wagging her finger, she continued "and what's more if you mention a word of this to anyone outside this house, I will remove you from the church choir. This is family business and if it gets out then what an embarrassment that would be to us all. Do you really want people to think badly of us after everything we've done for you?"She went silent and sat in the armchair looking across the room to Christine and Albert. She leaned forward and took a deep breath. "Look, it's in your best interest. I know you may not understand this but that's the way it has to be. Trust me I know what I'm talking about. It's better this way."

"How can you be so mean?" Christine said whilst looking to her dad for support. "I wish I had my real mother here. Maybe she would've loved me. Maybe she would never have been so cruel to me."

Her mother stood up and straightened her jumper. "Are you really going to let her talk to me like that Albert?" She stormed out of the room and went back into the kitchen.

Albert squeezed Christine's hand and gave her a sympathetic smile. She knew he wanted to talk but her mother would not let him so she left the room and ran upstairs to her bedroom. Her heart broke with every step she took. *How can my mother be so cruel? Is this really how my life is going to be from now on? Do I really have to live as some kind of shameful secret?*

Christine threw herself on her bed not knowing what she would do next. Despite all the hurt and anger, she knew she needed the choir. She needed to sing. Christine had no choice and decided she wouldn't say anything about this to anyone because she didn't want to lose the one good thing in her life.

***

The next day after school Christine called to see her Aunt Daisy and Uncle Fred. She couldn't wait to see a friendly face. As she walked up the pathway to her aunt and uncle's house, she wondered if they knew about her adoption. *Surely, they would have said something. They wouldn't have kept something like this from me. But how could they not know? They're family.*

The door suddenly flung open. Aunt Daisy was standing there with a big welcoming smile on her face. "Come on in out of the cold my dear."

Christine walked in past her aunt and for the first time in her life, she felt like maybe she was wrong about her aunt and uncle. Maybe they were as bad as everyone else and keeping secrets from her. *Is there anyone in this family that I can trust?*

Daisy turned and watched as Christine walked past her. "Ahem, what is wrong with you Christine? Did you have a bad day at school?"She closed the door and followed Christine into the sitting room.

"No, not really Aunty, I have just had a bad week,

that's all."

Daisy could tell there was something wrong. "Really? How was the rehearsal? Did something go wrong?"She had never seen Christine so quiet in her house. "My dear, please tell me what's wrong. If you don't tell me I can't help." Daisy beckoned Christine to sit down. "If it's not school then it has to be your mother? What has she done this time?"

Christine took off her coat and pulled her woolly hat from her head. She sat down infront of the open fire. Staring at the flames burning in the fireplace. She bowed her head then she explained what had happened. "I'm adopted. I was told by a stranger in the church hall." She lifted her head to see her aunt's reaction. "Did you know? Did Uncle Fred know? I bet I'm the very last person to find out. I feel like my life has been a lie. My family is a lie. Who am I?" Christine poured her heart out to her aunt who sat quietly and just listened. "I don't know what's real and what's a lie," Christine said whilst wiping a tear from her eye. "Of course Mother won't talk to me about it."

Daisy handed her a clean tissue to wipe her tears. Then she sat back and brushed some stray strands of hair behind her ears. Slapping her hands onto her knees, she asked Christine to come with her to the kitchen where she would get her some tea and cake and they could have a proper chat.

They both sat at the table. Daisy took a sip of tea. "I am so sorry you have found out that way. Yes, we did know about your adoption. We were told never to talk to you about it and that it was best for everyone if you didn't know. We were so afraid we would never be allowed to see you if we ever told you."Daisy took a bite of cake and her eyes softened. "Let me tell you something. You are very much our family. Family is not just about blood. Your uncle and I were never blessed with a child of our own but then you came into our lives. We adore you every bit as much as we would love a child of our own. You must know that's not a lie."

Christine looked at her aunt. Of course, she knew

deep down that Daisy and Fred loved her. She knew they cared and she understood that none of this was their fault. "I am so sorry Aunty. I love you and Uncle Fred as well. You've always been so kind to me. I know it's not your fault. I am just sad that's all. My mother has been pretty mean to me in the past but this time it really hurts." Christine could feel herself calming down and then remembered she should not be talking about this. "Aunty please promise me you won't say a word of this to anyone. If mother knew I'd been discussing it she would be so upset with me. She told me she would take me out of the choir if I talked to another soul about this and I couldn't bear that."

"Of course, you don't need to worry. I won't say a word. You can always trust me no matter what is wrong. Please always know I am here for you. I will never turn you away." Daisy tried to offer her reassurance, knowing that she was the only real motherly influence in Christine's life. "Now, if you are up for it let's go bake a cake. Baking always cheers me up. Eating one also works wonders!"Daisy said with a smile and a wink.

"Oh yes please," Christine said as she pulled up her sleeves.

***

The following two weeks went by in a blur and the night of the carol service had finally arrived. Christine was all dressed in her best clothes her hair was put up in two pigtails with ribbons flowing from them. She and her parents were among the first people to arrive at the hall.

"OK Christine run along now and find the vicar and remember your words," her mother said.

Her dad gave her a big hug. "You go and enjoy every second love. We are so proud of you." Albert smiled as she turned to walk towards the backstage room.

Soon everyone was standing in his or her place on the stage. Christine scanned the hall looking out for the woman who she had met at the rehearsal. She could not see her anywhere. *Oh, I hope she is not here. N mother wouldn't be happy, and what would I say to her anyway? But I have so many questions for her.* Christine could feel her heart beating faster and faster as she tried to work out how she felt about encountering the woman again. Then suddenly, silence fell across the hall. The audience applauded as the music started and the first Christmas carol was about to be sung.

The time came for Christine to sing her song so she stepped forward and stood centre stage. She had never been in the spotlight before. Her tummy tightened with nerves. However, as soon as she heard the music start, she began to sing and soon forgot all about her troubles. As the song concluded, Christine closed her eyes and opened them to the sound of a huge round of applause. She grinned from ear to ear when she saw her dad sitting in the front row clapping furiously with pride. However, her mother seemed more interested in looking around the hall. *I bet she is also looking for that woman,* Christine thought. The night went well and she got through it, as she knew she would. There were refreshments laid on afterwards which was a real treat for Christine. When she got home, she went straight to bed and fell asleep as soon as her head hit the pillow.

***

In March of 1954, Mother's Day was looming and because Christine was a child, she never had money to buy anything for her mother. Instead, her dad would buy a box of chocolates and bring her to the local park where she picked a bunch of flowers to give to her mother. This year Christine was dreading it. For the first time in her life Mother's Day held a different meaning to her. Why was she being forced to give presents to someone who did not care enough about her to give her a name?

The day before Mother's Day, her dad had a rare day off work. He bought Christine for an early morning walk to the park to pick the flowers for her mother. She knew this would be her only opportunity to speak to her dad alone about her predicament.

When she and her dad arrived at the park, she asked

him to sit with her on the bench for a chat and he agreed. "Dad, please tell me the truth about my adoption. Mother just won't say anything but it is eating me up inside."She patiently waited for his reply.

Her dad stared ahead, as if he was trying to find the words to answer her. "I'm so sorry you found out like that. It was unforgiveable of us. We should have been more honest with you. I honestly don't have the answers you're looking for. I don't know who your birth parents are but you can't ever go looking for them. You will get into big trouble if you do. You do know I would help you if I could. Don't you? Once we adopted you that was that. You became our daughter."He held Christine's hand in his and squeezed it tight. "I know it is not what you want to hear but that is the truth. All I know is that you are my girl. I am your dad. I love you and so does your mother. She just doesn't know how to show her feelings that's all."Albert smiled and winked at her. Then he put his arm around her and hugged her tight.

Christine smiled at him. "Thank you, Dad. Thank you for not shouting and for letting me ask questions. It means a lot to me to know you care so much. But maybe we can keep this conversation between just us two?"

"Of course love. I won't say a word I promise you. This conversation is between us. Nobody else needs to know."

Christine badly needed that hug. At least her dad understood and her feelings mattered to him. She knew he meant well and was trying to protect her. She needed him in her corner. She needed someone that would fight with her not against her. As for what he said about her mother, well, that had yet to be proven.

Chapter 7

Two months later Christine's teacher gave the class their homework, which was to write a story about their family. *Oh great, this is going to be fun. How do I write about my family when I have no idea of who my real mother actually is?* Christine pondered later that evening. She sat at her kitchen table with her pen in hand and her copybook open in front of her but she was stuck for words. What would she write? Everything she thought she knew about her family was wrong. It was a lie. She imagined what her teacher would think if she wrote the truth. Would she be shocked and disgusted or would she even believe it was true. She knew she could not tell the truth because her mother would take her out of the choir and she loved being in the choir. However, the truth was that she did not know who she was. How could she talk about her mother and father when she did not know who gave birth to her? This made her ponder over the meaning of the word 'Mother' and 'Father'. She always thought the only people in the entire world that you called 'mother' or 'father' were the people who gave you life. She decided the best option would be to imagine her birth family. It was supposed to be a story after all, and she was going to make it the best story ever.

She created the names Jane and Richard for her parents she loved those names. She wrote that her dad was a soldier who fought in the war and saved the King. She said her mother was a glamorous actress who was always singing to her, giving her nice clothes, and shared her makeup with her. In her story, Christine said she had four siblings. Two brothers, and two sisters and they all played together and loved each other dearly. They were not cruel or unkind to each other. She included Patch in her story. He was the only family member she did not have to imagine because he really was family to her. As she wrote her story, she wished that it were true. Christine thought that maybe her birth mother would one day come looking for her and whisk her away from the mess she lived in right now.

Christine sat on her bed and packed her schoolbooks into her bag for the next day. She picked up one book and the name she had once so carefully written across it stood out to her. She sounded the name aloud whilst carefully rubbing her finger along the lettering. *Christine.* A name she had been using for so long as she could remember. It was a name people associated with her. However, a thought entered her head. Who am I? She thought about everything she knew about herself up to that moment, who she was who her family were and even her name. Was any of it actually true? The name 'Christine 'felt like a mask some stranger had forced her to wear, hiding who she really was from the world. Her real name had to be different from the name given to her by the courts. Surely, her birth mother called her something different. What about her surname? That had to be different too. Her name was the only thing she had that was hers and even that had been taken from her by the courts.

She had never seen her birth certificate and wondered if there could be any information on it that may shed some light on what her real name may have been.

Suddenly, she heard the front door slamming shut. *Now is my chance. Mother and Dad have gone out for the evening.* She ran to her bedroom window and saw them both walking down the footpath and climbing into the car. As they drove away out of sight, she crept down the stairs and walked into the kitchen only to be greeted by Patch wagging his tail. In the cupboard above the sink, she pulled out a box where her mother stored all-important documents. *My birth certificate must be in here somewhere.* She emptied the box and leafed through all the papers that fell out of it. She soon found what she was looking for and stuffed it into her pocket. She then put everything back into the box and placed it back in the cupboard before running back upstairs to her bedroom. She threw herself on her bed and excitedly opened and smoothed out the certificate across the blankets. Her eyes slowly scanned its content.

This certificate says it is a 'Certificate of birth' yet it is my adoptive parent's names that have been written on it. Surely, it can't possibly be a real birth certificate. She thought a birth certificate was supposed to be a means of identification but this piece of paper told her nothing about who she was. She felt like her entire identity had been stolen from her and replaced by lies. Flinging herself back on the bed she wondered, who was I before I became Christine? She lay there in silence and closed her eyes as if meditating on her thoughts. Then, suddenly, an idea popped into her head. Grabbing the certificate and taking a pen from her schoolbag she looked at the name 'Christine' and without a second thought she changed the last 'e' to an 'a' making her name 'Christina'.

Her tummy tightened at the realisation of what she had done. There was no going back now. However, she decided to change her name further. *Many people shorten their name or have a nickname. Why should I be any different? Nobody, not even the courts, can stop me doing that.* Therefore, she decided that she was now to be known as 'Tina' if anyone called her Christine, she was going to ignore them. *If anyone asks me, I will tell them it is short for Christina that is the name they will see if they were to look at this certificate.* She could feel the adrenaline rushing through her body. She knew her parents may not approve but this was her life and she was prepared for her mother, or so she thought.

The next morning, she marched down the stairs

where her parents were sitting at the kitchen table eating their breakfast. Suddenly she was not feeling as brave as she was the night before in her room, but she could not change what she had done and she knew she had to stick to her guns. She sat down at the table and began eating a big bowl of porridge that had been dished up for her. Her nerves kicked in, but she knew she had to tell her parents before she left for school and whilst they were both in the same room as her.

"I have news for you both. I have made a decision." Her parents stared at her, looking perplexed. She cleared her throat. "I have decided that since nobody in this family could be bothered to give me a name, I have chosen one for myself. I want to be known as 'Tina' from now on". She could hear her dad trying hard not to laugh, so she looked at him scornfully and he promptly began eating his breakfast without saying another word.

"You're being foolish. Why on earth would you expect anyone to call you Tina when that's not your name?"Snapped her mother.

Tina was not listening. She had already made up her mind and nothing her mother said was going to change how she felt. "Well, that's my decision Mother. I've even changed my birth certificate," she said whilst reaching into her school bag and pulling out her certificate before boldly slapping it down on the kitchen table. Her mother almost choked on her tea when she saw what Tina had done. She told her mother she would ignore anyone who did not respect her wishes. She had never talked to her mother like this before and was feeling a little apprehensive about how she may react. Her dad just smiled and winked at Tina as if to give his approval. When her mother was not looking, she smiled back at him. She then grabbed the last slice of toast from the table before picking up her school bag and running out of the house as fast as she could.

When she got to school, she sat in her seat and the teacher did the usual morning roll call. When she called out the name, 'Christine' there was silence in the room.

The teacher became very frustrated because she could see Tina sitting at her desk just staring back at her in silence. All the other students were giggling and calling her. They thought she did not hear the teacher calling her. Eventually she stood up and told the teacher that from now on she was to be called Tina. At this declaration, the whole class laughed aloud. Her teacher told the class to keep the noise down and told Tina she would call her by her registered name and she had better answer. This got Tina into lots of trouble as she stubbornly refused to back down. Her name was now Tina. Why was that so hard to understand? Eventually, the teacher grew tired of being ignored so she had to back down and she stopped calling her Christine.

Chapter 8

Tina spent the next two years concentrating on her schoolwork. She never gave up on her dream to become a nurse. Her mother's family all laughed at her and doubted her. Her Aunt Ivy and Cousin Deborah never missed a chance to taunt her and knock her confidence but this only made her more determined to succeed. All her hard work was worth it when she passed her final school exams and was accepted into nurse training. This was an exciting new chapter in her life. It was an opportunity to get away from her hometown and away from her family. She would make new friends, real friends with people who did not know her. People who didn't know her secret and would not insist on calling her Christine.

***

On the Saturday after she received her acceptance to nursing Tina could not wait to see her aunt Ivy. She wanted to be the first to tell her the good news. Her aunt arrived as normal. "Hello Aunty Ivy how are you?" She was extra chirpy as she opened the front door to let Ivy in to the house.

"I'm good. Why do you ask?" Ivy replied with a suspicious look on her face.

"Oh no reason, I just wondered that's all. Mother is in the kitchen."Tina directed Ivy towards the kitchen and followed her in. She then told her mother to take a seat and offered to make them both a nice cup of tea.

"For goodness' sake, why are you making such a fuss?" her mother asked.

"Can I not just do something nice for you Mother, "she asked as she reached to get some cups out of the cupboard. "Oh Aunty, I have been meaning to tell you, I have been accepted in to nursing. Isn't that great."

"Hmmm, well, I suppose it's better than I expected."

That may well be the nicest thing aunt Ivy has ever said to me. She finished making the tea and placed the teapot and cups on the table along with the milk and sugar. "Well, I had better go now. I'll leave you both to your tea. But please give my best to Cousin Deborah and tell her not to be too down on herself. I am sure there are plenty of jobs out there for people who didn't pass their school exams, "she quipped as she said her goodbyes to Ivy. "Mother, I'm going to Aunty Daisy and Uncle Fred's house. They've invited me for tea and cakes to celebrate my news, isn't that nice of them," Tina said as she grabbed her coat and made her way out the front door.

***

Tina made her way to Fred and Daisy's house. Her dad

had already told them she had been accepted to nursing and they were genuinely happy for her. She walked in to their house and was met with a huge hug from them both.

"Come in, come in, take a seat and tell us all about it," Daisy said whilst directing her to the kitchen table. Tina walked in and saw they had laid the table with her Aunt Daisy's best china. She had made a beautiful sponge cake filled with real cream and pink icing on top. There were also plates with sandwiches and biscuits placed on them. Tina felt very special indeed.

She told them all about her nurse training and when she was due to begin. She also told them she would have to live in the nurses' quarters so she would not be able to visit them every week as normal.

Aunt Daisy stood up and went upstairs only to come down holding a blanket in her arms. "Here you are Tina. This is for you. I made it myself and was going to give it to you for Christmas but you may as well take it now and use it on your bed in the nurses' quarters."

Tina was speechless as her aunt opened up the blanket to show her. It was multicoloured and hand knitted with her name beautifully embroidered in the corner. She loved it. "Oh Aunty, thank you so much. I love it. You are just so kind to me."

After they all finished their tea and cakes Tina helped to tidy up and then she had to go. Her Uncle Fred offered to drive her home with the blanket and handed her a tin. She opened the tin and when she looked inside, she could see it was full of her Uncle Fred's favourite sweets.

"You take these with you and any time things get tough just have one of my sweets and know that we are always here for you," Fred said with a smile.

***

Six weeks later Tina was all set to begin her new adventure. Leaving her home felt strange to her. She never thought she would feel sad leaving but she did. She saw Patch hobbling around in the back garden. He was getting so old now.

Tina went up to her bedroom one last time before leaving. Her bedroom had been her sanctuary, her safe place for so long. She sat on her bed allowing herself to indulge in the recollections of her past and all the emotions she had expressed within the confines of her bedroom walls. She closed her eyes as her mind flooded with memories of her singing into her hairbrush or the sounds of her mother calling her down for her tea. She placed her hand to her cheek as she remembered the tears she had once shed after discovering her secret. She walked to her bedroom door and took one last look around and looking at the bed, she smiled at the memory of when she boldly dared to change her name all those years ago.

Suddenly her thoughts were interrupted. "Tina, c'mon love, it's time to go now." Her dad was calling her. She grabbed an old cardigan that she had left on her bed and brought it downstairs to put in Patch's bed. She thought it might comfort him to have her smell around him. After helping her dad put her bags in the car, she went into the kitchen to say goodbye to her mother.

"Here, I have packed you some sandwiches for the journey," her mother said. "Now go on, you go now and I'll talk to you soon."

Tina thanked her mother and took the sandwiches before leaving. She thought she saw a glimmer of a tear in her mother's eye but she could not be sure. As she made her way to the car, she heard her mother shouting to her from the kitchen.

"Goodbye Tina, good luck now and stay safe."

Chapter 9

As Tina and her dad drove further away from the house, she could feel a shiver flow through her as she said goodbye in her head to her childhood hometown.

"Are you OK love?" her dad asked.

"Yes Dad," she said as she opened her window to take in some fresh air. It was going to be a long journey but she was looking forward to it.

It was almost a two-hour journey by car from Orpington to London. They found somewhere to stop and eat their sandwiches and her dad had made a flask of tea as well. Soon they were on the road again and in no time at all they were in London.

The city was bustling. As she looked out of her window, Tina saw girls walking around looking very glamorous and draped in the height of fashion. Tina rarely went to London to shop

It was far too expensive. She could not believe this was going to be her home.

When they arrived at the training hospital in London, Tina got out of the car and stared in awe at the building in front of her. She was lost for words and could feel butterflies stirring inside her. Her dad got her cases from the boot of the car and put his hand on her shoulder.

"Are you ready love? I may not say it often enough but I am so very proud of you. I never thought that a child of mine could ever make something of themselves. I am going to miss you. The house will be quiet without you in it."

"Oh Dad, thank you but I couldn't have done it without your support. I will miss you too but I will write to you often. I promise."

They both walked inside the hospital building and into the large reception area. Albert waited until Tina had registered and signed in. They hugged again for the last time before he left as he had a long journey home ahead of him.

Tina stood and watched as her dad walked out of the hospital. She knew she would miss him but she was excited to begin this new chapter in her life. She took a deep breath and then looked around to take in her surroundings. The floors were grey marble and the walls were cold white stone and seemed to tower around her. She asked a girl behind a desk where she should go and she brought Tina to a luggage room where she could store her cases until she was taken to her accommodation. She then made her way through two big double doors that opened onto a long corridor that seemed never ending. Once she reached the end of the corridor, she pushed open another heavy door labeled 'Student area'.

As she opened the door, Tina was faced with a long staircase that had a big sign saying 'registration and learning centre' at the bottom step. Tina followed the sign and walked tentatively up the staircase. Luckily, there were just two flights of stairs. When she got to the top, she saw big open double doors leading into a huge room. A lady stood at the doorway holding a clipboard and pen. Tina asked her if she was in the right place and the lady looked up her name on the clipboard and told her she was, so Tina nervously walked in the room. She stood at the doorway glancing around at her surroundings. Tall rather grand looking windows adorned the far wall and each window had long heavy red velvet curtains draped from them. A beautiful chandelier hung elegantly from the centre of the ceiling. At the top of the room, there was a podium set up and behind that stood two long tables placed together with three chairs pushed into them. Long rows of chairs were placed facing the podium and the room was filled with groups of girls standing around nattering away to each other. As Tina turned to look around, she saw a girl standing in the corner looking a little lost, so she walked over and introduced herself.

"Hello, my name is Tina," she said whilst holding out her hand to the girl.

"Hello Tina, my name is Margaret," the girl replied and shook Tina's hand. "I'm from Ireland. It's my first time away from home. I've never been outside of Ireland before. I really don't know anyone at all."

Tina loved that Margaret accepted her name without question. "Well I'm feeling a little nervous as well so why don't we both sit together? I'm sure we'll be fine once we settle in. I'm so excited, are you?"

"Oh yes, I'm very excited. This place is so big and looks posh compared to some hospitals I have seen back home in Ireland. I would love to sit with you. Oh we will be grand. Let's stick together."

Grand? What does that mean? Must be an Irish thing!

The big double doors were closed and people were being asked to take a seat, so the two girls found a space up at the front of the room. They sat in their seats busily chatting and getting to know eachother when the doors opened and there was silence as a tall dark-haired man entered the room and quietly took his place at the speaker's podium. He introduced himself as Professor Wall. A rather stern-looking woman with big wide eyes that glared around the hall at everyone as she walked followed Professor Wall into the room. This lady was introduced as Matron. She sat on one of the chairs at the tables behind the professor. A small woman then walked in and smiled at everyone as she looked around the hall. She was introduced to everyone as Sister Ann.

Professor Wall talked the student nurses through his expectations as far as learning and teaching were concerned. He was a nice man and even cracked a few jokes, which Matron didn't seem to find funny at all. Sister Ann outlined what their initial duties would be and how they should conduct themselves when on the wards with patients. Sister Ann was small in stature but Tina could tell she was a woman who would not tolerate mistakes. Matron was the last to speak. The microphone screeched as she pulled it towards her and began to talk. Silence soon ensued. She scanned the room as if she was trying to look inside the heads of everyone sat watching her.

"Good afternoon. I am Matron and I am incharge of all aspects of patient care. I am also responsible for all of you." Matron stopped to gauge the student nurses' reactions. "I expect the highest standards of cleanliness and professionalism to be upheld at all times. When you wear a nurse's uniform you are representing the hospital and the nursing profession. You must conduct yourselves with the upmost of self-respect and professionalism. You must perform your duties exactly as directed by Sister Ann and myself or any doctor that should give you direction. We do not expect to have to ask you twice. I hope that is understood."Again, Matron paused and looked around the room. "We will hold a more formal introduction to your training and our expectations. However, there is one thing I would like to make clear to you all since we are together. I do not tolerate any foolishness in the nurse quarters at all. You must treat your rooms with respect and dignity and this means no parties and absolutely no boys are allowed in your rooms under any circumstances." At that, a few giggles emanated from the students. Matron paused, her mouth closed shut and she looked like she had sucked on a lemon. "Anyone who finds this humorous can put their hand up and share their humorous view with me now."

Silence fell across the room.

"Good, it seems we all understand eachother," Matron responded."There are booklets in your rooms outlining the rules so please read sign and return them to Sister Ann."Matron continued to outline her rules and then finished by wishing them the best of luck in their training.

Tina thought her mother seemed like a kitten compared to this woman.

Next, the new students were brought on tours of the hospital. They were shown around the learning centre and the main wards that they would be assigned to as part of their training. Once the tours had finished they were shown to the nurses' residence and given their room numbers and room keys. To enter the nurses' quarters the students had to go through a reception room. This room was located through a door to the left just inside the main hospital reception area and this was the only way a student could enter the nurses 'residence. There was a warden stationed in the reception room. One of his main responsibilities was to ensure all students abided by the strict etiquette of signing in and out of their quarters. He also had to carry out daily and nightly patrols of the corridors to ensure no rule breaking was going on. Matron would regularly inspect the 'Sign in book' and if any student was signed in after the curfew time of 10:00pm without a genuine reason or if they broke any of her rules they would face disciplinary action. There was a communal 'television room' which was locked at 10 O'clock every night without fail and only the warden held the key.

On the ground floor there was an inspection room. This was where the ward sister would carry out a uniform inspection every morning before the student nurses were allowed on the wards. As it transpired Tina and Margaret were both to share a room with eachother. A third girl called Linda was also assigned to their room, which was situated on the ground floor.

Tina never had any real friends and she certainly never had sisters so sharing her accommodation was going to be a real change for her but she was looking forward to it. The room Tina, Margaret and Linda were to share was a plain room with a set of bunk beds and one single bed. Tina jumped on the single bed and Margaret ran to the bottom bunk bed, which meant Linda had to take the top bunk bed. There was one large wardrobe, two sets of drawers, and two desks in the room that had to be shared between the three girls.

The girls found a booklet on their beds. It was the booklet that Matron had talked about in her introductions. The three girls sat in silence reading their booklets giggling at some of the rules but vowed they would not dare to break any of them. They did not fancy being in trouble with Matron.

The rules of the nurses' residence were very strict and outlined as follows...

1. *Under no circumstances are male visitors allowed within the nurses' residence.*

2. *No parties allowed in any area within hospital grounds or the nurse residence.*

3. *No romantic relationships permitted within the first three years of training.*

4. *Curfew is 10pmand students must be in their room by that time.*

5. *Students can avail of one late pass per week.*

6. *All students must sign in and out of the building at the warden station.*

7. *The warden will report any rule breaking to Matron*

8. *Anyone caught breaking the rules will face strict disciplinary action.*

Tina began unpacking her case. She took out the beautiful blanket that her Aunt Daisy had made for her and spread it out over her bed. The comforting smell of her aunt's perfume wafted around the room. She took her Uncle Fred's tin of sweets and placed them in her top locker drawer but not before sneaking a sweet out of the tin and placing it in her mouth. She had a picture of Patch and her dad, which she managed to sneak out of her mother's private box and stood it on top of her bedside locker. Linda had sneaked a radio into the room that her mother had given to her and the girls planned to listen to it with the sound down low so as not to draw attention to their room.

It had been a long day and eventually the student nurses were shown their eating quarters. They were fed with whatever food was left over from the main hospital that day. After dinner, they all retired to their rooms. Margaret, Tina and Linda sat chatting as a way to get to know eachother.

"Tina, do you mind if I ask you something?" Margaret asked.

"No not at all. Go ahead," replied Tina.

"Well, I cannot help but notice you have a hearing aid. I didn't really notice it before because you had your cardigan closed and your hair draped down over your shoulders hiding the cords. Do you have a hearing problem? I hope you don't mind me asking."

Tina was taken aback a little. "Yes, I do have a hearing problem. It is not too bad but my hearing aid helps me. I can lip read so I never miss a thing. Why do you ask?"

"Well, I know a girl back home in Ireland who was training to be a nurse here in the UK and she was sent home because she also had poor hearing. So I was just curious."

Tina had never let her hearing issues hold her back

in life. Thanks to deaf club she had learned to cope with it and she was very good at lip reading so it was rarely an issue for her. "Oh no, what will I do?" Tina asked the girls.

"You will do nothing." Said Linda. You say nothing. Margaret and I will help you, won't we?"

"Of course we will. If you sit beside us in lectures then we can tell you anything you may not hear. Plus, you can always use my notes to study from if you miss anything. You'll be grand." Margaret assured her. "It will be our secret."

"Oh, thank you so much girls it really won't be a problem. I'll find a way to hide my aids or maybe not wear them and rely on lip reading. Or I can clip the aid to my bra and stuff one ear piece into the bra with just one wire under my dress and around the back of my head. It will be well hidden by the nurse's hat if I pull it down low enough. I'll work something out," Tina replied, as they got ready for bed.

Chapter 10

Tina loved nurse training. She felt proud that her work would involve helping those most in need. As part of her training, she learned how to deal with the more sensitive aspects of a nurse's role. Like how to comfort patients who were suffering from injuries that would change their lives forever. They also had to learn how to cope with hearing a family's heartbreaking cries after the death of a loved one. She knew it would be difficult at times but she believed that nursing must be one of the most rewarding careers she could ever have wished to have.

In those days the life of a student nurse was tough and the days were long. All students had to wake at 6am every morning. They had to get breakfast be washed and dressed make their beds and ensure their rooms were spotless in time for uniform inspection by 07:30am.

Some of the most valuable learning took place in the wards. Sister Ann and Matron regularly carried out ward inspections. They were very strict. If a nurse made the slightest of mistake whilst making a bed, she would have to do it again from the beginning. Tina once had to make the same bed four times under the constant glare of Sister Ann until she finally got it right. Although Sister Ann was strict, she was nothing compared to Matron who ruled with a rod of Iron and nobody not even the most senior doctor dared to go against Matron and her rules.

A student nurse's primary responsibilities were

taking temperatures, making beds, giving bed baths plus administering and cleaning the bedpans. They were also responsible for making and serving all meals to the patients. These jobs were tiresome but Tina enjoyed them because she knew the patients needed her and every task she undertook was an important one in a patient's recovery.

***

Student nurses were subjected to numerous pranks from the more senior staff members. It was a sort of initiation into the hospital. On one occasion, whilst working on the ward one of the senior shift nurses called Tina over to her."Tina, I need you to go and locate a fallopian tube for me. It's most important. You may need to ask one of the doctors to give you theirs."

Tina was eager to please, so she went on the hunt for a fallopian tube as requested."Sorry Doctor but can I ask if you could possibly give me your fallopian tube as the senior shift nurse cannot seem to find hers."

The doctor looked from under his glasses across the

ward at the nurses who were huddled together eagerly watching Tina. "No, I do not have a fallopian tube but you will most definitely find one in the next ward as I specifically saw one there." Tina thanked him and made her way to the next ward.

The doctor on the next ward laughed when he heard Tina's request. "Oh my dear if the senior shift nurse could not find her fallopian tube I would seriously doubt her credentials."

Tina looked puzzled. "I'm sorry but what do you mean?"

The doctor placed his hand on her shoulder and moved in close to her. "My dear girl a fallopian tube is a rather important piece of female anatomy. It is not a medical instrument. I most certainly do not have one. I rather think someone is having a laugh at your expense." The doctor grinned and told her to hurry back to her ward in case Matron saw her.

Tina's face was bright red and the nurses responsible for her embarrassment laughed when they saw her walking towards them. She eventually saw the funny side and took it all in good spirit but swore to be more aware of the requests from other nurses from that day onwards.

When she told the girls what had happened, Linda told her a similar thing had happened to her the previous night. She had been on her first night shift. The senior nurse, Julie, had called her over to the nurse station where two other nurses were also sitting. "Linda, as a vital part of nurse training I am going to teach you the quickest and easiest way to know if a patient has a urinary infection."Julie then picked up a small clear plastic pot with orange liquid in it. "OK, so this is a urine sample from the patient in bed three. She has abdominal pain so I collected a urine sample from her in this pot." Julie had held the pot up to Linda's eye level and took off the lid. "Infected urine tastes sweet so you simply take a sip, like this." She took a sip from the sample pot. She then closed her eyes as if to focus on the taste in her mouth. Linda looked at her in shock.

She couldn't believe what she was seeing."So, now you take a sip and tell me how it tastes to you Linda. Go on just a quick taste will tell you all you need to know."Julie handed the pot to Linda.

Linda took hold of the pot but in her head, she was disgusted at the thought of having to drink urine. She put the pot to her mouth and as the liquid touched her lips, she could hear the two nurses laughing aloud. Linda realised the liquid was sweet but it was actually watered-down orange juice. She had been the victim of a prank just like countless other trainee nurses before her. She laughed out of pure relief that she had not actually drunk urine!

The nurses were laughing hard whilst trying not to wake the patients. "Oh my goodness, you did not really think I was being serious, did you? All you students are just too easy to trick!" Julie was very amused indeed. Just then, the unmistakable sound of Matron's heavy footsteps could be heard trundling towards the main door to the ward prompting the nurses to scatter and appear to look busy.

As time went by Tina and her fellow students found inventive ways to avoid Matron and break her rules without being caught by the warden. Linda loved partying until late as did many of the students. On party nights students in the nurses' quarters would leave the latch off a downstairs window so they could climb back in late at night and creep back silently to their rooms. Sometimes they would make noise, which would alert the warden who was not always quick enough to catch them so they hardly ever got into trouble. Sometimes, if the warden were in a good mood he would turn a blind eye and say nothing.

***

After the first four months all the student nurses were given a well-deserved long weekend off so they could go home to see family. Margaret was getting a ferry Thursday night to Ireland. She was so excited and even though she would only have three nights in Ireland she simply could not wait to see her family. She was feeling a little homesick so this break could not have happened at a better time for her. Tina was getting the train home to Kent on Friday morning and Linda was going to hang around the nurses' quarters because her parents were out of the country but she was looking forward to having the room all to herself!

Tina was excited to tell her parents all about her training. She just hoped they would be interested. Of course, she also planned to see her Uncle Fred and Aunt Daisy as she had missed them both so much.

She got the bus from the train station that stopped just five minutes away from her house. She got home to find her mother and father both sat in the sitting room.

"Great to see you love. Now sit down and I'll get you a nice cup of tea." Her dad made his way to the kitchen to put the kettle on.

Her mother asked how she was getting on so Tina told about all of her news.

"That's nice dear. Now I need to pop out, but I will see you later." Her mother then got up out of her seat and went into the kitchen to get her coat.

When her dad bought in the tea he listened intently as she told him all her news. He told her he was so glad she loved her new life and that he was proud of her. Tina asked if he had any news for her.

He shook his head."Oh actually, yes, yes, I do. You remember Alice Brown, don't you? Your old friend. Well, she has only gone and got married."Albert whispered as he spoke. It was as if he did not want people to hear him even though there were only the two of them in the house."But that's not all. She is also expecting her first child. Isn't that lovely. I am glad everything worked out for her. Mind you, it all happened very fast. She only got married a month ago and now she's pregnant. She most likely was already pregnant when she married. At least that is what your mother thinks." Albert sipped the last drop of tea from his cup.

"Yes, she most probably was Dad," Tina replied, shaking her head. This baby would not be Alice's first child. This would be her second child. *Why was her first child forgotten about? Was he less important just because he was born out of marriage?* She changed the conversation because she knew she would just get upset and she did not want that to happen. Looking around the room she wondered why she had not seen Patch yet. Usually, he would come to her as soon as she walked through the door. "Where is Patch Dad?"

Her dad nodded his head toward the kitchen. "Oh poor Patch is in the corner by the back door love. Lately, all he does is sleep. He's been at the vet's a few times and he thinks the tumours are back. I think he has just missed you. He's pining, that's all. Hopefully seeing you will perk him up." Albert smiled.

Tina walked into the kitchen to see her old furry friend. Patch was nearly eighteen years old. For a dog he was practically an old age pensioner. "Aw my poor little man," Tina said whilst rubbing Patch gently on his head. He opened his eyes briefly and looked up at her. His tail started to wag but he was tired so she left him alone. He knew all her secrets. He was her world and if anything happened to him she would be devastated.

Tina went to see her Uncle Fred and Aunt Daisy who were both excited to see her and hear all her news. Her aunt had baked a lovely sponge cake that they all ate with a nice cup of tea whilst Tina told them all of her news. She always felt so much love from her aunt and uncle. When she was with them, she felt safe. It made a nice change to be the centre of attention and she lapped it up. Her dad came to collect her, but before she left, her uncle gave her another bag of sweets for her tin, which Tina was thrilled about because her initial stash was all gone.

Later that evening Florence had made a lovely dinner. She even used the good china, which only ever got used on special occasions.

"Tina your father and I have news for you. Sadly,

Patch has to go to the vet tomorrow. He has not been well and lately he has not been eating his food. The vet had to do some tests. He'll give us the results tomorrow and if the tumours have returned then Patch will have to be put to sleep."

Tina put her knife and fork on her plate. "Put to Sleep?" She could not believe what she was hearing. "But surely he's not that bad. Surely there are treatments available like last time." She looked at her dad for some support. "You didn't say anything about having him put to sleep Dad?"

He looked up at Tina, "I am sorry love but you were only just in the door and I didn't want to upset you." He put down his knife and placed his hand on Tina's arm. "There are no more treatments. If this is the tumours again then we have no other option."

"Oh poor Patch can I go with him to the vets please? I can't bear to think of him being scared."

"Of course. You and your father can go together. I know how important he is to you. I'll say my goodbyes before you leave just in case he doesn't come home," her mother said softly.

They sat talking about Patch and their memories of him as a young dog. He had been such a huge part of their family and had touched each one of them in his own loving way. Tina was sad but managed to suppress her tears because she knew her mother wouldn't like it.

That night Tina decided if this was going to be Patch's last night in this world then he should not spend it alone. She went to her bedroom bought her blankets and pillow downstairs to the kitchen and set up her bed beside Patch. She sat chatting to her furry friend whose black and white patches of fur had now turned a dark shade of grey. She reminisced about all their times together and for the first time Patch did not have the strength to prick up his ears as she talked. She did not want him to feel her sadness so Tina did what she always did when she was feeling down. She sang to him.

In the morning she awoke to what felt like a sticky

damp cloth on her face. When she opened her eyes, she saw patch, who was licking her cheek."Oh Patch, what is the matter little man. I wish you could talk to me. I wish you could tell me how I can help you to feel better again."

***

After breakfast Tina wrapped Patch in a blanket and sat in the car with him on her lap. When Tina, Patch, and her dad got to the surgery they had to sit in the waiting room. As she sat with Patch on her knee, she remembered the early days when he was a young dog. He was a war survivor and if her dad had not seen him when he did Patch would have been put to sleep along with thousands of other animals. When their name was called, Tina and her dad walked into the examination room and she placed Patch on the table where Dr Munroe could give him a thorough examination. The silence in the room was stifling and made Tina very nervous. Poor Patch was so calm whilst Dr Munroe pressed his tummy. Suddenly, Patch let out a little yelp. The vet stopped and softly petted Patch on his head before continuing. Once the examination was finished, Dr Munroe looked at both Tina and her dad. He didn't have to say a word the look on his face said it all. Tina instinctively knew it would not be good news.

"I am so sorry but sadly Patch is very sick and all treatment so far is not working."

Dr Munroe spoke softly as he told them the devastating news. There was no more treatment available and Patch would most likely be in a lot of pain.

"Love, you know what this means. Patch will need to be put to sleep. It is the kindest thing we can do for our old friend. He has been such a great pet and brought us so much joy. So now it's our turn to do what's best for him." Her dad wiped his eye with the back of his hand.

Tina could see this was hard for her dad as well. It

broke her heart to know Patch was suffering but she knew her dad was right. She just didn't realise how hard it would be to hear it put into words. She wrapped Patch in the blanket again and asked if she could hold him. Dr Munroe agreed.

She picked up her furry friend and held him in her arms as she talked to him for the last time. "OK Patch my old pal, this will be our last walk together but you don't have to be scared. I will be with you every step of the way. I will hold you close my brave, brave little boy," Tina said whilst fighting her tears.

He had been there throughout her life. He had comforted her through some of the most difficult times. She didn't want Patch to feel her fear because this was not about her. This was all about him and comforting him in his hour of need. Tina felt privileged to be with him. It was the least he deserved.

Her dad put his arm around her and with his other hand he rubbed Patch on his head and said, "Goodbye, my boy." Patch lay in Tina's arms, staring into her eyes as Dr Munroe gave him the injection. Within seconds, his eyes slowly closed. Tina drew her head close to Patch and whispered gently into his ear. "Goodbye my friend."

And that was it Patch was gone.

Chapter 11

By the end of the second year of the nurse training in 1959 Linda had a boyfriend and was always going out on dates with him. Tina was far more refined and shy than the other girls. She worried for Linda because if Matron discovered that any student had a boyfriend, she would not be happy with them. Tina often went out with the girls, she loved to dance but that was all she did. When it came to the boys, she was not so confident. However, in her third year of training, there was a fine-looking junior doctor with blonde hair and blue eyes called Jonathan who was very taken with Tina. He was always asking her for help with a patient or he would magically appear in the canteen when she was on her breaks. He had asked Tina out on a date a few times and she always made excuses not to go. She had never been on a date before. She did not know how to talk to a man. Not in that way anyway. Linda told Tina if she kept saying no then he would give up asking and that would be such a shame. Eventually Tina said yes and Dr Jonathan brought her to the cinema with a promise to have her back to the nurses' quarters before the curfew.

The date went well. They saw a cheeky comedy called Carry on Constable and Tina loved it. As time went by, they saw more and more of each other and went on many dates. She was thrilled with her life until one day whilst in the canteen with Dr Jonathan she saw a side to him that truly shocked her.

He mentioned a junior nurse who had to leave the

hospital under suspicious circumstances.

"What do you mean by 'suspicious circumstances'? What happened?" asked Tina.

Dr Jonathan leaned in close. "Well rumour has it she's gotten herself pregnant," he said with a smirk on his face."Don't look at me like that Tina. It's all true. She was doing a line with one of my colleagues. She claims he is the father of her unborn baby. Can you believe that?"

Tina stared at him as he ate his lunch. *She didn't make the baby by herself. What did he mean she had 'gotten herself pregnant'?*"And what does your colleague say about it all?"Tina asked whilst placing her knife and fork onto her plate in anticipation of his reply.

Dr Jonathan seemed surprised that Tina would ask such a thing."Well of course he denies it. I mean if she slept with him then God knows who else she slept with. He has his career to think of in all of this." It was as if he thought the nurse was completely in the wrong and nothing could possibly be blamed on the junior doctor. "Luckily for him his father happens to be a very senior doctor at this hospital. His father has had a word with Matron and now the nurse has been told to leave. Talk about a life saver, eh?"

Tina's response was cutting. "Oh yes, a real blessing in disguise." *My god, who is this man? How could he be so unkind? I thought he was better than this.* "But did anyone stop to think she might actually be right? Maybe he is the baby's father," Tina said trying hard not to raise her voice. "She didn't make the baby by herself you know. It takes two. Surely being a doctor you know that much about human biology" Tina grew agitated and she could not bear to look at Dr Jonathan anymore.

"Why are you siding with the nurse? My colleague has a promising career. He really doesn't need this right now. No, the baby will have to go. It's not like he would marry her anyway. She's just a nur—" Dr. Jonathan stopped himself mid-sentence. He could see how upset Tina was.

"Oh, please don't stop on my account. Go on say it. She's just a nurse. That is what you meant to say wasn't it?" Tina blurted. "Well this nurse has somewhere else to be so please excuse me. I have to get back to work." Tina stood up and walked away leaving Dr Jonathan sitting stunned at the canteen table by himself. Nobody had ever talked to him like that or at least not a woman anyway.

As Tina walked out of the canteen, she could see people were looking at her. She did not realise how loudly she must have been speaking.

She was disappointed and angry with Dr Jonathan but she was also sad for the junior nurse. Tina hoped she had a kind loving and supportive family that would help her. Otherwise, she would most likely have to go to one of those awful mother and baby homes. *What about her unborn child? What will happen to her baby? Why does nobody seem to care about the baby in all of this?* Just thinking about it was heartbreaking for Tina as she felt old emotional wounds slowly opening once more.

Wounds she thought she would never have to deal with again.

She got back to her ward, straightened her uniform and put a smile on her face. She could not allow the patients to see that she was upset. For the first time since meeting Dr Jonathan, Tina felt she just could not be around him so she avoided him for the rest of the day. When he asked if they could meet later to talk, she lied and said she had a headache.

After her shift she went straight to her room, changed out of her uniform, unpinned her nurse's cap and brushed her hair. She flopped on her bed and as she turned on her side, she saw the picture of her old dog Patch. He always knew how to comfort her when she needed it as a child. She sat up and placed her hairbrush back into the locker drawer where she noticed her Uncle Fred's sweet tin. There were two sweets left so she picked one out and put it in her mouth thinking how much she would have loved a big hug from him and her Aunt Daisy in that moment.

Her aunt would know exactly what she should do in her current situation. She lay back down onto the bed and draped her Aunt Daisy's blanket around her for extra comfort.

Taking the edge of the blanket in her hand she rubbed her finger over the lettering of her name embroidered on the corner. *Tina*, she said the name in her head remembering when she was fourteen and had changed her name from Christine to Tina. She remembered how energised it made her feel. She was trying to make a point about who she was and ever since that day she had desperately tried to distance herself from her past. From all the lies hurt and secrecy that now seemed to have crept back into her world. However, now she wondered how Dr Jonathan would react if he knew her secret. Would he think she was a shameful unwanted child? Would he think I should have been gotten rid of? Does he have no compassion at all? Tina always believed if people truly cared about her then her past shouldn't matter. However, right now she was too scared to put that particular theory to the test and she did not know if she would ever be ready.

Suddenly she heard familiar footsteps nearing the door to the room. It was Margaret. She came bouncing in full of fun and laughter declaring she had heard some juicy gossip.

Tina sat up in the bed she looked at Margaret and asked her if her juicy gossip was about the same junior nurse Dr Jonathan had told her.

"Yes, it must be true!"Margaret looked at Tina and realised she had been crying. "Oh Tina, what is the matter with you? Are you OK?"

Tina did not know how to put her feelings into words. She wiped her eyes and pulled her blanket around her. "Oh Margaret, I have had the worst day. I don't know where to begin"

"How about you begin at the beginning," Margaret said with a smile.

"OK, well, it's just…" She was about to tell Margaret when Linda came bounding into the room with the same gossip spewing from her mouth. That was the final straw. Tina could not contain herself as a familiar anger took over her thoughts once more. "Oh for god's sake girls, have you nothing else to talk about. Surely you can find something better to do instead of picking on the unfortunate circumstances of someone else. What business is it if yours or anybody else for that matter?" Tina was visibly upset and wondered if she knew her friends at all.

Margaret and Linda were silent, not knowing how they should react. Linda turned and looked at Tina. Her eyes were open wide and her hands slapped against her cheeks. "Oh Tina, you aren't pregnant, are you? Is that why you are so obviously upset by this news?"

Hearing this only made Tina even angrier. "Really!" she shouted whilst throwing her hands in the air in frustration. Then she looked up and saw the shock and horror on her two friends' faces. She took a deep breath and tried hard to stay calm. "Is that all you can say? Do you honestly think that about me? Anyway, I am a virgin so it's quite impossible." Tina said whilst flicking her long black hair behind her shoulder.

At this point both Margaret and Linda glared at her. Neither of them knowing what to say or how to respond to that particular piece of information. After a few moments of awkward silence Linda turned away to get changed out of her uniform. She was hungry and was meeting her biker boyfriend for dinner. Margaret was getting changed out of her uniform and began sheepishly tidying around her bed. She could not bear the awkward silence that had filled the room and could see Tina was upset and deep in thought about something.

Linda said her goodbyes and left the room. "So what on earth is the matter with you Tina?"Margaret asked breaking the silence and sitting on the bed beside her friend. "We're best friends. You can tell me anything. Please, just tell me how I can help you."

With that, Tina broke down crying. *How can I explain my secret to my friend? What will she think of me?*

Tina asked herself. She took a deep breath, dried her eyes and pulled herself together. She began by telling Margaret the bare bones of her earlier conversation with Dr Jonathan and how shocked she was at his attitude. She told Margaret how he talked about the junior nurse and showed so little regard or thought for the baby that was yet to be born.

Margaret smiled. "Well that's just men for you Tina. They don't see things like us women see them. I come from a house full of men. Trust me they are a different species altogether. My mother always told me a man needs a good woman to keep him on the straight and narrow and she is right. Is that it? Is that all that has you so upset? It is not as if you are the one having to leave the hospital. How did you leave things with him? Will you be seeing him later?"

"Oh I walked away. I lied and told him I had a headache."

"Why did you do that? I don't understand." Margaret replied looking puzzled.

"No, I know you don't understand how could you? There is a lot you don't know and I am so sorry I snapped at you. That was very wrong of me," Tina said.

Margaret's eyes opened wide upon hearing her words. "So there is more? Tell me Tina, please. Help me understand because you are not making much sense," Margaret asked.

"OK I'll tell you, but before I do I need you to promise me you will not tell another soul. Do you promise me Margaret? I need to know I can trust you."

"I promise I won't say a word to anyone, cross my heart," Margaret said whilst making the sign of the cross upon her chest.

"I have a secret Margaret. It's one my mother forbade me from telling anyone, EVER." Tina opened up to Margaret and before she knew it she had told her everything. She told her all about her adoption and the lady she met when she was fourteen and how scared she was of people's reaction if they found out the truth. Strangely, she felt so much calmer after talking to

Margaret. She could not believe she had held it all in for so long.

At first there was silence and then Margaret wrapped her arms around Tina. "Oh Tina I know many girls back home who had to have babies in those homes. It is just shocking. But it is not your fault and if anyone gives you a hard time you come and get me and I will deal with them you hear me?" Margaret told her she could trust her and it would be their secret. "So what are you going to do about Doctor Jonathan?"

"Oh I don't know Margaret. I am not sure if I want anything more to do with him. I need to concentrate on my training so I think it may be best to end things with him." She wiped her tears and the girls began to giggle. They decided to lighten the mood in the room by turning on the radio and having a singsong into their hairbrushes. It was a very welcomed distraction.

Tina decided she never wanted to be in a situation where she would have to explain herself or admit her past to a man and be rejected because of it. She ended things with Dr Jonathan. She told him she needed to focus on her training. He didn't seem to be too bothered and just weeks later, she saw him with another nurse. He was rumoured to be seeing a few of the nurses at the same time, so she was happy to be away from him. As far as she was concerned she had a lucky escape and they were welcome to him.

Chapter 12

At last, Tina was in her final year of her training. The time had gone by so fast and it only seemed like yesterday she had first began her training. She and all the student nurses had studied hard. The last few months before the exams were the quietest the nurses' quarters had ever been. The months turned into weeks and the weeks into days and before she knew it, the end was in sight.

Tina had become very good at hiding her hearing

aids from Sister Ann and Matron. There had been some minor instances where she couldn't hear a patient or had to ask a doctor to repeat himself. Sometimes the other nurses on the ward had to tell her if a patient was calling her but so far, she had kept her hearing problems away from the attention of Sister Ann or Matron.

***

It was a Monday Morning and Tina was on a full twelve-hour shift on the ward. A young female patient, Jill, was admitted to the ward. It was Tina's job to care for her so she settled Jill in to bed two on her ward. Jill was in pain and Tina was busily tending to another patient when Sister Ann pulled Tina aside. "Tina what is wrong with you today? Your patient in bed two has been calling for you and you haven't been near her at all."Sister Ann was not happy. Tina turned to look at Jill who seemed in distress."I am so sorry Sister I will go to her now."

"Please do, and be more attentive in the future. The

patients rely on you. This is not the first time either. I have noticed you seem to ignore people when they talk to you. I have made allowances for you because you will make an exceptional nurse but this is the last time Tina." Then Sister Ann signaled Tina to go to Jill. Tina did as she was asked but she was worried that Sister Ann would discover her hearing problem. She had come so far and managed so well, or so she thought.

***

When her shift finished Tina sat in her room by herself. Margaret and Linda were still working on the wards. She thought about every experience she had throughout her training. Nursing was not the glamorous job she thought it would be. The hospitals were under-staffed and under-funded. After the war many nurses left the profession because of everything they saw during that time. This meant that staff were very hard to find and those who stayed had to do twice or three times the amount of work they used to do. Of all twenty-seven student nurses that had lived on the ground floor in the nurse quarters only fifteen of them remained. Some of the girls left because they didn't like Matron or they could not cope when patients died. Some left to get married and some just seemed to vanish or leave in 'suspicious' circumstances. Tina was glad she stuck it out. She felt so proud of how far she had come in her life.

Tina was worried about Sister Ann and the incident on the ward with Jill. *Was I fooling myself to think nobody would find out?* Just then, she heard laughter in the corridor outside her room as the door opened.

It was Linda and Margaret. They had finished their shifts and were full of chat about a new doctor they had seen. He was getting a lot of attention from the nurses. Margaret said that even Matron seemed giddy when she was around him. "Honestly Tina, you should have seen Matron whenever he was around. He asked for a patient's notes and she was completely tongue tied and went bright red in the face." Margaret and Linda were laughing out loud.

"Mind you I am glad we finished our shift before he left the ward because those nurses that were laughing in the corner will have felt the wrath of Matron once he was out of sight," Linda said. They all had a good laugh at the thought of Matron swooning over a doctor.

"So how was your afternoon Tina? Did you miss us?" asked Margaret.

"Oh it was lovely to just relax and do nothing."

"I thought you would be asleep after your twelve-hour shift. What has you awake?" Margaret asked.

"My thoughts, that's what!" Tina replied. Then she told them both about the incident on the ward with Sister Ann. "I hope she doesn't ask too many questions about my hearing. I would hate for her to find out."

"Don't be worrying Tina if she thought there was a problem, she would have said it by now so just relax. Training is nearly over now so keep calm. It will be just fine," Margaret said.

Margaret and Linda went to have some dinner but

Tina had already eaten so she had an early night and went to bed instead.

***

The exams crept up on them and the three girls were filled with nerves. They studied together, they supported and encouraged eachother and before they knew it, the exams were all over. All that was left now was to wait for their results. Tina knew she had done her absolute best and prayed it was enough to get her through. Margaret had studied as best she could but she always doubted herself. Linda spent more time with her boyfriend than studying but she tried her best.

The day of the exam results finally arrived and Tina had never felt so anxious in her whole life. All students had to take a seat in the very same hall they were sent to on their first day at the hospital. Someone would come in to the hall and call out ten names at a time. Those ten students were then shown to seats in the hallway outside the room where the results were to be given. As well as receiving their results they would also receive information about work placement opportunities. Margaret, Linda, and Tina promised eachother that no matter what happened they would always be friends. Even if they were placed in different hospitals they promised they would always visit each other and stay in contact.

One by one, the student nurses were called into the office where the professor and head of nursing and recruitment were meeting with them. The three girls were called together and they sat nervously waiting and watching as students came out of the office. Some came out with massive smiles on their faces and others with tears in their eyes. The first of the three girls to be called in was Margaret. It felt like forever but she eventually came out with a massive grin on her face and Tina and Linda both jumped up to give her a big hug. Next Linda was called in to the office. Eventually, she came out and walked past Tina and Margaret. She could not even look at them. Tina was called in just as she and Margaret were about to run after Linda. It was agreed that Margaret would go after Linda and Tina would go find them once she had been given her results. Tina walked into the office her heart beating harder and harder with every step she took.

She had dreamt of being a nurse her whole life. Even when the bullies and teachers said she would never make anything of herself she never allowed them to stop her. Their cruel words just made her more determined than ever.

The professor shook Tina's hand and invited her to sit down on the brown wooden chair that sat next to a big table. Then he sat down and shuffled a few papers before placing them on the table. The silence was deafening. "Tina it is a pleasure for me to say you have passed all your exams and therefore have now qualified as a nurse."

The head of nursing smiled and congratulated Tina on passing her exams. She was thrilled and could hardly contain herself. She did it, she had qualified and she was going to be an amazing nurse. The professor asked if she had any questions. She asked where she was going to be placed. At this point, the head of recruitment looked at her with an awkward smile and bowed his head, which confused Tina.

He then raised his head and leaned forward. He placed his two arms outstretched on the table clutching his hands together. "We have looked at your overall record with the hospital. You have proved yourself a remarkable and capable nurse. It is obvious to everyone you have worked with that you love working in patient care."

Tina knew she should be pleased to hear this but she felt like there was more to come and it was making her nervous.

The head of recruitment cleared his throat. "Tina, I have a serious question for you and I need you to be truthful with me."

Tina looked at him and was stunned by his question. *What have I done? What does he want to ask me?* "Of course you can ask me anything. I am always truthful," Tina said.

"As part of our assessment when considering future positions within the hospital we always ask for a written report from Sister Ann and the Matron. We need to ensure that every nurse in our hospitals conducts herself impeccably without limitations. Your report states that you have been outstanding in your conduct. Your focus and attitude have been outstanding. However, it mentions some serious concerns about your hearing. I need to know if you are aware of any hearing problems. If not, then before we can decide your future in nursing, we will need to arrange some hearing competency tests for you."

Tina could feel her heart pounding hard in her chest. Her mouth felt dry and she did not know what to say. She asked for a glass of water to help her speak more clearly. *How do I handle this mess? I can't lie. I'm not a liar. I have to be honest but this could be the end of my hopes and dreams.*

"Tina, I need to know. Your silence is not filling me

with confidence."

Tina placed the empty glass on the table infront of her and looked the head of recruitment in the eye. "I do have a hearing problem. I am hard of hearing. I am not deaf and it has never been a problem for me."

The head of recruitment looked at the professor."We thought that might be the case. You really should have told us sooner. We have discussed your particular future here in great detail. In view of what you have just told us I am so sorry but we cannot place you in a nursing role."

Tina stared in shock. "I'm sorry. I don't understand. You say I have qualified so surely that proves I am capable. My hearing is not a big problem. Please don't do this to me. You have no idea how hard I have worked for this. Nursing has been a childhood dream of mine. Plus I'm fluent in sign language so I can help with deaf patients." As she spoke her tears became more and more uncontrollable.

The head of recruitment handed her a tissue. He

told her to wipe her eyes and try to calm down. "This isn't the end for you. We have another exciting opportunity to offer you and we hope you will accept it. With your qualifications and experience you would be a perfect fit for an opening in social work that has become available." He stopped talking and waited for Tina to calm down.

"The position would include both office and hospital-based work. Of course there may be weekend or evening lectures and you will need to sit some exams but we have every faith in you."

"But I only ever wanted to be a nurse. I've never even thought about social work." Tina replied.

At this point Professor Wall raised his hand as if to ask permission to speak. "Tina, you are a very able, dedicated, and caring person. You have skills that are far wider reaching than just nursing. For example, there is a high demand for social workers who can communicate with those who are hearing impaired. You say you are fluent in sign language so you are already practically fully trained for the job of social worker. I know you may be disappointed but please, please do not dismiss what's being offered to you today. You have worked far too hard to just throw it all away." He told her she needed to make her mind up as soon as possible. Tina promised they would have her decision by the end of the week.

Walking back to her room felt like the longest walk of her life. There were still girls sat outside the office eagerly waiting to be called in to be given their results. She could not even look at them as she passed them by. *How can this be happening? It's just another rejection in a long list of rejections in my life. Why is it always me? What's wrong with me? How can I possibly explain this to everyone and would they even believe me?* She felt like a failure and it was becoming the story of her life.

When she walked into the room Margaret and Linda were both sat on Linda's bed with their arms wrapped around eachother. "Linda didn't pass. She didn't qualify," Margaret whispered. Tina joined them as they embraced eachother. She pushed her worries aside to comfort her friend whilst trying to hold in her own emotions but she soon felt the familiar stinging of tears in her eyes.

Linda sat back and looked at Tina. "What has you so upset Tina? It's me who failed. Surely you passed? Didn't you?"

"Oh yes, yes, I passed but they told me that because of my hearing problem I can never work as a nurse."

Margaret and Linda were both speechless. "But how did they find out about your hearing problem?" Margaret asked.

"Apparently Sister Ann and the Matron write reports on all student nurses and on my report there were concerns for my hearing. So that was that." Tina stood up walked over to her own bed.

"You should have denied having a problem," Linda said.

"They said if I was not aware of any problems then I would have to have hearing tests. So, there was no point in lying. I should have known this was gonna happen. It's the story of my life. Nothing good ever happens to me."Tina threw herself back on her bed and stared at the ceiling. She turned on her side to face the girls. "It's not all bad though. They did give me the opportunity to apply for a social work position. Second best is better than nothing at all."

Margaret told her that was fantastic news."Tina that's great news. The hospital must have been very impressed with you because nobody else was given that opportunity."

Linda also tried to cheer her up. "Margaret is right Tina. Look at me, I was simply told I could repeat but that's it. If I don't repeat then I have nothing."Linda was not as disappointed as Tina because she always said that nursing was not her first choice of career. Her mother wanted her to train as a nurse. "Plus, you still get to work with patients. You still get to work with people in need just like you always wanted to do. Oh Tina you'll be an amazing social worker," Linda said.

Tina perked up a little because the girls were right. She was just so upset because nursing had been all that she had ever dreamt of being from a very young age.

Tina and Linda both congratulated Margaret and told her they were thrilled for her. Now all Tina had to do was tell her parents.

Chapter 13

Tina had arranged to meet the head of recruitment to discuss her decision about the social work position. She entered his office and made herself comfortable in the chair at his desk. "First, I want to thank you for recommending me for the social work position. I have had lots of time to think about what I want for my future and although social work may not have been my first choice, I know it's a role where I can still fulfil my wish to help those in society that are in need of support."

The head of recruitment was pleased to hear her decision. He took an envelope from the top drawer of his desk and placed it in front of him. "Tina I'm so pleased to hear this and wish you all the best in your future career. You have come highly recommended so please don't worry. I am fully confident that you will pass the interview with no problems at all," he said with a wink, whilst handing her the envelope. "In this envelope you'll find the details such as the time and place for the interview. I have also included all the information you need to help you prepare. It has already been arranged with Matron that you can have the time you need to attend. Please don't hesitate to contact me if there is anything else you need."

With that, Tina took the envelope. They both shook hands and said their goodbyes. Tina had told her parents she passed her exams and qualified as a nurse, which was true but she just could not face telling them everything. Not yet. She was dreading the disappointment from her mother but she knew she would have to face them eventually. The plan was to get this interview out of the way, go home to her parents, tell them the news and then relax and celebrate in Ireland. Then, if she were chosen for the new job she would return to the UK and make the most of her new career.

The day before her interview Tina had to pack her bags and prepare for vacating the nurses' quarters as she would not have time after her interview. Once she was all packed the three girls went out for dinner together. They spent the evening discussing their plans for their future. Margaret was looking forward to going home and was thinking of looking for nursing work in Ireland. She was homesick and just wanted to be close to her family. Tina was sad to hear this because it meant she would not see her so often. Linda had no idea what she was going to do. She accepted the opportunity to repeat the exams but said she was only going to repeat once and if she still did not pass then she would rethink her career choice.

The next morning Tina got ready for her interview. Margaret loaned her a navy-blue knee-length skirt. Linda loaned her one of her respectable cream silk tops and a lovely pair of navy-blue shoes as well. She swept her hair up onto her head in a bun and applied some lipstick and blusher.

Tina felt very sophisticated as she entered the interview room. She answered the questions as best she could. The interviewers were lovely and put her totally at ease. Before leaving the lead interviewer told her she would have their decision before the end of the week. If successful, she would be required to start in five weeks' time. Tina was relieved to hear this as it meant she had lots of time to visit her parents and she could still go to Ireland. She gave them her parent's address because that would be where she was staying for the next week or so. She said her goodbyes and left the room feeling positive as her Aunt Daisy's words of wisdom came to her mind. *All you can do is your best, nothing more…*and she was so right.

***

Tina went back to the hospital where all the other student nurses were busily tidying their rooms and packing their bags before the Matron inspected the nurse quarters for the very last time. Margaret and Linda had already cleaned their room from top to bottom.

"So how did the interview go Tina?" Linda Asked

"I think it went well. I answered their questions as best as I could. They'll be intouch soon so hopefully I'll get good news."

"Oh of course it will be good news. Believe in yourself Tina. We believe in you." Margaret and Linda gave her a big hug.

Suddenly there was a knock on the door. It was Matron and Sister Ann. They were carrying out their room inspection. Matron walked around checking every square inch of the room whilst Sister Ann checked the furniture for breakages.

The three girls had to stand at their beds in silence. Linda struggled not to laugh and let out a giggle which made Matron spin on her heals. "What is so funny?" Matron asked.

"Nothing, Matron. Sorry," Linda said.

Tina and Margaret had to bite their lips to prevent them from laughing. Soon the inspection was over and Sister Ann and Matron found nothing to complain about. So they both swiftly left and could be heard banging on the door to the room next door.

As soon as they were gone Linda, Margaret and Tina all threw themselves on their beds and laughed out loud. They went quiet as they all turned to look at each other.

"This is it," Tina said. "It's over. Our training has finished and now we are going to leave and go our separate ways." The reality of their situation suddenly registered in her head.

"Oh Tina, only the training has finished, we have the rest of our lives to share. Even if it is from a distance we have to keep in touch with each other," Linda said.

"Absolutely. You bet your life we will all stay intouch. Shur aren't you coming to see me in Ireland soon?" Margaret said to Tina, "And shur why don't you come as well Linda?"

"I would love to but I can't just yet. In a couple of months maybe. Like I said, we have the rest of our lives."

"Let's write down our addresses so that we can write to each other," Margaret suggested. Linda and Tina agreed and did exactly that. Linda was meeting her boyfriend and spending the night with him before she went home to her parents in the morning. She had her bags packed and said her goodbyes as her boyfriend called to the hospital to collect her. Next, Margaret had to leave as her taxi arrived to bring her to the train station. She was travelling to the ferry port. Tina told her she would see her soon in Ireland.

Tina was alone in the room. Before going to bed she

stood looking out of the window at the view across the hospital grounds. There were traffic noises from the busy road outside the hospital gates and she could hear ambulance sirens and the faint sound of chatter from people walking in and out of the main hospital entrance. She knew she would miss this. She would miss the hospital life. As she looked up into the sky she could see the big moon shining bright surrounded by millions of stars. Just as she was about to turn away she spotted a shooting star. Her Uncle Fred always told her to wish upon a shooting star for good luck.

She closed her eyes tight. *I wish for happiness, health and good fortune for me and my friends Linda and Margaret.* She closed the curtains and hopped into her bed thinking about the next chapter in her life.

Chapter 14

The next morning, Tina woke up and turned expecting to see Linda and Margaret in their beds but they were gone. The room was silent. It felt strange being alone and she could not wait for her dad to come and collect her. He was driving down early so she did not have long to wait.

Tina had to get special permission to allow her dad into the nurse quarters as she could not carry her luggage by herself. It felt sad as she left the accommodation. It was her home for so long and she had made some great friends but she was taking some amazing memories with her as well.

As her dad put the last bag into the car boot, he could see Tina standing beside the car, looking around. He put his hand on her shoulder. "Time to go now love, are you ready?"

Tina took a deep breath. "Yes Dad, I'm ready." She smiled and got into the car. On the journey home, she thought about how she would handle telling her parents her news. How would she tell them she had qualified but would never work as a nurse? She thought that maybe she did not have to tell them everything. Maybe she could just tell them she had qualified and make them believe she was going to work as a nurse. After all she had qualified. She was an actual nurse – that bit was true. However, she had enough secrets in her life so she knew she had to be honest with them.

When she got home, Tina walked into the house unsure of what would await her. As she entered the kitchen, she saw her mother with a smile on her face and then she noticed some neighbours were also present. Tina desperately wanted to believe her mother was proud of her and that her smiles were genuine. However, she knew her mother was most likely just doing it all for show. Of course, her cousin and Aunt Ivy were also there. When everyone left she knew she had to sit her parents down and tell them the whole truth.

She sat at the kitchen table and asked her parents to join her. She looked at her dad. "You know I'm so happy to have qualified as a nurse. It was always a dream of mine and I did it." Tina took out her diploma to show her parents.

Her dad held it in his hand and he smiled widely as he read the words out loud. "I am so very proud of you. We always knew you could do it. Never doubted you for a second love."

Tina started talking and the words just fell out of her mouth. She couldn't control what she was saying. "I didn't tell you everything on the phone Dad." She couldn't look at her mother so she focused on her dad. "I have qualified but I was told that at this present time there were no nursing jobs available for me. But they will let me know as soon as a position becomes available." Her dad looked a little confused.

"But it's not all bad. The hospital offered me the opportunity of a very interesting position in social work. It's very exciting indeed and I am so happy, really I am."When she eventually stopped talking the room fell silent and as she looked at her parents, she saw shock and confusion on their faces.

"That's OK. You qualified. You did what you set out to do and social work is a fantastic opportunity for you," her mother said before standing up and leaving the kitchen.

Once her mother left the room, her dad put his hand on Tina's shoulder. "I'm so sorry you didn't get a placement love, but what an amazing opportunity for you. You have a kind heart so I know you'll be a wonderful social worker. As long as you're happy then so am I love?"

Tina smiled and thanked her dad. She couldn't lie, not to him, so whilst she had him to herself, she told him the truth that her hearing problem was the real reason she could not work as a nurse."Dad, I am sorry. I didn't tell you the complete truth." She bowed her head. She couldn't bear to see him disappointed.

"Love, I knew there had to be more to it. Well, it's their loss. I fully believe that what's meant to be will be. The world obviously has bigger and better things in mind for you."He pulled her close and gave her a hug. "Everything will be OK. Either way I am so proud of you. Now, don't you worry, we can keep this between ourselves if you wish. I won't say a word to anyone if you don't want me to." He winked at her.

"Oh thank you Dad. Yeah, let's keep it between just you and me. I don't think I could bear mother's reaction if she knew." She reassured her dad that she was happy and excited to have been given the opportunity in social work. She was relieved that he knew the truth because she knew he would never judge her and she could never deceive her dad.

***

The next day Tina had planned to visit her aunt Daisy and Uncle Fred. She was not worried about telling them of her change of career because she knew they would be happy for her no matter what she chose. After breakfast she got herself ready and left for her aunt and uncle's house.

It felt like forever since she had been to visit. She knocked on the door and her Uncle Fred opened the door to greet her. "Ah, there she is. How are you love? Come in and tell us all your news."

Tina walked in the house to find Daisy sat in the fireside chair knitting a scarf.

"Hello there, we've been waiting for you. Come sit down and tell me all about your news." Tina took off her coat and sat on the sofa whilst Fred went and made some tea.

"Aunty you're looking very well. Is that a scarf you are knitting?" she asked."

"Yes, it is. It's for Fred. He needs a fresh one for this winter so I thought I would start one now. But that's enough about me. How are you? We were both so happy when your father told us you had passed your exams. You must be so proud of yourself."

Just then, Fred walked in with a tray and three cups of tea on it. "Yes, Tina, we are both so happy for you."

"Oh, thank you. I qualified, but there has been a bit of a change of plans."

Daisy put her knitting down beside her when she heard this and both Fred and Daisy looked at her inquisitively. "What do you mean by a change of plan?" Fred asked.

"Well, because of my hearing problem the hospital has told me they cannot give me a job in nursing. But they were so impressed with me and that's why they 'highly' recommended me for a position in social working." Tina took a sip of her tea to give Daisy and

Fred a chance to respond.

"Oh, OK. So you're going to train as a social worker. That's a very noble profession and your nurse training will always stand to you," Daisy said.

"Well, aren't you a woman of many talents. My niece a qualified nurse and social worker! I am very proud of you Tina. Well done my darling girl," Fred said with a smile.

"Thank you so much. Social work was not my first choice but it is exciting. I have had the interview but should know in the next day or so if I have been successful. So I am trying not to get too excited until I know for sure."

"You will get it. I'm positive of that," said Daisy.

***

On her last morning with her parents, Tina was sitting at the kitchen table eating her breakfast when she heard the letterbox flap. She rushed to the door and picked up the letters that had dropped on the floor. As she shuffled through them, she saw one addressed to her.

Stuffing the letter in her pocket, she quickly rushed in to the kitchen and left the remaining letters on the kitchen table. She ran up to her bedroom to read her letter in private. Her hands were shaking as she opened the envelope. She knew if she did not get the job there would be nothing else for her. She could hardly believe her eyes as she read the first sentence.

'Dear Tina, we are delighted to inform you that your application for the role of trainee social worker has been successful'.

Her parents were very pleased for her and wished her well. She rang her Aunt Daisy and Uncle Fred who were also happy for her. A new beginning was hers for the taking and she could not wait for it.

Chapter 15

The plane journey to Ireland was a short one. Tina looked out the window at the misty rain hitting the small round glass window. The plane landed on the runway of Dublin Airport with a huge thud on the tarmac. As the plane taxied along the runway she could feel a real sense of calm washing over her. The plane slowly came to a halt and the pilot spoke on the loudspeaker giving the usual welcome to Ireland speech. Next, the plane filled with the sound of passengers' busily unlocking seatbelts and opening the overhead lockers as they prepared to leave the plane. Tina had already done everything she had set out to do in the UK and now all that was left was to enjoy a stress-free holiday in Ireland.

As she walked through the gates in the arrivals hall of Dublin airport she could see Margaret's dad Sean standing in the distance. He stood with a huge smile on his face. She loved this. She loved that he was happy to see her. They both got in the car and were soon pulling out of Dublin Airport. Margaret's family lived in a lovely place called the 'Curragh' in County Kildare. Margaret had three sisters, four brothers and lots of aunts, uncles, and cousins. Their door was always open and there was always a pot of tea on the stove. Margaret's mother, Bridie, believed there was not a problem in the world that could not be put right over a nice cup of tea.

As Tina sat in the car looking out the window Sean asked her how she was feeling about leaving the hospital. "So, Margaret told us about your great exam results. Well done and congratulations."

"Thank you, I appreciate that but…"

"I know, I know all about the social work opportunity and we are all so happy for you. You will make a wonderful social worker. The world needs more social workers like you," Sean said as he turned the car radio on. "You just relax now Tina. You must be tired with all the travelling."

"Aw you are very kind. I have been so looking forward to seeing you all," Tina said.

"And we are always happy to have you with us. But be warned, Bridie has a big dinner ready for you. You know how she likes to feed everyone who comes in to the house!"

Soon they were pulling into the driveway and Sean beeped the car horn to let everyone know they had arrived.

Tina got out of the car and the front door to the house flung open. Margaret's mother, Bridie, was standing there beckoning her to come in out of the rain.

As soon as she walked into the house she was greeted with the tightest of tight hugs and Bridie told her she was so happy to see her. "Now come in the dinner is made. I want to hear all your news and plans."

Tina loved her visits to Margaret's family. She visited Ireland with Margaret many times during her nursing training. Bridie and Sean were always so warm and welcoming to her and treated her just like one of their family. They had even bought a spare bed for Margaret's bedroom especially for Tina when she would visit them. She believed Margaret must have told her mother about her secret because not once did any member of her family ever ask Tina about her family life or parents. They knew it was a sensitive subject for her and did not want to upset her.

Over the years of coming to Ireland Tina had made many friends in the Curragh. Of course, she connected with the local church choir and whenever she was visiting, she would join them. The vicar's children were friends of Margaret's brothers so she had met them on practically every visit. Margaret had arranged a night out at the local dancehall to celebrate their graduation from nursing school.

They all spent the evening getting ready. As they did each other's hair and makeup the room soon filled with the sound of giggles, the smell of perfume and the hazy mist of hairspray.

Tina walked into the dance hall with Margaret and her sisters. There were many people in the hall and it was going to be a great night. She would spend the whole night on the dance floor. She even agreed to a cheeky dance with a young man which was brave of her but she was out to have fun and that is what she did.

The next morning, Tina woke up and stretched her arms open wide. She slowly opened her eyes against the glare of the morning sun shining through the window and flashbacks to her antics from the night before crept into her mind. *Oh my goodness, what was I thinking? My legs feel like I've run a marathon after all that dancing.* She then heard a thud coming from Margaret's bed. When she turned to look, she saw Margaret had rolled over and fallen out of her bed. Tina laughed aloud as Margaret quickly stood up rubbing her arm and looking very confused about what had just happened to her.

"Oh you can laugh," Margaret said.

"What on earth do you mean, Margaret?" Tina said with a giggle.

"I saw you dancing with that bloke on the dance floor. You looked like you were having fun." Margaret laughed and inspected her leg for bruises after her fall.

Margaret's words resonated with Tina who suddenly remembered dancing away to the Hucklebuck on the dancefloor. "Oh my goodness Margaret why didn't you stop me?" Tina said whilst placing her hands to her forehead. "But it was a great night, wasn't it? I don't remember ever having more fun on a night out!" Tina said with a smile.

Margaret and Tina laughed as they mulled over the

details of the night before. They then got dressed for the day and went down to the kitchen for breakfast.

***

Tina never lost her love for singing and whenever she visited Margaret she always joined in with the choir in the local church. So after breakfast she was going to call to the vicarage and talk to the vicar about possibly joining the choir for the duration of her stay. When she arrived at the vicar's house his son let her in and told her someone was with his father and asked her to come in and wait.

Tina was conscious of the time as she had to be back by 12 O'clock. She and Margaret had agreed to make lunch for everyone. She walked into the kitchen with Mark the vicar's son and noticed another young man sat at the table who she had never met before. He was introduced to her as Neville who was a cousin visiting from the UK. Neville pulled out a chair and beckoned her to sit down beside him. She thought he was a nice-looking man with dark black hair and a lovely smile. She felt her face getting redder and redder as she sat there chatting to him. Although Neville was visiting from the UK he was actually born in Ireland, in a town called Athboy in County Meath. He told her he lived in the UK and was a trainee farm manager but had studied horticulture in college.

She eventually managed to talk to the vicar and it was arranged for her to sing on Sunday in the church with the choir. When she was finished talking to the vicar Neville offered to walk her back to Margaret's house, which she accepted. As she and Neville drew close to Margaret's house, Tina could see Margaret standing at her front door. She had seen her with Neville. *Oh no, I am never gonna live this down now that she has seen me,* Tina thought. She said goodbye to Neville and then turned to walk in to the house. No sooner had she walked through the front door when she was bombarded with questions. "So, go on Tina, tell me was that the vicar's nephew that you were walking with? I think his name is Neville, I've met him, but I never really pay much attention to my brother's friends and he doesn't always visit. When are you seeing him again? What's he like? Do you like him?"

Tina was trying not to let her excitement show. "Oh Margaret, he is lovely. He lives in the UK. He is the vicar's nephew and I don't know if I'll see him again." She went upstairs to pick out her clothes for church tomorrow before helping to make lunch.

Margaret followed her up the stairs. "What do you mean? Did he not ask to meet you again? Oh please tell me you didn't say no."

The two girls got into the bedroom and they sat on their beds. Tina grew impatient with all the questioning but she knew Margaret was just being her usual curious self. "Neither Margaret, we've only just met you know and maybe he was just being friendly. I don't even know if he has a girlfriend. He most likely does. A man like him just cannot be single." Tina

Blushed.

Margaret giggled. "Well, maybe he will be at church tomorrow. If he is you better point him out to me do you hear? I need to suss him out!" Margaret wagged her finger at Tina as she spoke with a smile on her face.

Tina smiled and looked into her suitcase for some clean clothes. "I will, I promise Margaret. Now can we please talk about something else?"

Margaret threw a magazine at Tina. "Here, look at this. There's an interview with your favourite singer, Jim Reeves. He's thinking of doing a tour in Ireland. You will have to come over for that. Maybe Neville will come too!"

They both made lunch for everyone and then they just lazed around the house talking about Neville and the next dance due to take place the following week. They were both early to bed that night as they were still tired after all their dancing the night before.

***

The next morning, Tina and Margaret were still giddy

and chatting about the events of the previous day. They decided to write to Linda. She had given Margaret her parent's address, so they found a pen and paper and wrote down all their news. They told Linda to write back to them at Margaret's house and put Margaret's address at the bottom of the page.

The following week a letter arrived addressed to both Margaret and Tina so they knew it had to be from Linda. They sat at the kitchen table and held the letter between them. At first, they were full of giggles in anticipation of Linda's news. As they read the letter their giggles stopped and their eyes filled with tears. They put the letter down and hugged each other in silence. Margaret's mother walked into the kitchen and saw the two girls crying. She picked up the letter from the table and read it. She took both girls in her arms and without saying a word she held them both tightly.

The letter was from Linda's mother telling them Linda had been killed in a road accident. Her boyfriend visited her on his motorbike and brought her out for a spin against her parent's wishes. The road was wet and the motorbike skidded causing her boyfriend to lose control. Luckily he survived and was left with a badly broken leg. However, Linda was not so lucky and she died in the hospital three days later. She died in the hospital she had trained in, the very hospital she had called home for so long. The last couple of lines stuck out to Tina and Margaret.

I am so glad you two girls seem to be having fun. Linda would be so pleased for you. Please do not allow grief stop you from having even more fun. She would not want to see you sad. She talked about you both with such affection. You were her true friends. I have enclosed two pictures that Linda had in her belongings of all three of you together in your nursing quarters and hope you will keep them as a memory of the good times you all spent together.

All my thoughts,

Susan (Linda's Mother)

Margaret and Tina picked up the pictures and went for a walk. They decided to go to a wooded area near Margaret's house. It was quiet there and they could both sit and talk and think about their friend. They found an open space and sat down with their backs leaning against a tree. They took out the pictures and reminisced about the good times they had with Linda.

Tina wiped her eyes as she felt tears welling up. "Margaret, I can't believe she is gone. She was so young and so full of energy. It seems so cruel."

Margaret pulled some grass out of the ground and threw it in the air. "I know Tina. To think we were all strangers four years ago and look at us now. So much has happened, so much was yet to come to us and now she's gone it's just us two left."

There was silence as the two girls became lost in their thoughts and allowed their tears to flow. Then Tina sat up straight. "You Know, they say it takes all kinds of characters to form a strong and lasting friendship. I think I'm the sensible one," said Tina.

Margaret looked at Tina. "Well then I would be the agony aunt. The one who listens to everyone's troubles. But what was Linda?" Margaret asked.

Tina laughed. "Oh that's easy. Linda was without a doubt the adventurous one. She was fearless, she was the rule breaker," Tina said.

They both laughed as they reminisced about all the times Linda had broken Matron's rules and never seemed to get caught.

"She lived her life her way. I remember her telling me 'You only live once,' she was dead right," Margaret said whilst wagging her finger in an effort to mimic the way Linda spoke that day.

Tina thought for a moment. "Oh Margaret, what are we going to do? Linda's last words to us were that we have the rest of our lives to share but we're never going to see her again. She's gone. Linda has gone. I just can't believe this is happening," Tina said as her thoughts drifted back to the present day and the heartbreaking reality of what had happened to her friend.

Margaret looked up at the sky. "Yeah and she also said she would visit Ireland in a couple of months. But that will never happen now either."

The girls sat crying and hugged each other as they agreed to remember Linda in everything they did from that day onwards.

***

Over the next two weeks Tina saw Neville almost every day. Before she left for the UK, they met up one last time. There was a wooded area close to the vicarage. They had a particular tree that they would meet, and on this last day, they spent hours sitting under its massive bows, just chatting and laughing together. They were sharing a picnic. Neville made the sandwiches, and Tina bought some orange juice and fruit.

"Can you believe it has been just over two weeks since we met," Tina said.

"I know. Time flies when you're having fun," Neville laughed.

"Isn't it strange how things happen? I mean, if I had not wanted to talk to the vicar, then we may never have met."

Neville looked at Tina with a smile and his face. "Well, I am glad you did call to the vicar's that day."

Tina blushed. "Me too."

"Look Tina, we're both leaving for the UK soon. You're going tomorrow. How about we exchange addresses and write to each other? I would like to stay in touch with you. If that's what you want?"

Tina was glad he suggested this. "That would be lovely Neville. It would be nice to hear from you again."

Neville dug into his coat pocket where he had a pencil and Tina had some paper in her handbag. They both wrote down their addresses and exchanged addresses.

"Now Promise you will write. Promise me," Neville asked.

"I promise," Tina said.

Neville walked Tina back to Margaret's house and as he said goodbye, he leaned in to kiss her. Feeling embarrassed she allowed one peck on the lips and they both said their goodbyes.

She walked into the house and entered the kitchen. Margaret and her sisters all sat at the table giggling. Even their mother had a smile on her face.

"Did you honestly think we wouldn't see?" laughed Margaret. "Is he a good kisser?" she whispered in Tina's ear.

"What do you mean?"Tina said defensively but there was an outburst of laughter.

"Don't you be minding them, Tina." Margaret's mother said whilst pulling a spare chair out from the table and directing her to sit down. "Now let me get you a cup of tea and you can tell us all about it."

Tina could feel her face getting redder and redder. *How embarrassing*, she thought.

Chapter 16

As the plane landed back in the UK Tina was filled with excitement and could not wait to begin the next chapter in her life. She was sad about Linda's death, but she knew her friend would not want to see her moping around. She would want her to have fun and enjoy her life. Linda would have loved Neville and she could almost hear her friend telling her to *"go for it."*

Neville was a welcome addition to Tina's new life. Every time she thought about him, she could not help but smile. He was a funny and kind man. He had a good job with great prospects and he made her laugh which was the icing on the cake.

She finally arrived home and for the first time in quite a while, she actually enjoyed her parent's company. Of course, she went to see her Uncle Fred and Aunt Daisy. Her aunt noticed Tina had a spring in her step and asked all about her trip to Ireland.

"So Tina, tell me all your news. How was your trip to Ireland?"Daisy asked.

"It was very relaxing, although sadly I learned that my friend Linda, who I had trained with, had tragically died in a motorbike accident. She died just days after we all left the hospital."

Daisy placed her hands over her mouth."Oh my dear, I am so sorry to hear that. You must be devastated."

"Yes, yes, I am. But Linda was full of energy. She loved life and would not want me or Margaret to mope around."

"You're right. There's no point to that. You have to move on. It's not always easy but what choice do you have?" Daisy made a pot of tea and they both sat chatting.

"I have met a new friend as well. A man, his name is Neville. He's lovely Aunty you would love him."

Daisy sat up in her chair to take notice of what Tina was saying. "Oh really? Well, you enjoy your new friendship but remember you're a lady." Daisy said with a wink. Tina asked her not to say anything about Neville to her parents, especially her mother. Aunt Daisy was aware of how difficult her mother could be so she promised not to say a word to anyone. Tina valued her aunt's advice and promised to give regular updates on how things were progressing with Neville.

*****

Soon it was time to pack for London. Tina was going to rent a room in a shared house with some old friends she had met during her nursing training. Her wages were not worth much. She was only on a basic starting wage but it was enough to get her by.

When she arrived at her accommodation she was shown to her rather small bedroom. However, the house was just one bus ride away from the office where she would be working so she was happy to take a small room. She was sharing a house with four other girls who were working shifts at the hospital. This meant the house would never be over crowded at any one time. Tina was going to be working nine-to-five Monday to Friday and to supplement her wages she got part-time work in a local bar. She would work in the bar Thursday and Friday nights plus Saturday and Sunday when needed so the extra money came in very handy.

The first morning of work was nerve-wracking. She wore a blue pair of trousers with a nice new cream silk blouse. Her lovely long dark black hair was swept back off her face under a blue silk headband. She felt very smart indeed. Picking up her handbag and her neatly packed lunch, she left the house to the nearby bus stop.

As the bus moved, Tina stared out of the window looking at the busy morning traffic. Luckily, she only had two stops to wait before arriving at the office. The bus soon stopped at her stop and as she stepped of the bus onto the footpath, she took a deep breath and looked at her surroundings. She heard the sound of doors opening and when she turned to look behind her, she saw a café where a lady was putting out the menu boards and singing to herself as she worked. Tina turned back around and looked across the road at the office block where she was going to be based. It was six floors tall with a grey stone front and seven large windows on each floor. She crossed the road and made her way through the main entrance. There was no hospital smell and the floors were carpeted, not marble. This was a complete change for her and she was excited to get started.

Tina was told in her letter to ask for 'Mary Jones' so she walked up to the reception area and did exactly as she was asked. After some time, a woman came out of an office and walked towards her. The woman had lovely blonde hair held back off her face by a big yellow headband. She was wearing a knee-length yellow and white sleeveless dress with a long-sleeved blouse underneath. As she walked closer to Tina, she held out her hand and introduced herself

"You must be Tina. My name is Mary. It's lovely to meet you."Mary beckoned Tina to walk with her. She brought her into an office where two other girls were working at desks busily typing away. Mary pointed at an empty desk beside the window.

"This is your desk, Tina."

Tina sat in her seat and took a minute to take in her surroundings. Mary then gave Tina a big pile of forms and information booklets and asked her to take her time and read them all. She told Tina her sign language skills would be needed after lunch as Mary had a client who was deaf and Tina would have to act as an interpreter for the meeting.

Her first day was a shining success. Although there

was a lot to learn, she was pleased to be working and earning her own money at last.

When Tina got home, the house was silent as one housemate was sleeping before her night shift and the others were all working so she had the house to herself? She made herself some dinner and then sat down in a comfortable chair, where she began reading a book that Mary gave to her about the role of social work. After about an hour of reading, Tina thought about Neville. It had been two weeks since she left Ireland and she had not heard from him yet. She had his address but she was an old-fashioned girl and thought it should be him who wrote to her first. Then, she realised he had her parent's address not her London address. This caused a major panic because what if he wrote to her parent's house and her mother opened the letter. That would be a total disaster. She had images in her head of her mother opening the letter and running to her Aunt Ivy who would not waste the opportunity to make nasty comments and tease her when she saw her again.

Tina quickly got out her writing paper and started the first of many letters to Neville. She told him all about her new home and job.

The letter was three pages long and before signing off she told Neville she hoped he was well and advised him of her new address. She addressed the envelope and planned to post it the next morning on her way to work.

The first week in her new job went by so fast. The bar work was great fun too and she made many new friends. Life could not have been better.

The following week, she came home from work and saw someone had pushed a small white envelope under her bedroom door. The writing was not familiar to her so she opened the letter and glanced at the name written at the bottom of the last page. It was from Neville. She was so happy to hear from him. His letter was full of humor and made her giggle. She lay back on her bed and held the letter close to her chest. She had never felt this way before and could not believe that

Neville had actually replied to her.

As time went by she and Neville continued to write to each other weekly without fail and after six months Neville asked to come and visit Tina in London.

Tina replied immediately telling him she would love to see him. She told him the name of a local guesthouse that he could stay in. A date was set and Tina was excited but a little nervous as well. What would she wear? Where would they go? What would they do? What if things went terribly wrong? It was times like this she wished she had Margaret with her to help calm her down. She panicked. Tina didn't know the rules about first dates. She had not been on a proper date since Dr. Jonathan in her student nursing days. She bought a magazine with articles about dating etiquette. She sat in her bedroom on her bed and read the dating rules.

The main rules, according to the magazines, appeared to be as follows:

    1. Do not apply makeup at the dinner table.

2. Laugh at the man's jokes even if they do not seem funny to you.

3. Ask him about his work and always appear interested in what he tells you.

4. A woman should never appear more knowledgeable than the man.

5. Absolutely no kissing on the first date. No matter how tempted you may be.

After reading the article, she threw the magazine on the bed beside her.

Oh my goodness, how am I ever going to remember all of this? So, I'm supposed to wear long lasting makeup, laugh at his jokes, appear stupid but interested in pig farming – off all things – and run a mile if he tries to kiss me. This is going to be a disaster. I just know it. What ever will he think of me?

The weekend of Neville's visit soon came around. She had bought a lovely new blue dress and knee-high boots for their date. She did her hair and makeup and waited nervously for him to arrive. The doorbell rang.

She opened the door and there was Neville standing there dressed in a very smart suit. He had not changed one bit. He was still as handsome as she remembered him – maybe more than that even.

Tina had booked a table at a local restaurant and if the meal went well, she planned to suggest a dance in the local dance hall.

They arrived at the restaurant and once they were sitting at their table the waitress gave them a jug of water and the menus.

They ordered their food and Neville poured water into their glasses. His hand shook slightly as he poured."Tina, you look lovely by the way."

Tina blushed. "Thank you Neville."

Remembering rule three, *ask him about his work and always appear interested in what he tells you*, Tina asked, "So Neville, how is your work? Pig farming sounds so interesting."

"Oh, really, well yes it can be interesting I suppose," Neville said as he placed the jug back on the table.

"Apart from the times when I end up face down in pig muck of course!"

Tina remembered another of the rules to *laugh at the man's jokes* so she laughed out loud and a little too hard. She could feel her face getting redder and redder as she looked around and saw people looking at her. *Oh, my god did I really laugh that loud?*

Neville was looking at Tina as if he was not sure what he had said that was so funny. "Tina, are you OK?"

What do I do now? Where is the rule for this one? "Oh, Neville I am so sorry. I am just a little nervous. It has been so lovely writing to you and reading your letters. I always look forward to hearing from you. Honestly, I do. It has just been so long since I have actually seen you that my nerves have got the better of me. I even bought a magazine with dating rules but I have messed it all up haven't I." Tina was talking so much she failed to notice how hard Neville was trying not to laugh.

She eventually stopped talking and made eye contact

with Neville as he began laughing out loud.

"What Neville, what's so funny?" Tina asked whilst looking around again.

"Oh Tina. I'm sorry, I am not laughing at you. I'm laughing at us."

"Us?" Tina asked.

"Yes, you have no idea how nervous I am. I spent all day yesterday convincing myself that you'd take one look at me and tell me to go home. Honestly, what are we like? As for rules, forget them. Just be you because it's you I've come to see. So why don't we start again and just be ourselves?"They both laughed at how ridiculous they had been.

After a rocky start the meal was a total success. The conversation flowed with ease and the laughter was never ending. It was a lovely night. They had chatted for so long it was too late to go dancing so Neville walked Tina back to her house. It was half-past eleven at night and she had never been out so late.

At the doorstep Neville leaned in for a kiss. This

time Tina did not step back after just one peck. She was breaking all the rules, but she didn't care.

They said their goodbyes and Tina went inside her house. That night in bed she was on cloud nine. She was so very happy with her life and could not wait to tell Margaret all about it.

***

Tina knew if she was to keep seeing Neville, she would have to tell him about her secret but the thoughts of it scared her. She could not bear the thought of losing him. She talked it out with Margaret who told her to tell him when she was ready. Margaret told Tina if Neville really were *the one*, then he would love her no matter what she told him. Tina knew Margaret was right, she was just so nervous.

Chapter 17

Just one month later, Neville bought a car. He had bought a blue Morris Minor and he could not wait to show it off. Tina couldn't drive but seeing Neville in his car gave her the push to learn. Two weeks after buying his car, Neville drove down to visit Tina. They planned to go for a picnic. It was the summer of 1963 and they had now been properly going steady with eachother for about twelve months. She had packed a picnic basket and sat waiting for him to call for her. Even though she was excited to see him, she could also feel a familiar feeling of nervousness flood her body. This feeling became one of the legacies that her secret had so cruelly bestowed upon her. *I hope he won't think badly of me when I tell him my secret. I don't think I could bear that,* Tina thought as she sat in the silence of the kitchen.

She heard Neville pulling up outside, she picked up the picnic basket and made her way to the front door where she stood watching as he got out of the car. He was smiling from ear to ear while wiping the wing mirror with his sleeve. She made her way out to meet him. "Let's go," she said.

Neville promptly took the picnic basket and put it in the boot before opening the passenger door for Tina. "Take a seat madam," Neville said with a grin.

They were on the road in no time and enjoying the scenery as they drove. They soon began looking for somewhere to stop and eat and eventually came across a lovely big public park, so Neville parked up and they found the perfect spot on the grass to set up their picnic. Tina was enjoying herself so much and nearly said nothing to Neville, but she could not put it off any longer.

After they had finished eating, Tina went quiet and Neville asked her what was wrong. "You seem distracted Tina. Is something wrong?"

Tina looked at him, unsure of what to say. "I'm sorry Neville. I'm having such a lovely time, but I do have something I need to talk to you about. I'm just not sure how you will feel after I tell you."

The color slowly drained from his face. Tina had a whole speech prepared in her head, but when the moment came to speak, she drew a blank and her words were lost. "I'm adopted. There, I said it now, and that's it." She couldn't even look at Neville as she threw her hands up in the air and looked away.

"Is that it Tina? Seriously, is that all you wanted to say to me?" Neville asked, sounding a little relieved.

"Yes, that's it." Tina replied eventually looking up at him to see his reaction. "You must think I'm awful but

I had to tell you."She did not know what to expect, but she was surprised at how calm he appeared to be upon hearing her news.

He simply took her hand and just as she was about to speak he squeezed her hand in his."Tina, I have never been so happy. I don't care about that stuff. I only care about you, me and our future. Our past is not important."Neville smiled softly trying to offer reassurance. "You know, I do have some understanding of that kind of thing. My sister had a baby before she was married so I get it, really, I do. My sister kept her baby much to the disgust of our family. She was sent away and refused to be parted from her daughter."

Tina felt a huge sense of relief. He knows my secret and cares about me anyway. He didn't judge me or look down on me. Could he be any more perfect?

"You don't really talk about your sister. Why is that?" Tina asked.

Neville smiled. "Well, sadly, our mother died when we were just children. My sister and I were separated because the family it felt my sister needed a female in her life. As a result we became very distant and to be honest we don't have a sibling relationship. She and I never talk or write or anything."

Tina thought that was so sad. She had spent her life craving a sister and there he was with a sister but never allowed to know her. "I am so sorry to hear that Neville, life can be so hard."

They both sat in the sun eating their food and talking about their childhoods. They realised they were actually more alike than they knew. Once they had finished eating, they packed everything away and went for a walk, hand in hand, like so many other couples they passed along their way.

I am such a lucky girl, finally I feel like I belong. Nobody has ever made me feel like this before. With Neville I am safe. My god is this what love feels like. As this thought entered her head, Neville let go of her hand and put his arm around her and she put hers around him.

I love you Neville, she thought with a big smile on her face.

***

The following day, Neville and Tina were driving to Kent. Tina was going to introduce Neville to her parents and her Aunt Daisy and Uncle Fred. She was nervous about how her mother would react, but she knew it had to be done sometime. She had told them about Neville on her previous visit and her dad was eager to meet him, so she promised she would bring him with her to meet them. Neville called early that morning to collect Tina as they wanted to make the most of the day ahead.

"How are you feeling about meeting my parents?"

"I am fine Tina, how hard can it be?" Neville said with a smile.

"Well, my father is lovely. You will love him and he will love you as well. My Mother can be disagreeable at times but ignore her. I'm sure she doesn't know she is even doing it most of the time."

"Don't worry Tina, everything will be just fine."

They soon arrived and Tina could see her mother standing at the window watching them. As they parked the car and made their way up the garden path, her dad opened the door and welcomed them both in to the house. He gave Tina a hug and then shook Neville's hand.

"Pleased to meet you, Mr Vousden," Neville said.

"Oh please, call me Albert. Mr Vousden makes me feel old."

"Where is Mother?" Tina asked.

"She should be in the kitchen. Go on in and we will all have some tea." Albert directed them towards the kitchen and Florence then appeared. "Hello Tina, how are you? You're early," her mother said.

"I know mother, I wanted to have a whole day here to go and see Uncle Fred and Aunt Daisy as well. Mother, this is Neville."

Florence wiped down her apron and shook Neville's hand "Pleased to meet you Neville, we have heard all about you."

"Thank you I have heard all about you as well. Tina has talks highly of you both," he said.

"Hmm really," Florence said. "Now take a seat and we will have some tea."

Albert laughed at his wife's reaction but soon snapped out of it when Florence gave him one of her looks. "Tina tells me you studied horticulture Neville. Can I borrow you for a few minutes as I have something in the garden that I could do with some advice on?" Albert and Neville went out to the garden and were soon deep in conversation.

"He seems nice Tina."

"He is Mother, he's lovely," Tina said

"Well, it is about time you met a man and he has a good job with prospects so you would do well to keep him. You're not getting any younger."

"I know Mother but things are different today than they were in your day. We're in no rush."

Soon Albert and Neville came back into the kitchen

and Neville sat beside Tina at the kitchen table. They all drank their tea and Albert and Neville were chatting away to eachother. Tina was happy to see them getting on so well. Once tea was over Tina suggested they go for a walk around the area. She wanted to show Neville some of her childhood haunts.

They walked through the park that she had spent so much of her childhood making daisy chains and walking Patch. Then, when they left the park, they walked up the road a little and Tina stopped at the church hall. There were signs outside advertising a jumble sale.

"I love a jumble sale," Tina said. So they both went in for a look. Tina had so many childhood memories of this hall. "Neville, this is the hall I used to attend as a child for choir practice. The deaf club that I was a member of used to meet her as well." Tina went quiet. "It is also here that I learned I was adopted."

Neville rubbed her back. "Well, it is still standing and so are you Tina. Let's have a look around and see what we can find."

They both walked around the hall and Tina bought a few small cakes from a cake stall. Neville found a table adorned with all kinds of nick knacks. Picking up a plastic bag, his eyes opened wide with delight. "Oh I like these," he said. The bag was full of stamps.

"They're stamps Neville?" Tina looked a little perplexed

"I know what they are. I collect stamps. I have a huge album of stamps at home. These could be valuable one day. I have to put something by for my retirement!" Neville laughed as he paid for the stamps and put them in his pocket.

"Now let's go back to my parents and then we can drive to Aunt Daisy and Uncle Fred." They both returned to Tina's parents' house. They said their goodbyes and made their way to Daisy and Fred's house.

When they arrived, Tina knocked the door and Daisy welcomed them both in to the house with her arms outstretched and a huge smile on her face. "Aunt Daisy, this is Neville," Tina said.

"Hello Neville, it is so nice to meet you. Tina has talked about you on many of her visits. All good, of course," Daisy said with a wink.

They made their way into the house, and Fred came into the kitchen from the garden. "Ah hello Tina, so this must be Neville," he said. "Please make yourself at home. Daisy has some sandwiches made. I hope you're hungry."

They all sat eating their sandwiches and drinking tea and Tina was happy with how accepting everyone had been of Neville. She watched as Neville chatted away to her Uncle Fred. *He really is amazing. I am so lucky to have him in my life.*

Soon it was time for them both to leave but they promised they would visit again soon. They both made their way back to Tina's parents' house to say their goodbyes and then they left to make their way back to London.

The weekend had been a complete success and Tina hated having to say goodbye to Neville that night. It would be another two weeks before she would see him again and she was already counting the hours.

***

Over the next two years, Neville travelled to London every second weekend to see Tina. They both spoke almost every day by phone and wrote to each other often. It was true love.

Chapter18

By 1966 the UK was bustling with activity and brimming with talent. The Beatles were storming the charts and had released their Revolver album. Some of the greats, like the Rolling Stones had released their first album. Jimmy Hendrix had also found fame in the UK music charts. By 1966, the UK fashion had an explosion of color with the more flamboyant fashion designs. Miniskirts, knee-high boots, bootleg jeans and paisley shirts were all the rage. In 1966, England won the football world cup with their famous 4-2 win against Germany, so the UK was in celebration mode.

Tina was happily settled into her job. She felt like her work was really making a difference to people's lives. She had become a member of a charity for deaf children and adolescents and signed up to teach sign language in her spare time. She did this because when she was a child, she had learned so much from 'Deaf club' and this was her way of paying that help forward. She had made many friends within the deaf community, and everyone who met her seemed to love her. Finally, life was working out for her in ways she never thought possible.

***

On Valentine's Day of that year Neville came down to London. He was taking Tina out for the night. They were going to get something to eat and then go dancing. Neville knew Tina loved to dance. He on the other hand was not so enthusiastic but he liked to make Tina happy so he never said no. The meal was lovely and the dance hall was packed with eager partygoers. Neville knew Jim Reeves was Tina's favourite singer so he requested the song *I Love You Because* to be dedicated to the most beautiful woman in the room, Tina. Tina was shocked and flattered at the same time. Neville took her by the hand and lead her onto the dance floor. Still holding her hand, he wrapped his other arm around her waist and pulled her close as they both danced to the music. "I love you Tina," he whispered into her ear.

She blushed. "I love you too Neville."

They finished the dance and walked back to their seats. Neville was looking a little red in the face and Tina wondered what was wrong with him. Suddenly, he got down in front of her on bended knee. He was holding his hand out to her as if beckoning her to take hold of his hand. Tina was dumbfounded. She did not expect this at all. Neville told her he loved her and that she was his one and only. Then he asked her to marry him.

Tina blushed again. She looked around the room and noticed people were staring at them, eagerly waiting to hear her reply. She looked at Neville, told him to get up and with the biggest smile on her face, she said yes. She flung her arms around his neck not caring who was looking, and kissed him hard.

She could not wait to tell her parents so she rang her dad the next day, but her dad already knew.

"How do you know?" Tina asked with surprise.

Her dad laughed. "Because Neville called me a few weeks ago and asked for my blessing. Your mother and I are both thrilled for you love. As long as you are happy that's all that matters to us."

"Oh, Dad, thank you. How did you manage to keep it to yourself?" Tina asked.

"I made a promise to Neville and I never break my promises. Although it was so hard not to blurt it out to you."

Of course, the next call was to her Aunt Daisy and Uncle Fred who were both delighted to hear her news.

***

Tina had entered full wedding planner mode. Ever since the day she watched the Queen's coronation as a child she dreamt of her own big day. She longed for the day when she would find the man of her dreams and walk down the aisle in a big white dress with a long veil. Of course, as a child, she dreamt of her wedding taking place in Westminster but as she grew older, she lowered her sights and settled for the local church instead.

The first thing she and Neville had to do was set the date, so they contacted the local vicar and booked their wedding for April 1st, 1967. The year passed by so quickly and wedding plans were all she could think of. They had booked a church wedding with lots of singing involved. She was a traditional girl and her dad and her aunt Daisy helped her with the *"something old, something new, something borrowed and something blue"* wedding tradition. Her Dad gave her his mother's clean white silk handkerchief for her handbag (something old). She had her wedding dress made (something new). Her aunt Daisy loaned her a necklace given to her by Uncle Fred (something borrowed) and she gave Tina the blue garter she wore on her wedding day (something blue).

Tina's wedding dress was full length with pure white lace detail. She boasted to her mother and her mother's family that her wedding dress was being handmade using the same lace used to make Princess Margaret's wedding dress. She bought a long veil with a beautiful diamante headpiece. Her bridesmaid was of course her old friend Margaret, who was to be dressed in a lime green sleeveless dress. They booked the local dance hall for their reception and planned a huge buffet with a band for the evening entertainment.

***

The day before the wedding Margaret had arrived from Ireland. She stayed with Tina and the two girls sat up till the early hours talking about all the good times they had together. They talked about nursing; they talked about their old friend Linda and they laughed about when Tina first met Neville. Life had been a rollercoaster for Tina but Margaret had been her one true, constant friend. She had been her calm in many a storm and she was so glad to have her with her on her big day.

The girls were in their beds chatting. "Can you believe I am actually getting married Margaret?" Tina asked. "Who would have thought that I would be the first, eh?"

"I know, but I am so happy for you. I wonder, if Linda was still alive would she have been first?" Margaret said.

"I doubt it. Linda would be too busy partying." Tina and Margaret laughed.

"And what about you Margaret? You have been with Brian for some time now. Do you think you will be married soon?"

Margaret smiled. "Well, I wasn't going to say anything to you just yet as this is your weekend, but

Brian and I have been talking about marriage."

Tina sat upright in her bed. "Tell me more."

"Well, my birthday is next week and I have a feeling he is going to ask me then."

"What makes you think that, Margaret?" Tina asked.

"Well, he keeps taking my ring and trying it on, so surely that's a sign. He's not good at hiding things. I can always tell when he is up to something. We shall see!"

"Well, you will have to let me know straight away Margaret. Do you hear me!"

"I will, I promise," Margaret said.

"Right, now let's try to get some sleep. I need to be well rested for tomorrow."

With that the two girls said goodnight and turned in their beds to go to sleep.

As Tina closed her eyes, she thought of Neville and wondered what he was doing at that moment. This time tomorrow night I will be Mrs Neville

McClaughry. We will be spending our first night as man and wife and I cannot wait. Then her eyes closed and she drifted into a deep sleep.

Chapter 19

On the morning of her wedding, Tina woke up early, full of excitement for the day ahead. Margaret was fast asleep on a fold up bed. Tina threw a pillow at her. "Wake up sleepy head."

Margaret turned around and looked at Tina. "What has you so excited? You'd swear it was your big day," she said with a grin. "OK, you have my full attention. I'm all yours for the day," Margaret said whilst jumping out of her bed.

They both had breakfast and soon it was time to get themselves ready for the day ahead. Excitedly, they did each other's hair. Margaret's hair was mid-length, she swept it off her face with a flowered headband. Tina had her beautiful but very long black hair put up in a bun on top of her head. Next, it was time for makeup and then the dresses.

Tina looked stunning. She beamed from ear to ear and as she looked at herself in the mirror, she could not contain her emotions.

Margaret rushed over and placed her hand on Tina's shoulder. "Whatever is wrong Tina?"

Tina turned to look at Margaret. "Nothing is wrong Margaret. For the first time in my life, I can honestly say these are tears of joy. I've never felt so happy."She grabbed a tissue and dried her eyes because she did not want her mascara to run down her face.

Margaret hugged Tina. "I'm over the moon for you. You deserve this happiness."

Tina heard her dad calling out to them, "OK girls

are you ready? Time to go now."

They went downstairs together and into the sitting room. Tina's dad was standing at the fireplace, waiting for her to come into the room.

"Oh my dear girl," Tina's dad said as he lifted his hand to his mouth. Margaret left to get into the car. Tina's mother had already gone with Ivy to the church and was meeting them there. "You look beautiful. I suppose you're no longer my little girl. You're a grown woman now. Neville is a lucky man, but always remember, I love you too." Albert held his arms out to Tina to give her a hug.

Tina smiled softly. "Thank you, Dad. I love you too."

The driver beeped the car horn, prompting Tina and her dad to leave the house. As she walked down the garden path, she saw her neighbours standing at their doorways clapping her and wishing her well. She had never felt so special before and she enjoyed every moment. As the car made the Journey to the Church

Tina felt butterflies in her tummy.

They soon arrived at the church. Tina took her place with her dad by her side and looped her arm through his arm. The church doors opened and they could hear the organ playing the wedding march prompting them to make their way down the aisle with Margaret walking behind them. They had invited over one hundred and fifty people to the church. Tina had invited everyone from the deaf society that she knew and had special permission to allow an interpreter for the deaf to interpret the service. Her heart raced as she entered the church with everyone looking at her and smiling as she passed them by. Then Neville stood out into the centre of the aisle and turned to look back at her as she walked toward him. He was looking very smart in his wedding suit with a top hat and tie. He was smiling from ear to ear. As Tina reached Neville, her dad placed her hand on top of Neville's hand and stepped to his left where he sat with her mother. Margaret sat beside Tina's parents.

"You look beautiful Tina," Neville whispered into her ear as they turned to face the vicar.

The service went by without any issues and at last Tina heard the words she had longed to hear the vicar say.

"And now I pronounce you man and wife. You may kiss the bride." With that, Neville turned to Tina and gently kissed her before they both signed the register and walked back down the aisle hand in hand as man and wife.

*****

The reception was held in a large dancehall that was just big enough to hold all the guests. It had been beautifully decorated with balloons and the tables were all covered in lime green and white tablecloths. There was a big buffet laid out and in the evening the tables were pulled back to make space for the dancing.

For their first dance they had chosen Jim Reeves, *I love You Because*. That was the song Neville had requested when he proposed to Tina. As the song began Neville held out his hand to Tina and they both made their way to the dancefloor.

He pulled Tina in close to him. "So Tina or should I say, Mrs McClaughry, did I tell you how lovely you looked to day?"

"Well, thank you Mr McClaughry you look fine yourself."

"This is the beginning of the rest of our lives and I promise I will work every day to make you happy." Neville said before wrapping his arms around her waist and sweeping her around the dancefloor.

Tina placed her head on Neville's shoulder and enjoyed her first dance with her new husband.

***

For their honeymoon, Tina and Neville went to Ireland. That was where they had met and it felt like the perfect place to spend their first holiday as man and wife.

Neville left the farm he was working on and got a higher paid job as a farm manager in a piggery near

Surrey. Accommodation was provided by the farm so Neville and Tina lived in a farm cottage. It was small but perfect and although Tina had a slightly longer commute to work; it meant they could save for their future. Tina worked hard to try juggling her work and running her home. She always had a cooked meal every day for Neville when he came home from work and although married life had its challenges, she loved every second of it. The extra money meant they soon had enough to savings for a deposit on their first home.

Tina had never had her own home before. She loved picking out the furniture and wallpaper and Neville had the job of painting and decorating. They made a great team and soon they had the perfect place to call home.

*****

The first year of marriage flew by. Neville had booked a table at their favourite restaurant for their first anniversary. They sat at their table and ordered their food. Tina wanted to talk to Neville. She had something she wanted to discuss. "So Neville, happy anniversary. Can you believe it has been a full year already?"

"Happy anniversary to you my dear. I know it really has flown by. Plus, we have our new home, life is great."

"Yes, the house really is great isn't it Neville? Except…" Tina felt nervous for the first time in a long time.

Neville looked at Tina. "What's wrong? Except what?" he asked as the waitress placed their food in front of them.

"Oh this looks nice, doesn't it Neville?" Tina tried to change the subject and hoped Neville would just forget she was trying to say something.

"Yes, it looks lovely. What were you saying before the food came? I am curious now."

Tina put her fork down. "OK, I was going to say I love our house except the rooms are so quiet. There are just us two rattling around and it seems so quiet."

"I know it is but that is just because you are so used

to the sound of farm machinery but now we are away from the farm we have peace and quiet at last," Neville said before taking a bite of his food.

"I know Neville, but I just think our home is missing something. You know something that may help fill the quietness."

"Tina if you want a dog then you know I will agree. I love animals as well so let's get a dog."

Why does he not get it? I'm gonna just have to say it straight, aren't I? "No Neville I'm not talking about a dog. I'm not talking about farm noises, I'm thinking maybe now we could try for a family of our own. You know, fill the house with the sound of children." Tina promptly picked up her fork and began eating.

Neville sat looking at Tina with a huge smile on his face. "Really Tina? Do you really want a child? A family of our own is everything I want and I have been thinking about it for a few months now."

Tina felt an enormous sense of relief that Neville agreed. "Yes Neville, let's start trying. We can begin tonight if you like," Tina blushed. She had no objections from Neville.

"But about the dog, we can get a dog as well, right?" Tina giggled. In July 1968, Tina and Neville were both thrilled and excited when they discovered Tina was pregnant with their first child. Their family home was about to get noisier and they could not wait.

Chapter 20

Tina had learned from early on that the bond between a mother and her child begins long before the birth. She loved every pregnancy milestone – feeling her baby kick for the first time or when her belly made funny shapes as her baby grew and stretched inside her. She felt like she was recreating the same bond that her birth mother must have built with her when she was pregnant. It was a special feeling that Tina grew to cherish with all her heart.

Choosing a name for their new baby was a real dilemma for Tina. She was six months pregnant when she approached the subject with Neville. Tina had cooked Neville's favourite dinner, a homemade steak and kidney pudding with all the trimmings. "Neville, we need to talk about baby names. We have only three months to go and we have no name picked. Do you have any suggestions?" Tina asked as she then ate her dinner.

Neville thought for a few minutes. "I don't know love. I'll leave that to you. You pick the name. After all, you're doing the hard work so I'll be happy regardless."

"What do you mean you'll be happy 'Regardless'?"

Her reaction surprised Neville. "Nothing love. I just mean I don't really mind what we call our baby. I am not good with names. That's all. You seem upset Tina?"

Tina was not impressed. "Hmmm, OK. Look at me," she said, placing her knife and fork on her plate and throwing her hands in the air."I have no idea what my birth mother called me. I don't know my birth family name. All I have is the name the courts gave me because my adoptive mother could not be bothered to change it. So yes, I am upset. I need you to understand that to mea name is everything."

Neville nodded his head as he listened to Tina speak. "OK love so explains it to me. I'm listening."

Tina smiled. "I'm sorry Neville. I know it is unfair of me to expect you to understand but I'll try to explain. To me, a name is not just a label. It's a person's identity– the first true gift of love that we can give our baby. I was denied that gift so I want our child's name to be special because they will carry it with them for their entire lives and I want them to know that we chose it together and that their name mattered to us."

"But Tina the name will be given by us no matter what we decide."

Tina could feel herself becoming upset again although she understood it was not Neville's fault. How could he possibly understand such a thing? "But

Neville, it's important to me that we both choose a name that means something special. Don't leave it up to me alone."

Neville reached his arm across the table and took hold of Tina's hand. "I'm sorry love. I didn't realise how important this is to you. You know how important you and this baby are to me, don't you? One name I would love is Iris for a middle name if we have a girl. My mother died when I was a child so that would be meaningful for me."

"OK, that would be lovely. And maybe if we have a son we could use Albert as a middle name after my dad?"

Neville smiled. "That sounds perfect love. So now we have middle names let's take some time to think about a first name. Like you said, it needs to be special and not rushed. We can talk about it again once we have some ideas."

"OK," Tina agreed with a smile and they both finished their dinner.

In time, they agreed that if they had a boy they would name him Neville. However, if they were to have a girl Tina did not want to name her after herself because she knew in her heart that Tina was not her birth name. So after much discussion they both agreed that if they had a girl they would name her after the midwife. After all, what better name to give your child than the name of the person who helped bring them into the world?

***

On March 8th, 1969, Tina gave birth to a beautiful new baby girl. Ironically, the midwife was called Christine. Surprisingly this did not upset Tina because now the name Christine held a different meaning to her. It was a part of her baby girl's birth story and she was not going to take that away from her because she knew how that felt.

When the midwife came to check in with her she told Tina that baby Christine was the first baby she had delivered unsupervised and she was honoured to know her first delivery was being named after her. This made the name even more special. At last, the name had a real birth story attached to it and Tina knew she had made the right choice.

The midwife smiled and made a fuss of baby Christine. "Oh, look at you with those beautiful big eyes just like your mother." The midwife turned to Tina with a smile. "You have a beautiful baby girl. She has your eyes. Now, it's time for you to get some rest, you'll need all your energy to look after this little bundle of fun."

Tina smiled and placed her hand on the side of baby Christine's cot. "Thank you. She really does look like me, doesn't she?"

The midwife was called away so she said her goodbyes and promised to check in with them again the next day.

Tina was twenty-nine years old and it suddenly dawned on her that for the first time ever she had someone in her life that was biologically part of her.

'She has your eyes.' The words of the midwife whirled around her head. As she lay there looking at baby Christine another thought came to her, *I wonder whose eyes I have.*

At that moment baby Christine woke up so Tina picked her up to give her a cuddle. "There's my baby girl. It's so nice to have you in my arms all to myself. I'm your mother and I promise you I will never stop loving you. I will never let you down."Tina gently kissed her baby's forehead.

In those days, all newborn babies were taken to a nursery at night. Tina hated to see her baby leave but was glad of the night's rest.

In the bed beside Tina was a young woman who appeared to be alone. No husband seemed to visit her. The nurses were not especially nice to her so Tina introduced herself one evening after all babies were taken to the nursery.

"Hi, my name is Tina. I see you've given birth to a beautiful little boy. I've just had a baby girl." Tina sat on the girl's bed.

"Hello, I'm Jenny. Yes, thank you. My son was born today. He's my first and to be honest, after my labour experience he may be my last," Jenny said with a giggle.

Jenny and Tina sat chatting on Jenny's bed. Jenny was twenty-four years old and was not married to her baby's father although they were due to get married the following month. She told Tina her pregnancy was an accident.

"We had not planned to have a baby. It was a complete shock to us both. Of course my father was not happy and wanted me to 'get rid' but I could not do that. Then he wanted me to give the baby away but that was also not something I could do. It would break my heart."

Tina sat listening to Jenny talk about her pregnancy and was so glad to hear that she had stood up to her parents and kept her beautiful baby. "That was very brave of you Jenny."

"Thank you but I have heard lots of stories about

young girls going into those homes and I just could never do that to my baby. Plus, my boyfriend and I are getting married and will provide a good stable home for our son." Jenny sat up in her bed and puffed out her pillows.

"Your boyfriend sounds like a really nice man," Tina said.

"He's the best. We have been together for three years. I'm a very lucky girl. Of course, some of our friends shunned us when I became pregnant. You would swear we had the plaque. We decided they can't have been real friends so we just forgot about them." Jenny leaned in close to Tina. "What do you think of this hospital Tina?"

"It seems fine to me. I have no complaints really. Why do you ask?" Tina asked.

"Oh well I suppose it is different for you because you are married. I see your husband visits all the time."

Tina smiled. "Yes, he comes every day. I never see your boyfriend at all. Does he live far from here?"

"He's not allowed to visit us. It's against hospital rules. Only married women can have their husbands visit them. If I had known about that rule I would have lied and said we were married. I just so badly want to see him and he wants to see his son."

Tina could not believe what she was hearing. "That is just awful Jenny."

"I know, and some of the nurses are horrible to me. Honestly, you would not believe the way some of them have treated me. All because I'm an unmarried mother. They look down on girls like me. But I'll be going home soon so I'll just bite my lip and then I can get out of here."

Tina thought Jenny was very brave. She was glad to see women in Jenny's situation standing up for themselves against the social norms. It gave her hope for the future of the world that her baby girl would be living in. On her last day in hospital, Jenny gave Tina her address and they both promised to stay in touch with each other.

***

When Tina and Neville brought baby Christine home the once quiet house was soon filled with the sound of a family at last. They were both happy and loved every second of their time with their new daughter.

Tina took to motherhood very well. Spending so much time with baby Christine reminded her of everything her own birth mother had missed with her. She felt a familiar sense of longing creep back into her life. Most women share the happiness of motherhood with their mothers but Tina did not have that. Having Christine in her life brought back her need to find her birth mother. She did not want her secret to deny her own children of ever knowing their true roots. So two weeks before she was due to go back to work part time she put Christine to bed and sat Neville down and discussed her feelings with him.

"Neville, I have loved my time with Christine. Being her mother has reminded me of how important family truly is. I have also been thinking about my birth mother. My secret has caused me so much hurt throughout my life and I don't want it to do the same for our children. No child should ever be denied the right to know where they truly come from."

"So, what are you going to do?" Neville asked.

"Well, I work in social work and there had to be a social worker involved in my adoption. I am hoping my manager may be able to help me locate the records for my adoption file. I don't have access to those files but she must know how I can go about this. I know once a child is adopted the records are supposed to be sealed. I have been told nobody can ever access them but there has to be a way. I have to try," Tina said.

"Look, love, I'm behind you all the way. If you need to do this then of course I will support you. But please don't get your hopes up. I'd hate to see you hurt so please just remember it may not be possible."

"Thank you, Neville, I know you're right and it may not be possible but like I said, I have to try."

***

She returned to work after her maternity leave and asked for a meeting with her manager

The meeting had been arranged for the next day, which gave Tina time to write down all of her questions. When she met with her manager, Mary, she asked if she could speak in confidence and Mary assured her she could trust her with anything she needed to discuss. Tina was nervous. She had only ever discussed her secret with Margaret, Neville, and her aunt Daisy. They were the only people she had ever fully trusted and so this was a big deal for her. However, Mary was a social worker so Tina was sure nothing could shock her. She began by telling Mary about her adoption. She told her she wanted to find her birth mother and asked how she could locate her records.

Mary sat in her chair behind her desk. At hearing Tina's request, she leaned forward with a puzzled look on her face. "What makes you think you can access your records Tina?" It was clear from her body language that Mary was uncomfortable with Tina's request for help."Of course there are adoption records but you know as well as I do that all adoption records are sealed and stored in a secure office."Mary paused to consider her words. "Remember, your adoption took place during wartime with the majority of records lost in fires during the bombings. I'm sorry, but there most likely is nothing left for you to find."

Tina didn't like the tone of Mary's voice. Why is she speaking to me like this? "Mary, I just feel like I need to know who my mother is. After having my baby, I have realised that I want my children to know who their grandparents are. I want to know who I am. I don't expect you to understand this and it is hard for me to explain. I just need your help. Please, will you help me?" Tears brimmed in her eyes.

Mary was confused."Tina, I don't understand. You have the parents who adopted you. They are your children's grandparents. Forget about finding your birth mother and get on with your life."She handed

Tina a tissue to wipe her tears. "As a social worker you know all birth mothers should and must remain protected. When a woman gives up her child, she has a right to remain unknown. We cannot go against her wishes. I know this isn't what you want to hear but that is just the way it has to be." Mary stood up out of her chair and walked to the window. She stared silently out at the street below and then spoke without even looking at Tina. "I'm afraid if you insist on finding your records then you would be putting your entire career on the line."

Tina felt threatened by this. She could not believe what she was hearing. She left the office feeling so let down and frustrated. *What about my rights? Do my feelings not matter at all?* She never discussed the subject with Mary again. However, no matter how hard she tried she just could not let go of her need to know who she was.

***

She spent the rest of the week wondering if her mother

and father would have any information for her. Her mother had forbidden her from ever discussing the matter when she was younger but Tina thought maybe now she was an adult things might be different. That weekend, Tina visited her parents and was determined to ask for their help one more time. The following Saturday morning, she set off for Kent. Neville wished her luck and agreed he would stay home to look after Christine. It was a long drive, but it gave Tina time to think about what she would say to her parents. As she turned onto the road where her parents lived, a wave of nerves washed over her. She hadn't talked to her mother about her secret since she was a child.

As she entered the house she heard her mother in the kitchen. Tina walked in and said hello. Her mother said her dad was working in the garden so she called him in for a cup of tea and a chat. Her dad walked into the kitchen surprised to see her. "Ah hello love this is a lovely surprise. How are you and my beautiful grandaughter did you bring her with you?" he said as he looked around the kitchen.

Tina placed the tea pot and cups on the table. "No Dad, I wanted to call up to see you both by myself. It's good to take a break sometimes." She noticed her mother's look of indignation at her words. "Anyway, let's sit down and have a nice cup of tea. There's something I want to talk to you both about."

Her dad grabbed a chair from the table and sat down. "What's wrong Tina?"

Tina cleared her throat. "OK, well, this is a difficult thing for me to talk about, but I really need your help with something. I need you both to give me answers. I have nobody else that I can turn to". Tina went quiet and waited for her parent's reaction.

"Oh Tina, please stop talking in riddles. Just tell us what is on your mind please," her mother snapped.

Tina felt like she was a child again but saw her dad glaring at her mother and could tell he was not impressed by her mother's attitude."It's OK love you take your time. You can ask me anything," her dad said sympathetically.

Tina shuffled in her chair. "OK, well, since having Christine and becoming a mother I've been thinking about my birth mother."

Her mother let out a loud sigh and threw her hand in the air. "Oh not this again. Tina. I thought you'd put all that behind you?"

Tina refused to allow her mother to dismiss her like this. Not now. She was an adult and needed answers. "Look Mother I know you don't like me talking about it but I need to know who I am. I've spent my whole life wondering why I was given away and why I wasn't wanted. I held my new baby girl in my arms when she was born and I could see my eyes in her eyes. It made me wonder who I look like. My daughter Christine is the only person in my life that has my genes. She's my only biological family member that I know. That's unfair and cruel."

Her mother was not going to entertain her questioning. "Oh for god's sake Tina, you always were overly dramatic. Anyway, Christine looks nothing like you. She's the spitting image of Neville. Anyone can see that."

"Stop," Tina's dad snapped. He looked at his wife whilst thumping his hands on the kitchen table in anger. Tina had never seen her dad so upset."Do not speak to Tina like that. She has done nothing to deserve this from you." He took hold of Tina's hand and squeezed it tightly."My dear, I am so sorry for everything your mother has just said to you. It was nasty and uncalled for. I understand what you're saying and I hate to see you hurt." Her dad was upset and trying his best to be understanding."Love, we can't help you because we don't know anything. We were never told a thing about your birth mother or father. I don't think you'll ever know the answers to your questions. It's time to forget about it. You have your own family to look after now. You need to look to your future and stop chasing your past."He threw a look at his wife, who was now busy at the kitchen sink ignoring Tina and Albert completely. Tina finished her tea and changed the subject. She knew her dad thought he was helping her. He was just too old and set in his ways to understand how she was feeling. Her mother barely raised a hand to say goodbye when she left to go home so Tina hugged her dad and made her way out to the car.

***

She walked into her house and picked Christine up in her arms.

"How did you get on with your parents love?" Neville asked.

Tina turned to face Neville and tears streamed from her eyes. Neville just put his arms around her and held her in silence. Tina then put Christine back in her pram and left her to sleep. She and Neville both sat in the sitting room to talk.

"Neville, nobody wants to help me. My mother was her usual cruel self. I felt like I was fourteen again. She shouted me down back then and she did the same thing today. I have spent so many years trying to make that woman love me, like me, even." Tina took a tissue from a box on the coffee table and wiped her eyes. "I honestly thought she had changed. But no. She has not changed one little bit. All I want to know is who gave birth to me. It sounds so simple doesn't it? Surely I should be allowed to know that much about my life. Why does nobody care about my feelings in all of this? I thought the world was changing. I had some hope for the future of our children. Now that hope has been misplaced. It is as cruel today as it was when I was born." Tina leaned in to Neville as he put his arm around her.

"Tina I am so sorry that this has happened. I don't know how to make it better. If I could take away your hurt then I would."

"I know you would. You're the only one I can truly rely on. I just feel like I'm letting Christine down. Like I'm the reason she and any child of ours will never know their true roots."

Neville gave her some more tissues. "You're not

letting anyone down. Our children will always know love. They will always have us in their lives. Neither of us had great childhoods. We can't keep looking at our past. We have to look to the future not just for us, but for Christine and our future children."

"I know you're right Neville it just hurts that's all. I will be fine. I guess some people are never meant to be found. Some secrets are meant to stay a secret forever."

Christine woke up and started crying so Neville went into the kitchen and picked her up out of her pram. He brought her in to Tina and placed her in Tina's arms. "Here, here is our future. Our daughter. Look at her she is your flesh and blood Tina."

Tina smiled at Christine. *My future, my world, my everything*, she thought as she gently bounced her daughter in her arms. She knew Neville was right and so she decided she had to move forward and try to let it all go. The longing to know her true identity never fully left her but she learned to live with it.

Chapter 21

On April 24th, 1972, Tina gave birth to another beautiful girl who they named Linda Margaret, in honor of Tina's two old nursing friends. Now they had two daughters to look after. Life was busy but great. They had little money and every penny they had was spent on their children, but they never complained because their little family was worth it.

Tina went to see her parents and brought Christine and baby Linda with her. When she arrived, her parents were both sitting at the kitchen table as always but this time Tina thought they looked different. She could not put her finger on it but something felt wrong. Tina's mother looked in at Linda who was fast asleep in her pram.

"So, this is Linda. Why did you choose that name?"Tina's Mother asked indignantly.

Tina knew her mother would ask this and explained that she and Neville named Linda after her good friend and fellow student nurse that had died just after they had finished their training.

At hearing that, her mother just threw her nose in the air."Hmmm well it would have been nice if my family was remembered, but it's your choice I suppose," Her mother was unsteady on her feet and Tina noticed she was holding on to the table as she moved back to her chair. Tina stood up reaching out her hand to offer assistance."Are you OK Mother?"

Her mother waved Tina's hand away. "I'm fine, stop fussing."

Her attention switched to her dad as he began coughing."Dad, are you OK?"

Her dad turned to look at her and smiled softly. "I'm fine love. I just have a bit of a bad chest. The doc has given me tablets and they should see me right again."

Tina was worried but she thought maybe she was over thinking things, after all, they were both getting older now. However, four months after this visit both of her parents were diagnosed with incurable stomach and lung cancer. They were to receive treatment but the treatment would only prolong their lives for a short time. Tina was devastated. Her nurse training taught her that cancer was scary and she should expect the worst. Her focus turned to her parents' health.

She spent almost every weekend travelling to Kent. She had two children to care for, a house to run and a job to hold down as well as having to look after two sick parents. She also had to deal with her mother's family interfering and criticising her every move. It was a struggle but she could not let anyone see she was not coping. She had to put on a brave face.

***

In January 1973, Albert was rushed to the hospital. A neighbour had called in to check on him and noticed that Albert was struggling to breathe. Tina was called to the hospital. She could feel her heart beating out of her chest as she braved the snow-covered roads to the hospital. When she arrived, the ward sister told her that Albert had been struggling with his breathing. He had dramatically deteriorated and may not survive the night. "He's been asking for you," she said whilst gently rubbing Tina's arm. "I must warn you to prepare yourself for the worst. The next twenty-four hours could be very difficult for your dad."

Tina knew what she meant. "Thank you, I understand. Can I stay with my dad? If this is going to be his last night then I don't want him to be alone."

"Of course, you stay as long as you want," the ward sister said before being called away to assist a nurse with a patient.

Her mother was also in the hospital. She had a relapse and was very ill. Tina decided to focus on her dad as he needed her the most at that time. Fighting back her tears she sat with him and held his hand. She didn't want him to see her falling apart. He needed her to be strong and she did not want to let him down. Eventually he opened his eyes and gave a big smile as he saw Tina sat beside him.

"Hello love. It's great to see you."His face was very pale, his breathing was weak and he looked like a skeleton because he had lost so much weight."I'm afraid I'm not feeling so good today." Taking hold of Tina's hand, he pulled her close. "I need to talk to you and this may be my only chance so please just listen"

Tina drew close to him. "What's wrong Dad? Take your time."

He composed himself and asked to have his pillows plumped up so he could sit up in the bed. "I'm sorry for everything you have had to endure because of us. I want you to know that I would not blame you if you packed your bags and walked away," he said, taking a break to breathe. "When I'm gone you walk away. You owe her nothing."

When he said her Tina knew he was referring to her mother. "Dad, don't worry. I won't leave her. I'll look after her because no one else would be brave enough to do it," she said with a hint of sarcasm. She saw the vague outline of a smile appear on her dad's face as if he understood why she would say such a thing.

"I love you Tina. I always have– never forget that."Her dad closed his eyes and fell into a deep sleep. She pulled the blankets up around his chest and told him she loved him too. She never doubted that he loved her. They had their own way of communicating with each other despite her mother's attempts to keep them apart.

As she sat at her dad's hospital bed the enormity of what was happening hit Tina like a bag of bricks as her dad slowly slipped into unconsciousness. She sat at his bedside unable to contain her tears any longer. She knew her dad would not make it through the night. He was dying and there was nothing she could do except hold his hand.

The doctor was carrying out his rounds with the senior ward nurse and when he got to Albert, he pulled the curtain and looked at his patient notes. Tina stood at the foot of the bed watching as he examined Albert. Her dad began struggling to breathe and then suddenly there was silence. The doctor listened to his chest and then turned to look at Tina. "I am so sorry but your father has passed away." Tina felt like the world around her was fading away and the doctor's voice sounded slurred and distant. She could feel her heart pounding as she clutched her chest and cried out loud. "But I'm not ready. I thought I was but I'm not." Tina looked at the doctor and pleaded with him. "Please, please can you do something? Please help him."

The nurse put her arm around Tina and helped her walk around to her dad's bedside so she could sit on the chair. "I'm sorry but there really is nothing we can do." The nurse and doctor then left Tina alone with her dad. As she sat with her dad she kept expecting him to open his eyes and shout 'just joking love' but that did not happen.

She pulled the blankets up closer to his chin and gently stroked his cheek with the back of her hand. She sat on the chair beside the bed and closed her eyes to stop her tears from falling. Her head filled with all the words she wanted to say to him. *I love you Dad. I am going to miss you. I will miss our chats, your laughter, your cheeky winks and most of all I will miss your cuddles. You were my dad no matter what. You were always here for me and now you are gone*. As she opened her eyes she saw the curtain being slightly pulled back and a nurse was standing there.

"I am sorry, but isn't your mother also a patient in this hospital. Is that correct?" The nurse asked.

Tina wiped her eyes. "Yes, yes, she is."

"OK, well, would you like me to tell her what has

happened?"

"No, no, I will do it." Tina stood up and gave her dad one last kiss on his forehead before pulling herself together and making her way to her mother accompanied by the nurse for added support.

She walked onto the ward and saw her mother laying on her bed. She looked old and frail and was obviously in pain. Florence saw Tina standing in the doorway to her ward and beckoned her to come over to her.

"What on earth is wrong with you Tina? Have you seen your father? I want to see him but they won't let me out of this bed." The nurse and doctor made their way over to her. "What are you doing here? I have already talked to the doctor today." Florence was looking between the doctor and Tina and clutching her tummy with pain.

"Mrs Vousden I—"

Tina raised her hand and interrupted. "It's OK Doctor I will tell her."

Tina sat beside her mother and took hold of her hand. However, her mother pulled her hand away and tucked it under the blankets. "Oh for god's sake, will someone tell me what is happening."

"Mother I have just been with dad. He was talking to me and drifting in and out of consciousness. I am so sorry to have to tell you but Dad has just passed away. He's gone Mother."Tina could feel tears streaming down her face as she spoke.

Florence lay back on her bed and turned to the wall unable to face the doctor or Tina. She cried uncontrollably while clutching her stomach with the pain of her cancer gripping hold of her. Tina wanted to hug her but knew her mother would not want that so she pulled the curtain around her bed to give her privacy before making her way home. That was the first time she had ever seen or heard her mother cry.

***

Three Months later Tina was still trying to cope with the loss of her father and look after her mother who had to be taken back into hospital many times. The grief of losing her husband was too much for her to bear and she simply gave up fighting for her life. On her last admission to hospital the doctors told Tina her mother was dying. There was no more they could do except keep her comfortable. Tina kept her promise to her dad but her mother was a very difficult and ungrateful patient and made it clear she did not want help from anyone.

Tina sat beside her mother's hospital bedside as she always did. Her mother wanted to write a letter so Tina placed a pen and paper on her bedside locker.

"So how are you feeling today mother?" Tina asked. Her mother opened her eyes and grabbed hold of Tina's hand digging her nails deep into her daughter's skin. "How do you think I'm feeling? I'm in pain and I am so tired. Where is Ivy? I need my sister, my family."

Tina's hands burned. "You're hurting me mother. Aunt Ivy couldn't make it today so I came instead." Tina tried not to raise her voice. She knew she had to show compassion although her mother made that a very difficult task.

With a firm grip on Tina's hand Florence spoke and the cruelest of words fell from her mouth. "Let me tell you something girl. I never wanted you then and I still don't want you now."

These words seemed to flow from her mother's mouth with such despicable ease despite how gravely ill she was. Tina stared at her mother stunned at what she was hearing. Tears fell from her eyes as she pulled her hand away from her mother's grip. She did not want her mother to see how much her words had hurt her. Instead, Tina decided her silence was the greatest defense. She composed herself and without saying a word she stood up, gathered her bag and coat and walked away from her mother's bedside.

As she turned to walk away, she noticed the ward sister standing at the foot of her mother's bed. She could tell by the look on the sister's face that she had heard everything her mother had just said to her.

As Tina walked towards the door to leave the ward, she heard the sister talking to her. "My dear, your mother is gravely ill. She didn't mean what she said. It will have been the medication. It can do terrible things to the mind. Don't walk away. You don't have long left with her now – she may not make it through the night."

Tina looked at the ward sister. "Thank you. I know you're trying to comfort me. I assure you my mother knows exactly what she's saying. Trust me when I say she means every word. I have heard it my entire life. So, I am done. I can't listen to it anymore," Tina said, trying to hold back her tears. She glanced back through the doorway at her mother who was lying helplessly in her bed. Her eyes were closed and she was calling for the nurse. Tina thought how sad it was that a woman of her mother's age had nobody by her side in her dying moments. She didn't feel guilty about leaving her there. She had tried her best throughout her life to make her mother proud – to make her happy. She had spent her entire childhood craving her mother's love but even being so close to death her mother could not find a kind word to say to her. As she walked down the hospital corridor, she could hear her father's last words to her in her head. You owe her nothing love. She no longer cared what or how her mother was feeling. Tina was glad her nightmare was finally going to end. That was the last time she saw her mother. Florence died alone in the hospital that night.

Tina went back to her parent's house. Neville had the children in bed. She just fell into his arms with her mother's words playing in her head."She is dead Neville, she is gone". They both sat silently in the sittingroom as Tina told Neville what her mother had said to her. Neville put his arm around her. "You are home now love, I have you. It is all over now." Neville did not know what else to say.

***

A few days after her mother's funeral, Tina arrived at her parent's house and spent a whole weekend packing away their belongings. Neville offered to come and help but Tina wanted to do it by herself.

She walked into the house and sat on the old brown leather sofa. The house seemed so silent, so empty and as she sat back, she could hear all the echoes of her past swirling around her. Patch barking in the kitchen the sounds of her parents talking in hushed muffled tones behind closed doors. She smiled as she could hear her dad's voice echoing gently telling her to "ssshh" whenever he gave her sweets behind her mother's back. She could see her dad in her mind's eye giving her one of his big smiles and a wink as if he was there letting her know he was OK.

She thought back to all the conversations and secrets buried in the walls of her childhood home. If walls could speak this house would have some tales to tell. She felt like the house would forever be haunted by the secrets of her past. It was as if no amount of cleaning would ever be able to remove the stains that had tarnished it for so long.

Eventually, she began packing boxes. She had arranged for local charity workers to call and take the big furniture. She knew from her social work that there were families who could benefit greatly from her parent's furniture.

She had called her aunt Ivy and asked if there was anything she would like of her mother's. Her aunt arranged to meet her at her parent's house the next day. She dreaded seeing Ivy, but knew it was the right thing to do.

When Ivy arrived, Tina knew by the look on her face that she had something on her mind. Of course her cousin was with her.

"I want to talk to you Christine," Ivy exclaimed as she marched into the house.

Tina hated that even now after all these years her aunt still could not respect her wishes and call her Tina but she decided to ignore the woman's ignorance.

Ivy stood tall in the kitchen. "The family have been talking and we feel it's only fitting that since you are not our real family by blood, you should not get anything belonging to my sister so you can go and we'll handle things from here."

Tina's cousin, Deborah, stood there with a big grin on her face. Tina wanted to punch them both. *How dare they speak to me like this. Who do they think they are?* She could feel a whole lifetime of hurt and anger bubbling inside her and it was about to hit the surface. She had enough of them and their cruel remarks. Tina was not going to let them do it to her anymore.

"How dare you speak to me like this. I will decide what I take from this house. Not you or anyone else." Anger burned inside her. "I have already packed a box for me to take but I want nothing more of my mother's belongings. She was a nasty, bitter, cold, and uncaring woman with you as her teacher. I'm glad I'm not related to you by blood because that means I can walk away and never look back. However, you lot are stuck with each other. So, as far as I am concerned, I don't want anything to do with you ever again." Tina could not believe the words coming out of her mouth. She had never stood up for herself like that before especially not to them but she could not help herself. They had gone too far this time. Her aunt became very agitated and her cousin was just about to speak when Tina raised her hand in the air as if to silence her."You can stop right there. Don't you open your mouth. You've spent your whole life looking down on me. Well, I'm the one with a career a husband, two beautiful children and my own home. What do you have?"Tina asked.

"You failed your schooling you have no husband and you are a grown woman still living with her parents. Your words can't hurt me anymore."Tina was not about to be hurt by her mother's family. Not now and not ever."Please, will you both just take what you want and leave. You are not welcome in this house while I'm here." Tina pointed towards the front door.

Both her aunt and cousin said nothing – they were stunned into silence. They had never been spoken to like that before and did not know how to deal with it. They gathered themselves and left the house as quickly as their feet could carry them. They did not even wait to take anything with them.

Once they were both out of sight Tina fell into the kitchen chair. She took a deep breath and felt like a lifetime of hurt had been lifted from her shoulders. She did not know she had it in her to be so assertive but she loved that she finally stood up to them and wondered what they must have been saying about her on their journey home. That was the last time Tina ever saw of either them or any member of her mother's family. She decided she did not need them. She had everyone she needed at home in Neville and her children.

Suddenly her thoughts were interrupted as she heard the doorbell ring. She thought it was her aunt coming back for another argument so she tried to ignore it but it rang again. She composed herself and opened the door. She was surprised to see Alice Brown standing there. Tina had not seen Alice for many years but was glad to see her old friend.

"Hello Tina, I hope I'm not bothering you, but I just wanted to pay my respects at this sad time."

"Please come in Alice. You're not bothering me at all. In fact, it's lovely to see you."Tina beckoned Alice to come into the house. "It's nice to see you after all these years. Please take a seat and I'll make us a nice cup of tea."

Alice sat at the kitchen table."I was so sorry to hear about your parents. It must be so hard for you. I can't imagine how I would feel if I were in your position," Alice said sympathetically.

Tina smiled and placed a fresh cup of tea in front of Alice. "It's really good to see you. It only feels like yesterday that we were both young girls playing on the street or making daisy chains."Tina laughed.

"Oh Tina, those days were a lifetime ago. We did have fun though even if life was difficult. We both made it through and look at us now. We're all the better for it."

We both made it through. Tina wondered what Alice meant but she thought Alice must have been talking about her baby and her own difficulties.

"Tina, I want you to know that you are not alone and can always call on me if you need a chat. I know you have had your struggles but now you're free to move on from it all."

"What do you mean Alice? What do you know?"Tina asked, feeling a bit baffled.

Alice went silent for a few seconds. "Do you remember a long time ago there was a Christmas choir rehearsal? Oh it was a long time ago. You were there singing in the choir with my sister."

Tina nodded."Well, I saw a woman talking to you afterwards and you ran out of the hall crying so I approached her and asked what she had said to you to make you so upset."

Tina was shocked to hear this and a bit baffled as to why she was saying this to her all these years later. "And what did the woman tell you exactly?"

"Oh she just told me she had told you the truth about yourself. I didn't understand what she meant. I told my mother and she told me she thought you were adopted because one day your parents had no children and then suddenly you arrived. She assumed that must have been what the woman was talking to you about. However, I couldn't possibly say it to you because I didn't know if it was true. But it's OK. I promise I didn't tell anyone. I would never do that."

Tina didn't know what to say. Part of her was annoyed that Alice was telling her this right now but she also remembered that Alice had her own secret to bear so she did not react with anger. Alice was right. She was now free to move on from that part of her life. "Oh my goodness Alice, all this time has gone by and I never knew that you knew about my secret. Actually, I only discovered my adoption not long after you and I sat in the park talking about your baby boy. Do you remember that, Alice?"

"Oh yes, yes, I remember that day and you're still

the only person who I ever talked to about that. You were such a good friend to me back then. I tried calling to your house but your mother always told me you were out. Then I got the job in Nottingham and time went by and before I knew it, we had lost touch. Time just goes by so fast."

The two women sat talking to each other about their lives and their childhood memories. Tina asked if Alice ever thought of her son after all these years.

Alice placed her cup on the table. "Every day – especially on special days like Mother's Day or his birthday."

"Really? I always wonder if my mother thinks of me because I think of her all the time. Like you said, Mother's Day and birthdays are special days but also when I became a mother I thought about her regularly," Tina told Alice."I tried so hard to find my birth parents, but I was told the records are private. Apparently, I could go to prison if I even try to look for my birth records. I have had no help at all so eventually

I gave up."

Alice seemed surprised to hear Tina say this."Do you want to find them Tina?" asked Alice.

Tina nodded her head. "Not one day goes by that I don't want to find them. I just don't know how or where to look. Do you want to meet your son one day?"

"It is my dearest wish and dream and hearing that you want to find your birth parents fills me with the hope that maybe my baby boy will want to find me one day," Alice replied, holding her hands to her chest….

"It has been lovely being able to talk to you about this Alice, I wish I had talked to you years ago. I honestly think you and I are the only ones who truly understand how we're both feeling. Our stories are like the opposite side of the same coin," Tina said with a smile.

"Ah, but in those days, we weren't allowed to talk to anyone about family business. Our secrets were meant to be kept forever but thankfully times seem to be changing now Tina and maybe more people will be on our side at last."

"I really hope so Alice. In my work, I see so many people in similar situations to us and I pray they find their answers. The world is so unfair sometimes," Tina said.

Just then, the doorbell rang. It was Alice's mother to tell her that her lunch was ready. Alice and her husband and four children were visiting for the day.

Alice stood up to leave and she put her arms out to Tina to give her a hug. "Don't stop searching until you find them." She whispered in Tina's ear.

"I promise. And don't you give up either," Tina whispered back.

Alice smiled and left the house linking arms with her mother. The house was silent again, and Tina got ready to leave. She washed the cups, put them in a box with all the other cups and plates for the charity shop and loaded the car.

Tina went for one last walk around her family home. It was one last goodbye to a home that held so many difficult painful memories but it was her home all the same. She picked up her coat, walked out the front door and pulled it shut behind her. As she walked down the garden path, she was thinking about her conversation with Alice. She thought about how life was so strange at times. She and Alice were more alike than either of them realised. As she drove away from her parent's house for the last time, Tina felt like she had just closed a massive chapter in her life and she felt relived by that.

She had not said anything to Neville yet but she was sure she was expecting again.

Chapter 22

Three months after her mother's funeral, Tina discovered she was pregnant again. At first, she was excited. She felt great having some good news for once. After the events of the last twelve months, she finally had something to look forward to again. However, she really struggled with her grief. Being a mother of two young children, pregnant and dealing with the aftermath of so much loss took its toll on Tina. Then in October 1973, she was heartbroken once more. Her

Uncle Fred called to tell her that her aunt Daisy had been taken ill in the night and had sadly died. She had been having headaches but Fred told Tina that Daisy collapsed on her way up to bed and he had to call an ambulance. She had suffered a stroke and never recovered. Tina was beyond devastated upon hearing this news. Her Aunt Daisy was like a mother to her.

A month after her Aunt Daisy's funeral, uncle Fred asked Tina to help him store away some of Daisy's belongings. She called over to his house with boxes and bags in hand. As she arrived, she noticed for the first time that Fred looked frail and old.It was sad to see him so heartbroken. He was lost without Daisy.

"I have been looking through some of Daisy's things and wondered if there is anything you would like to keep. I know how much she meant to you and I am sure she would love for you to have a few keepsakes," Fred asked.

"Thank you, Uncle Fred. I'd like that." Tina and Fred were in the sitting room and in the corner stood her aunt Daisy's old sewing and knitting stool. Tina had fond memories of her aunt and her sitting by the fire, knitting or sewing. Daisy stored her wool, knitting needles and all kinds of craft materials in that little stool.

"Uncle Fred, would you mind if I took this little storage stool? I have so many happy memories of this. But if you want to keep it, I understand."

Fred smiled as he walked over to the corner of the room and picked up the stool. "Of course Tina, Daisy loved this. It was like her little treasure trove of crafty bits and bobs. I know she would love you to have it." Fred placed the stool in front of Tina.

It was a beautiful dark brown solid mahogany stool, which doubled as a storage box. Tina rubbed her hand across the top of the stool. Her hand gently traced the ornate decorative carvings that were covering the hinged lidded seat. She opened the lid and ran her hand around the lining of blue and pink silk lace. As she rubbed her hand across the base of the storage space, the padded lace cushion came away and underneath was a piece of paper folded in half. Tina took the paper in her hand and opened it out. As she looked at it tears filled her eyes. It was a hand drawn picture of what looked like a lady and a little girl with knitting needles in their hands and across the bottom were the words Me and my Aunt Daisy. Again she felt the sting of tears as she realised it was an old picture that she had drawn many years ago for Daisy. Tina clutched the picture to her chest as her Uncle Fred sat beside her on the sofa. Realising that she had found the picture, Fred put his arm around Tina.

"Aw love, Daisy adored you. This was one of her favourites." Fred smiled and Tina placed the picture back in the stool.

"Thank you, Uncle Fred. I will treasure this and I promise I will take good care of the stool as well."

***

She adored her Aunt Daisy and her death brought Tina to her knees. She had lost so much in her life already that her mental health could not handle any more grief and so Tina suffered an emotional breakdown. She spent four weeks being cared for in the hospital where she spent most of her days just resting. She was classed as low risk and because of her pregnancy she was placed in a general and maternity hospital where psychiatric care was also provided. She felt safe there. She had twice weekly sessions with a psychiatrist who allowed her to talk whilst he listened. She opened up to him completely and told him all about her secret. She found that once she started talking, she could not stop.

On her first session the doctor asked her what was her earliest childhood memory. Tina thought for a few minutes. "My earliest memory is of me sitting in a pram looking around at my surroundings but I have no idea of where I was or who was with me. I try so hard sometimes to remember more details from that time but it's like my mind is blank."

The doctor sat forward in his chair. "Why is that memory so important to you, Tina?"

"Because maybe if I could remember where I was or if I could remember who I was with, then maybe I could see my birth mother's face. Maybe then I would know who she was." Tina bowed her head.

"Why is it so important to you to know who she was Tina?"

Tina looked up at the doctor. "Because since the age of fourteen I have walked around this world not knowing who I am. Feeling like a fraud, a fake or imposter. Nobody wanted me. Why? What was so bad about me? I was a child. What could I have possibly done that was so bad? Even my adoptive mother did not want me. Her family didn't want me. The nursing profession didn't want me." She stopped talking as tears stung her eyes.

The doctor handed Tina some tissues. "You say you felt this from the age of fourteen. Why fourteen?"

Tina wiped her eyes and after taking a deep breath she stood up and walked to the window, which looked out over a beautiful garden. "Because I was just fourteen when I discovered I was adopted. I was just fourteen when my mother forbade me from ever discussing my adoption with anyone. Even she would not talk to me about it. I was fourteen when my entire world came crashing down around me. I have never felt pain like it in my entire life." Tina went silent in her thoughts and then took a deep breath before returning to her seat.

"Before I discovered my adoption, life was hard enough for me. My mother and her family were never kind to me but at least I thought I knew who I was. At least I had my dad who I adored but even he was not my real dad. Even he was just 'standing in'." Tina stopped again and dried her eyes as more tears fell.

The Doctor was quietly writing notes into his notebook and then looked up at Tina. "What do you mean when you say your dad was 'standing in'?"

Tina sat quietly searching for the words to answer this question. "Until the age of fourteen, I may not have had the happiest of childhoods. My mother was not the most maternal woman in the world but I had my dad. He was my rock, my calm, my safe. However, when I discovered I was adopted I felt like everything and everyone in my life was not real. My mother and father felt just like actors in my life, 'standing in' for my birth parents. Like caretakers and nothing made sense to me. But then that made me feel guilty as well"

The doctor continued making his notes. "Why did you feel guilty Tina?"

"I feel guilty because I loved my dad and it really hurt to feel badly about him because he was the one person in my life that had my back."

"And how do you feel now?"

Tina had to think. "Now I feel lost because everyone is leaving me. I lost my dad my mother and now my Aunt Daisy. I don't know how to cope. How do I deal with this? Uncle Fred is the only one I have left and once he's gone that's it. I'm alone. I'm scared. How can I be a good mother or wife without my Aunt Daisy to advise me? I feel like I'm letting everyone down."

The doctor put down his notebook and looked at his watch. "OK, let me just say I have heard you talk at length about how difficult your life has been. I have heard you talking about your fears and worries. But when I look at you this is what I see. I see a young woman who has had the cruelest of starts to life. I see a woman who has been let down by almost everyone in her childhood. However, I also see a woman who, despite every knock back, has picked herself up and kept going. I see a strong, intelligent woman who has not allowed life stop her from achieving her dreams. You are a wife, a mother and a good friend. You are stronger than you realise."

"Thank you, Doctor, I wish I could see the woman you see," Tina said.

"My dear, she is there and before you leave this hospital you will see her too. I promise."

The session ended and the doctor told Tina he wanted her to think about all the things that were bothering her. He asked her to write it all down and gave her a small notebook to keep notes.

Over the next four weeks she filled the notebook with her thoughts and discussed them with the doctor on each session. In her last session the doctor handed her a piece of paper and an envelope and told her to write a letter to herself. He asked her to write about all the things that mattered the most in her life as well as her own hopes and dreams. He then told her to put it in the envelope and store it somewhere safe at home so that when things get her down she could take out the letter and remind herself of what matters most.

***

Tina had been surrounded by so much death in her life that she became convinced her unborn baby was dead. It was a fear that she just could not shake. During her time in hospital, she had many chats with a young nurse called Claire. She spent many hours trying to calm her fears.

On Tina's last day at the hospital she sat at a table writing her letter to herself as the doctor asked her to.

She struggled to find the words so she wrote just a few sentences.

Dear Tina,

If things get you down, just remember your husband loves you, your children adore you. You do not need anyone else in your life and although you may never have riches in gold you have all your wealth you need in your children.

You cannot keep looking back because then you will never move forward. Do what makes you happy and remember, letting go is not defeat. Sometimes letting go and moving forward, leaving the past behind, takes more courage than holding on, but you can do it.

Remember that brave fourteen-year-old who defiantly changed her name and told the world how she wanted to be addressed? Well, that fourteen-year-old may have grown up but her bravery is still there deep within you. You got this and as Aunt Daisy always said, 'All you can ever do in life is your best and if your best is not good enough for some people then that is their problem, not yours'. Make change happen in your own time.

Love from me.

She signed her letter and placed it in the envelope. Nurse Claire dropped by her bed to say goodbye and wish her luck.

"So Tina, this is your last day. How are you feeling about going home?"

"Oh Claire, I'm so grateful to you and the hospital for everything. But I'm also looking forward to seeing my family again. My husband has been fantastic in looking after the girls but they need me home with them where I belong."

Claire smiled. "Absolutely Tina, you have done so well you should be proud of yourself. And don't worry about your new arrival. I guarantee that when your little one is born he or she will be just fine. I know it. Just have faith."

Tina gave Claire a hug and promised she would stop worrying.

Nurse Claire was right and, on the 14th March 1974, Tina gave birth to a beautiful, strong and healthy baby girl. As soon as she gave birth Tina thought of Nurse Claire and she and Neville both agreed to name her Claire. They were the proud parents of three baby girls, Christine, Linda and Claire.

***

Cutting ties with her mother's family was scary, but it meant she no longer had to put up with their cruel remarks or comments ever again. She did however stay in touch with her uncle Fred, and visited him regularly with the children. However, Tina felt like she needed a complete change. She loved her job, but there were aspects she found hard to cope with. Especially the adoption cases. She felt she had come so far in herself since her stay in the hospital that she did not want anything to set her back. So just two months after having baby Claire she sat Neville down for a chat.

When the children were in bed, she and Neville were both in the sitting room watching television. Tina asked Neville to turn the TV off so they could talk. "Neville, I think we need to talk. Or rather, I need to talk to you."

Neville got up to turn off the television. "OK love, what's up?

"Well, I've been thinking for some time now that I need a change. I need to move jobs."

"But I thought you loved your Job Tina?"

"I do, but there are aspects that are just so hard for me and I cannot cope with it any longer."

"OK love, so what will you do?"

"Well, the courts are looking for someone to work as an interpreter for the deaf and dumb. It would be part time but it is good money and a lot less stressful. Plus, I could teach sign language classes."

Neville smiled. "OK Tina, if that is what you want, then I will support you."

"Thank you Neville. I Don't know what I would do without you."Tina handed in her notice at the office and signed up with the courts for interpreter work. Life became a lot easier for her.

***

In October 1976, Tina received a phone call from the hospital. Uncle Fred had been taken ill and admitted to hospital. Things were not looking good for him.

Chapter 23

Tina rushed to the hospital to be by Fred's side. He had been unwell for some time. In June of 1976 the doctors diagnosed him with lung cancer. Tina had watched her dad, Fred's brother, suffer and die with the same disease. Fred was told there was nothing that could be done for him, but the doctors thought he would have another twelve months of life.

When Tina arrived at the hospital, she was shown to a side room and the doctor came to speak to her.

Tina was recorded as Fred's next of kin. "Mrs McClaughry, your uncle is very sick," the doctor said whilst taking a seat at his desk.

"Please call me Tina. What is the matter with my uncle? Is it the cancer?"

The doctor leaned forward in his seat. "Your uncle Fred's neighbour knocked in to check on him as he had not seen him all day. When Fred failed to answer the door, his neighbour looked through the front window and saw him lying on the floor. When he was brought in to the hospital, he was struggling to breathe and we believe he is gravely ill. I am so sorry, but your uncle may not make it through the night."

Tina sat back in her chair. She knew this was coming but she thought she had more time. "But when he was diagnosed you told him he would have twelve months left before he would get seriously ill?"

The doctor sighed. "Yes, we did, but unfortunately, it's sometimes hard to be sure. Sadly, your uncle's illness has progressed much faster than we thought it would."Tina understood what the doctor was saying and of course it was not their fault.

Uncle Fred never got over losing Daisy and his grief must have exacerbated his illness. "Can I sit with him please?" Tina asked.

"Of course, I will get a nurse to show you where he is. If you need anything please just ask the nurse."

When Tina got to Fred's bed, she could see he was slipping in and out of consciousness. She sat with him for an hour before he opened his eyes long enough to see her sat at his bedside. He was too weak to speak but he smiled to acknowledge her presence.

"It's OK Uncle Fred, you don't have to talk. I'm here and won't be going anywhere." As Tina spoke she saw a tear fall from Fred's eye. "Shhh don't cry Uncle Fred. I'm OK. Don't worry about me. All that matters right now is you." Tina took hold of his hand and held it in hers. "I love you Uncle Fred. Thank you for everything you've done for me in my life. I want you to know that I'm OK. You don't need to hang on here for me. It's OK for you to go now." Tina struggled to hold back her tears. "It's time for you to go meet Aunt Daisy. No need to be afraid. She'll be waiting for you with the kettle on and one of her cakes freshly baked just for you." Fred managed a faint smile at hearing this. He tried to squeeze Tina's hand and then he closed his eyes and drifted away. Tina was heartbroken but it brought her comfort knowing he was no longer in pain and was with her Aunt Daisy where he belonged.

Tina was the closest relative to Fred so two weeks after his funeral she took on the task of emptying his house. Every room held special memories for her. She walked into the kitchen where she could still smell the faint smell of fresh baked bread. In her mind's eye she could see them all sat around the table chatting and laughing whilst eating delicious home cooked cake and drinking tea. In the sitting room, she could picture Uncle Fred sitting in his armchair. On the shelf was his sweet tin. She opened the lid and saw there were two sweets still inside. She could swear she heard her uncle speaking to her. "Go on, have a sweet. Our secret." Tina smiled to herself as she looked at the window where the Christmas tree stood every year. She could see herself as a child opening her brand-new doll and Uncle Fred carrying in the handmade cradle that he had made for her. Those were happy times — memories Tina knew she would have with her forever.

***

When Tina arrived home from Fred's house, she noticed that Neville seemed quiet. It was not like him to not ask Tina how her day was or offer to help with cooking dinner. Tina just thought he must have had a bad day at work. By the time the children were in bed, Tina could not stay quiet any longer. Whilst Neville sat quietly watching television, she asked him what was wrong.

"Neville are you OK? You seem very quiet today?"

Neville looked up from the television. "I'm sorry Tina. I have something to tell you. I Just don't know how."

Tina was worried at hearing his. "Look Neville, just tell me. It can't be that bad. Can it?"

"Well things are not good at work. I've been told that I am being let go. I am sorry love. I promise I will snap out of this mood and I will find work somewhere."

Tina tried not to let her worry show. "Look Neville don't worry we'll be fine. We always manage and this will be no different. There is work out there."

Neville was true to his word and found work in a security firm. He settled in to his new role that saw him spend three days on the road driving money transit vans to the banks and for two days a week he worked in the office as part of the recruitment team. He also had lots of overtime at weekends. Life was good again and the extra money came in very handy.

The company also had an office in Ireland and he was told of work opportunities within the Irish office. It was more money and as it was a new office there would be good opportunities for promotion. When his manager told him of the openings Neville was told that he could easily transfer if he wished. Neville thought about nothing else over the next week. He was born in Ireland but he had spent the majority of his life in the UK. When he left Ireland as a young man, he always planned to move back there eventually. However, he met Tina and settled down with a family so the opportunity never arose until now. He had told his manager he would let him know soon if he was interested.

On that Friday he bought a bunch of flowers for Tina on his way home. They were going out for a meal that evening so he was going to bring up the subject of Ireland with her then.

"Oh they're lovely Neville. It's not my birthday you know."

Neville smiled. "I know. Can I not treat my wife to flowers now?"

Tina smelled the flowers and placed them in a vase. "The babysitter will be here soon," Tina said as she filled the vase with water.

Neville ran upstairs to get washed and changed and they were soon being seated at their table in the restaurant.

Tina could not help but notice that Neville seemed a little different. "Neville, what is up with you today? You seem to be in an extra good mood. Was your day that good?"

Neville smiled. "Well, it is funny you should say that Tina. I wanted to run something past you."

Tina looked at Neville as she asked the waitress for the food menus. "OK, you have my attention."

Neville began fidgeting with the knife and fork on his placemat. "OK Tina, I know this may come as a surprise to you, but I was wondering how you'd feel about moving to Ireland?" The words fell out of his mouth so fast he did not notice the waitress handing him the menu. His face blushed as the waitress smiled and looked at Tina as if she was waiting to hear her reply. They both promptly made their food choice and the waitress left.

"Sorry but what did you say Neville?" Tina asked him to repeat himself.

Neville stuttered. "I – I was just wondering how you would feel If we were given the opportunity to move to Ireland. That is all."

"Why are you asking this now Neville? Why Ireland? Is there a problem with your job?" Neville took a deep breath. "OK, sorry I should have explained. There's no problem with my work so you have nothing to worry about there. However, the company has a new office in Ireland and they are looking for staff. It is good money with real opportunity for promotion. I know this is a shock for you but I have always told you I would like one day to return to Ireland. There is no pressure on you at all. If you do not want it then we won't go."

The food soon arrived at the table and they began eating. Tina could not ignore what Neville had said. "Neville are you serious about this? Have you thought what a move like this would mean? We'd have to sell the house here and find a new house in Ireland. Then there are the girls to think of. We would be moving them away from their schools their home and their friends. It's not just about you and me anymore."

Neville wiped his mouth with his napkin. "I know Tina, I know and I've thought about all those things. The girls are young they are the perfect age for this. They will make new friends easily. Like I said if you do not want to go then we won't. All I ask is that you think about it that's all."

"OK Neville, I will think about it, I Promise."

The rest of the night went by without a hitch. Neville was excited and glad he had told Tina what was on his mind. Whilst Tina was not sure what to think she knew she owed it to Neville to consider his feelings after all the support he had given to her over the years.

***

The next day Neville was out in the front garden digging a flowerbed and the girls were all playing in the back garden. Tina had just finished the housework and was going to sit with a nice cup of tea and do some knitting in the sitting room. She pulled her Aunt Daisy's old storage stool over towards her and opened the lid. Sticking out from under the padded cushion was the picture she had drawn her aunt as a child. She took it in her hands and opened it up once more. The crayon was fading but the picture was still there. Tina went to put it back when she also found the letter, she had written to herself in the hospital before having Claire. She had almost forgotten she had that letter and that she had put it in the stool for safety. She opened the envelope and read the words quietly to herself.

As she read the letter she thought of Neville and their conversation last night. She had no family in the UK now so she had nothing to keep her in the UK. Her friend Margaret was still living in Ireland. *Maybe a change is what I need. What am I waiting for?* She took another look at the letter in her hand one line in particular stood out to her.

'You cannot keep looking back because if you do then you will never move forward.'

Tina thought maybe moving to Ireland could help her move forward. Maybe Ireland could be a complete fresh start. It could be the beginning of a brand-new chapter for Neville, the girls and me. Then the last line caught her eye.

Make change happen in your own time.

Tina felt excitement for the first time in a long time. She put the letter back in the stool and watched Neville through the sitting-room window. He was busy digging in the garden. *Look at him, he never complains. He never stops trying his best for us. He has sacrificed so much of his life and now it's my turn to support him for once.* Tina smiled and felt a flurry of nervousness flood through her body.

She went to check on the girls and stood at the back door watching them. They were having a teddy bears picnic in the back garden. Christine had sat Claire in a doll's pram. She and Linda were laughing and giggling whilst busily pushing her around the grass. *Once they have us and each other they will be fine no matter where we live.* That night when the girls were in bed, Tina told Neville that she would agree to the move to Ireland. Neville went to work on the Monday and asked his manager to apply for a transfer for him. The decision was made and all that was left to do now was to sell the house, which took time.

By April 1978, Neville, Tina and their three girls were all packed and heading to the ferry for Ireland

***

Tina and Neville bought a brand-new house in a small sleepy country town called Navan situated just outside Dublin. The girls started school and soon made friends. Tina became involved in animal welfare. She became a member of the I.S.P.C.A and took many unwanted animals into her home until new homes could be found for them.

Money was tight. Neville was working for the same security company that he had worked for in the UK and Tina looked after children in their home. She also taught sign language to earn some extra money. Everyone who met Tina loved her and all the children on the housing estate affectionately called her Aunty Tina. She even offered to hold birthday parties in her house for children whose parents could not have one in their home. Poor Neville always dreaded a birthday party in his house. As soon as he came home from work lots of sugar-filled excited children would tackle him to the ground. Tina loved being around children, singing songs and talking to them. Despite all she had experienced in her own childhood she was the most loving caring and kindhearted woman anyone could have met.

Life had just moved on so much and for the better. However, soon Tina was to discover that some things can never be left behind or forgotten about.

Chapter 24

In May 1986, Tina had been out shopping and when she returned, her daughter Linda, who was fourteen at the time met her at the front door. "Mum, while you were out I took a phone call from a lady claiming to be your sister?"

Tina quickly ushered Linda through the front door. "Well, it must be a hoax call," Tina said, dismissing her.

Linda ran after her mother into the kitchen. "I don't

think so Mum. She knew your name and everything. I took her name and number and told her I would give them to you so you can call her."

Tina could not quite take in what she was hearing. "OK, OK Linda. Put the details on top of the fridge and I'll think about it."

Linda couldn't understand why her mother did not seem excited by all of this. "But why don't you let me unpack the bags and you can ring her now, aren't you excited mum?"

"Oh it's most likely a prank or someone has me mistaken for someone else. How could anyone in Ireland possibly be my sister?" Tina asked.

Linda threw her hands in the air. "OK but what if she's telling the truth? I could have an aunty out there!"

Hearing this upset Tina. *Why does Linda want an aunty? She has me. Surely, I'm enough.* A familiar feeling of rejection washed over her. She tried to put it all to the back of her mind but for some reason she just could not stop thinking about it.

Who was that woman? How did she get my number and what does she know about me that makes her think I could possibly be her sister?

Later that evening the three girls were tucked up in bed and Tina told Neville about the phone call.

Neville turned the television off and gave Tina his full attention. "I will support you whatever you decide but please be careful. I have seen you hurt by all of this before and I can't bear to see you hurt again love."

Tina nodded and smiled. "I know Neville. I honestly thought moving here to Ireland would mean a new start. I thought finally I could leave my past behind. Now, here we are almost seven years have passed and it's found me again. Why can't I just have some peace in my life?" Tina sat back in her chair, closed her eyes and got lost in her thoughts. *I don't know what to do, but what if this is real? What if she is my sister? I can't ignore it, I know I can't.*

She was conflicted. Her mind wandered back to the woman she had met in the church hall as a child. She always regretted not staying to chat with her for longer and now here she was all these years later with another stranger trying to make an appearance in her life. Somehow her secret had quietly crossed the ocean with her lying dormant like a volcano and now it was about to erupt yet again. She knew that not knowing would eat away at her so she decided she would call the woman the next day when the girls were at school and Neville was at work.

***

The next morning after breakfast, Tina picked up the piece of paper with the woman's name written on it. There it was. The name was Orla Evans. She could feel her nerves building inside of her. What would she say to Orla? How would she even know if this woman was telling her the truth? She waited until ten O'clock because that seemed a decent time to call someone. She dialed the number and just as she was about to hang up a woman answered.

Tina felt her heart race and nearly hung up. "Oh

hello can I talk to Orla please?"

"This is Orla speaking."

Tina's hand felt sweaty as she held the phone to her ear. "My name is Tina, Tina McClaughry. I believe you spoke to my daughter, Linda, yesterday. I was out shopping at the time and missed your call. I am sorry about that but how can I help you?" Tina asked.

There was a moment of silence and Tina thought Orla had hung up. "Oh Tina, I am so glad you called. Yes, yes, I spoke to your daughter. I hope I didn't say anything to upset her," Orla said.

"Oh no she was fine a little excited but that's all."

Orla laughed. "OK, well I have a story to tell you. I hope you do not mind me calling you out of the blue like this. I know it must be a shock to you?"

Tina relaxed a little. "Yes, yes, it was. You have to understand that my past is not an easy subject for me. I really didn't know what to think and have thought about nothing else since your call yesterday."

Tina could hear someone in the background with

Orla and asked her if now was a good time to talk.

"Oh Tina, I am sorry. My daughter is here with me. I can understand your worry. I have my own fears but I would love to meet you in person. I hate talking over the phone. So maybe we could arrange a time and date to meet for lunch? You could call to my house if you like. I will make sure we are alone and have privacy to talk properly."

Tina was reluctant. She did not want to get her hopes up. However, she knew she would regret it if she refused. So they set a time and date and said their goodbyes.

Later in the day Linda burst in the door after school."Mum did you ring that lady yet? Did you? What did she say? Is she really your sister?"

Tina did not want to discuss the conversation with Linda. She was not even sure if Orla was genuinely her sister."Linda, calm down. Don't get too excited. Yes, I called her but I don't know anything yet. It will take time. When I have news I will tell you, I promise."

This led to many questions from Linda about Tina's childhood and how she discovered her adoption. Tina was as open and honest as she could be but her past was a subject, she had kept to herself for so long that she didn't know how to explain it to her daughter.

They both sat at the kitchen table. "I was your age when I discovered I was adopted. Imagine if you went to a rehearsal and a stranger walked up to you and blurted out that you were adopted. How do you think you would feel?" Tina asked.

Linda flung herself back in her chair. "Wow Mum that must have been a shock for you. I don't know how I would feel. I just can't imagine that. What did you do?"

Tina took a deep breath. "I confronted my mother who admitted I was adopted but she forbade me from ever discussing it ever again so it became a secret." She leaned forward in her seat moving closer to Linda. "I became a secret. My mother told me it as family business and not to be discussed with outsiders."

Linda was shocked. "So, did you never want to find your real mother – the lady who gave birth to you? What if you have sisters and brothers? I think I would definitely want to know those things."

Tina sighed. "Oh Linda, I have never stopped wondering about those things ever since I found out. However, whenever I tried to search, I was told that nobody could help me. I was told repeatedly to forget about it and move on with my life. If only it were that simple." At that moment the kitchen door opened and Claire walked in full of chat asking for help with her homework.

***

Tina and Orla had arranged to meet the following week. On the morning of their meeting, Tina dropped the girls to school and made her way to Orla's house. She was not far from the house when she felt a wave of nerves rush through her body. Her heart began racing and her hands were sweaty. She pulled in and parked the car along the road.

What am I doing? I must be crazy putting myself through all of this again. This woman could be a liar. She could be wrong.

Tina took a deep breath and looked out the car window. But she could be right. She may be the sister I have always wanted. Why is this so hard? Why after all these years can the world not leave me alone?

Tina sat back in her seat and closed her eyes. She took a few deep breaths and could feel her heart rate returning to normal. She was beginning to calm down.

I can do this. If I go home now, I will never know if she is my sister. Plus, she has my telephone number so she will just keep ringing me. Let's just do it. Let's go.

So, she turned the key in the ignition and continued on her way to Orla's house. When she arrived, she got out of the car and saw a woman standing in the doorway watching her.

The woman reached out her hand to Tina and introduced herself as Orla. She was about the same height as Tina with shoulder length light brown hair and brown eyes. She was wearing a blue apron over a pair of brown trousers and a cream jumper.

"Come in Tina," Orla said beckoning her to come in to her house.

Orla lived in a small but beautiful country cottage not far from where Tina lived. As Tina walked in the front door, she was shown to the kitchen, which was to the right. Tina did not know what to say and felt a little awkward.

"Would you like a cup of tea Tina?" Orla asked.

"Yes please," Tina said.

"I have just made some scones as well. Take a seat and I will put the kettle on."

Tina pulled out a seat and nervously sat down."

Soon, Orla had the tea and scones on a tray and placed them in front of Tina.

"Tina, I know this seems strange to you.I was adopted as a baby and have been searching for what seems my entire life for my family."

"Oh, me too, but what makes you think you are my

sister? I was born in England, not Ireland?"

Orla poured out the tea and passed Tina's mug to her. "It's a long story, but I will try to explain as best as I can. I was born in England and then illegally adopted by an Irish woman and her husband." Orla stopped to see Tina's reaction.

"That is a little confusing. If you were born in England, how did you become adopted in Ireland?" Tina asked.

"No, my mother and her husband were living in England when they adopted me and moved back to Ireland as soon as they had me in their care."

Tina took a sip of tea. "OK, I understand now. But what makes you think you were illegally adopted?" Tina questioned.

"Well, I discovered my birth certificate was actually that of a dead baby. A sum of money was passed and I took the place of that dead baby."

Tina was shocked at what she was hearing. "So you mean no actual adoption took place, no courts or social workers were involved? How was that even possible? In the UK I worked as a social worker and I can assure you in my day that would never have happened," Tina exclaimed.

Orla smiled. "Trust me, the things I could tell you about adoptions back in our day would turn your hair grey."

She must be mistaken, Tina thought. "OK, so, again, can I ask what makes you think I am your sister? I don't understand how you found me," Tina asked.

Orla stood up to take her apron off and sat back down at the table. "I eventually traced my birth back to a baby home in a place called Chatham in Kent the UK. My adoptive mother confirmed that she got me from there. I was a year old and she was told I was 'hard to home' so my parents came to an 'Arrangement' with the orphanage and I went home to Ireland with my new parents." Orla took the last drop of tea from her mug and poured herself another one. "They had sadly lost their baby girl at ten months old, so they used her birth certificate and moved back to Ireland and told everyone here that I was their own baby. Nobody knew any different because their family had only seen their baby girl as a newborn so it was easy to pass me off as their own." Orla went quiet and bowed her head.

"But surely your grandparents knew your parents had lost their baby?"

"Yes, they knew. But they helped my parents keep their 'secret'. There were lots of secrets in our day. I am sure you do not need me to remind you of that," Orla said.

Tina did not know what to say although she knew Orla was right about Secrets, she knew very well how right she was on that score. Of course Tina knew Chatham. She had many childhood memories from there. "OK, so you discovered your own birth story and I will tell you Chatham is very familiar to me. I grew up in Kent. My family lived in Orpington which is just next door to Chatham."

Orla smiled. "I know Tina. I know where you grew

up."

"How? How do you know all that?" Tina asked.

"Because when I traced my birth, I came across a record of a baby who had been taken in to the same orphanage just two years before I was born. That baby had been abandoned in a garden right behind the house where my birth mother lived. In Chatham"

Tina placed her mug on the table and began fidgeting with her scarf which she had sat on the table. Abandoned, she thinks I am an abandoned baby, Tina thought."And how did you see that record? All records are private?"

"Yes, they are private. But for some reason there was a page of information along with mine. Most of the ink on the page had faded or the text was unreadable but I could just make out the words "Found in garden June 1939 Chatham. I was not meant to see it as when I asked one of the secretaries in the records' office about it she grabbed the page from me and told me to forget about it and that it was obviously an admin error"

"Are you OK Tina? I didn't mean to upset you but I do not know how else to tell you."

Tina held her hand in the air and interrupted Orla. "Stop talking, please. I don't know how you connect that baby to me and I don't want to hear it either. That baby was not me. Everything you have discovered is just a coincidence. I don't know how you found me but you are wrong. I was most definitely not abandoned."

Tina felt like the room was spinning around her head and she could not breathe. She wanted to run as far away from Orla as she could. "Now, I wish you all the luck in the world but please do not contact me again." Tina jumped up grabbed her coat and scarf and left Orla's house. She could not get out of there quick enough.

She got home and ran up to her bedroom. There she lay on her bed in the silence of the room. Her head filled with the childhood memories. Suddenly she was fourteen years old again and that woman's words played repeatedly in her head like a song on repeat.

You were abandoned across the road from a hospital and then your parents adopted you. Those words began haunting her every thought. Then she remembered her mother was adamant that was all lies. Why would my mother have lied to me? She had nothing to lose or gain from lying to me. In fact if it were true my mother would have delighted in telling me. No, my birth mother loved me so much she gave me up for adoption. She would never have abandoned me. Orla is wrong, she is wrong and cruel. I never want to see her again.

***

Orla did call her repeatedly until Tina finally asked her to respect her wishes and leave her alone. Tina just could and would not accept that she was abandoned. She had felt abandoned by everyone in her childhood but she always clung to the belief that her birth mother was the one person in the world who truly loved her. To Tina abandonment felt cold and uncaring and that was unbearable for her to think about.

However, her encounter with Orla had stirred up

her curiosity again. She suddenly found herself desperate to find her birth family. If her life had taught her anything it was that secrets and lies haunt you forever and she was not about to allow hers to haunt her any longer. She knew she could not do it alone so she opened up to her friend Breda who became one of her biggest supports. Breda told Tina to take a break. She advised her to step back and promised she would help her when she was ready.

Chapter 25

It was not until 1993 that Tina decided to search again. The girls were older by then and busy with their own lives. Breda kept her promise and agreed to help her in her search. After her encounter with Orla, she had become convinced there was an Iris connection to her birth family. Breda arranged for them to both go to the public records office in Dublin and search through all the birth records. Tina did not really know what she was looking for or where to begin but she knew her date of birth so that was a good start. Breda suggested they look for all birth records for females born on or close to Tina's date of birth. They stumbled across one birth record in particular that caught their eye. This record related to a baby girl born in a mother and baby home in Ireland. The baby's surname was Vousden, which was Tina's maiden name, her adoptive parents' surname. Tina was convinced this record was hers and as far as she was concerned that was the case closed.

She came home so happy with herself that day. First, she talked to Neville privately and then she called the girls into the kitchen and asked them to sit down.

"Well girls. After many years of searching for my birth family I believe I have found them." Tina looked around the table to see her three girls looking at her a little confused. "I found my original birth certificate. Look" Tina said passing the birth certificate to Christine.

Christine studied the certificate. "Mum, your birthday is May 31st1939 but the date of birth on this certificate says the 19th February 1940?"

Tina smiled. "Christine, the 31st of May was obviously a lie to stop me finding my real certificate. They did not want me to know the truth. This means I am really nine months younger than I thought I was." This actually cheered Tina up.

Linda looked at the certificate. "Mum, the surname on this certificate is Vousden. Does that not seem a little odd to you that your real surname is the same as your adoptive parents?"

Tina was upset. She felt like the girls did not believe her. "Look, all this proves is that I was obviously adopted within the family. It means I'm related biologically to the Vousden name. People always said I looked like Uncle Fred." Tina said this as if it should be obvious to everyone. "Now I know why."

Claire looked a little puzzled. "OK, but how come you were adopted in the UK Mum?"

Tina threw her hands in the air in frustration. "Oh for god's sake why do you all have to ruin this for me?

Why is it so hard to believe? It was very common in those days to send unmarried pregnant Irish girls to relatives in the UK and have their babies adopted there." Tina threw her hands in the air in frustration. *Why do they not understand? Why can they not just be happy for me?*

"Or maybe I was born here and my parents travelled to Ireland to adopt me and then brought me back to the UK. There are so many perfectly reasonable reasons and explanations for all of this. Why can't you girls support me? Why can't you be happy for me?"

The girls looked at eachother not knowing what to say or do. Christine broke the silence."Mum, we do believe you. Of course we're happy for you. We just didn't understand a few things that's all. Please don't get upset. This is good news." Christine looked at Linda and Claire for support. All three girls gave their mother a hug and left her and Neville to discuss the matter further.

Neville moved to the seat beside Tina. "Don't upset

yourself Tina. The girls just don't understand that's all. But that doesn't mean they're not happy for you."He rubbed her back and gave her time to gather herself again. "So, what happens now?"

Tina composed herself. "Well, on my birth certificate it lists my mother's address as what looks like a mother and baby's home. I found a phone number and made some enquiries. To cut a long story short, I've managed to get the name and number of her son-in-law who looks after her. She's still alive. Can you believe that? My mother is alive. Plus, if I have the number for her son-in-law that means I must have a sister. She's just a phone call away." Tina felt a sense of excitement at this thought because she had craved a sister her whole life.

"I have to be careful. If I tell her over the phone, it may be a shock for her. I want to look up their surname in the phone directory to see if I can find their address and then who knows maybe we can visit?"

Neville stood and reached into a kitchen cupboard.

He pulled out the Irish telephone directory and placed it on the table in front of Tina. "Here you go love. Let's find your sister, shall we?"

Tina leafed through the directory until she found the surname she was looking for and then narrowed it down to the Christian name, which lead to just six entries. From these listings she identified one in particular that matched the phone number she had been given. The names were James and Katie and they lived in Waterford. It seemed strange to her that she could be looking at the name of her sister. Neville gave her a pen and paper and she wrote down the details. All that was left was to decide when to visit. Neville told Tina he would go with her whenever she was ready. The woman she believed to be her birth mother was called Annie. She knew Annie would be elderly by now so she did not want to wait too long before making contact. However, she didn't want to turn up on her doorstep either in case the shock was too much for her.

Tina and Neville made the journey to Waterford

two weeks later. They had driven past Katie's house three times. Tina's body flooded with nerves as she contemplated knocking on Katie's front door. She had waited so long for this moment and now it was here she was filled with fear. Fear that she would be rejected or that Katie would not want to know her or talk to her.

However, she did knock on the door and was greeted by Katie's husband.

As the door opened a man appeared. Tina and Neville both stood there with smiles on their faces. "Hello, you do not know me and I don't know you but I believe I am Annie's daughter," said Tina.

The man stood in silence. "Annie's Daughter?" He asked.

"Yes. Sorry, I should have said my name is Tina and this is my husband, Neville."

"Hi Tina, my name is James. Please come in. I'll get my wife."

Tina and Neville stepped inside and he showed them into the sitting room. James said he would be back. He was going to get his wife. Minutes later James and his wife returned. "This is Katie. She's also Annie's daughter."

"Hi Katie." Tina thought her heart was going to burst. She was so excited but could see that Katie seemed hesitant.

"James tells me you think you are Annie's daughter, my sister?"

"Yes, Yes, I do. I have done a lot of research and I am sure of it. She has the same surname as my adoptive family so I was adopted by her family in the UK. Annie must have had me and then sent me to the UK or maybe my adoptive father travelled to Ireland to get me. It all makes perfect sense,"

James and Katie looked a little baffled. "I am sorry if we seem a little shocked, but we honestly thought we knew all of Annie's children. She had many in the mother and baby home and they were all given up for adoption. Well, all apart from one who was the child she had to her husband."

"Well, it looks like I am another member of the family. What is Annie like?" Tina asked.

"She's a real character. I am going to see her later. Would you like me to mention you to her and maybe if you are around for the next few days, I can introduce you if you wish?" Asked James.

Tina felt excited at the thoughts of meeting her mother. "Yes, oh yes, that would be lovely. Thank you so much. I know this is a lot to take in, but I am so happy to meet you both. Neville and I will be in Waterford for the next three days, if I give you my mobile number maybe you can call me and let me know when I can meet Annie."

"Of course, that's no problem." James got a pen and paper and wrote Tina's number down. "I'll call you as soon as I get back from Annie's house."

Tina and Neville said their goodbyes and left to go back to their hotel. In the car Neville asked Tina how she was feeling. "So Tina, how are you now? How do you feel after meeting your sister?"

345

Tina had a big smile on her face. "Neville, I'm so happy. I have a sister at last. My whole life I have wanted this. Do you think they were pleased to meet me?"

"That's good love. I'm happy for you. Yes, I think they were pleased to meet you. It will take time to get to know them but you have the rest of your life."

"Yes I do," Tina replied.

Later that evening, Tina and Neville were sitting in the hotel lounge having a drink after their dinner and Tina's phone rang. It was an unrecognisable number. "Hello, Tina speaking."

"Hi Tina, James here. I have spoken to Annie and she would like to meet you tomorrow at twelve if you're available."

Tina looked at Neville with a huge smile on her face barely able to hold in her excitement. "Yes, James, tomorrow is great. Thank you so much for arranging this for me. We will see you at your house at 11:30. Neville can drive us over."

"No problem Tina. However, you need to know she could not remember you. I don't mean to say that to upset you. I am just preparing you."

"That is OK James. She is elderly and if she had a number of children, it may just take her time, that's all."

Tina told Neville and he was happy for her. They had a few more drinks and went to bed. Tina lay in bed thinking about Annie. She had thought about her birth mother since she was fourteen years old. Every birthday, every Mother's Day and when she herself became a mother for the first time. Meeting her birth mother always felt like a fairytale or a story that would only live in her head and yet here she was just hours away from actually meeting her. It was a dream come true.

***

The next morning, Tina awoke to the sound of people in the hallway outside the hotel room. She sat up in the bed and looked around the room for her phone. She was so worried she would have had a message from James telling her that Annie had changed her mind. She looked at her phone sighed a sigh of relief as she had no missed calls or messages. Neville woke, and they both went for breakfast and before they knew it they were on their way to James and Katie's house.

James answered the door when they arrived and soon, they were on their way to Annie's house. Tina sat in silence as James directed Neville.

"OK Tina, we're here. How are you feeling?" James asked.

"I'm fine thank you. Nervous and excited all at once." *What if she doesn't want me? What if she has changed her mind and rejects me?* These thoughts swirled through Tina's head as she knocked on Annie's door. Suddenly, she could hear the shuffling of feet moving closer. Tina did not know what to expect or how to react. When the door opened, Annie was standing there. She was a small woman bent over slightly. She was wearing a knee-length plaid skirt with a long brown cardigan. She had shoulder length grey hair and blue eyes.

"Well, come in, come in." Annie said holding the door open. Tina walked into the sitting room area and Annie followed. Tina could feel Annie's eyes scanning her as she looked straight at her. "My name is Tina. I believe you are my mother." Tina felt emotional as her words came out. But this was not the emotional reunion that she had in her head for all these years. She always imagined her birth mother would open the door and fling her arms around her. There would be tears, lots of warm smiles and hugs. Instead, Annie didn't speak. She looked silently at Tina. "Are you not going to say hello Annie," James said.

Annie looked at James. "She is not my daughter." She turned to look at Tina. "My daughter died. They told me she died."

Tina smiled. "Well, they were wrong. I'm very much alive."Tina's stomach churned. This cannot be right. How can she say this? I know I'm right. I have to be. I

349

just have to be.

Annie said nothing and sat down in silence still staring at Tina. Tina could feel tears welling inside of her but fought not to let them show.

I am her daughter. She's old maybe her memory isn't good. Or maybe they told her I had died. That must be it. Oh, the poor woman this must be a shock to her as well.

There were many uncomfortable silences. Annie made a cup of tea for everyone. Once Tina had finished her tea they all said their goodbyes to Annie and they left. Tina sat in the car in silence as Neville dropped James back to his house and then he and Tina drove back to the hotel.

Tina convinced herself that Annie was going senile and having forgetful moments. After another visit Tina told everyone that Annie had finally admitted to being her mother in an attempt to convince everyone she was right. She knew people didn't believe her and deep down she knew she could be wrong but she was not emotionally strong enough to admit this to herself or anyone else.

Tina's children never fully believed she was Annie's daughter. They always had their doubts but for the first time in their lives, they were seeing their mother happier than they had ever seen her before. They could not break her heart so they left her alone to believe what she wanted to believe.

***

In 2003, Annie died still denying that she was Tina's mother. Shortly after Annie's death, Katie and James had invited Tina and Neville to their home as they said they had something they needed to discuss with them both.

James asked them in and put the kettle on to make them all some tea. They made their way to the kitchen, and Tina asked how they all were.

"We're fine Tina. However, there's been a bit of a development."

"A development?" Tina asked.

James looked at Katie. "Yes we have just discovered some news of our own regarding Katie and her birth."

"But I don't understand. What do you need to know about your birth?" Tina asked Katie.

"Well, we've received definite proof that Annie was not Katie's birth mother."

Tina looked at Neville and laughed. "But that cannot be true. How do you know this James? Why would you say this?"

"I assure you it's true. We've had it all verified with DNA so there is no mistake. But just because you are not a biological sister to Katie does not mean you are not the best of friends. Nothing has to change."

Tina did not know what to say. She went quiet and sat back in her chair trying to comprehend what this meant. So now I've lost my mother and my sister, I'm back to square one. How can this be happening? Why am I always the one that gets dirt thrown in my face every time I find a little bit of happiness. "Neville, I need to go, I need to get some air."

Neville was obviously feeling awkward. "OK love, just try to calm down and don't get soup set."

"I am not upset. I just need to go. Please Neville."

James and Katie both sat looking at Tina not knowing what to say. "Tina, I'm so sorry if I've said anything to upset you. Why don't you sit and we can talk about it? Please stay," James said.

"No, sorry, I will be in touch. Right now, I just need to go."

Tina sat in the car in silence for most of the drive home. She felt like her world was falling apart. Like a loose piece of wool hanging from a scarf that was slowly being pulled and her life was unraveling before her.

Neville allowed her to calm down before asking if she was OK. "Tina, are you alright love?

"I'll be OK Neville. I always am. You would think I should be used to all this by now. Life just seems to love giving me a good kicking. Like someone 'Up there' is reminding me of my place in life. I was never good enough for anyone. Not good enough for my birth mother, my adoptive mother, nursing and now I have lost Katie and all her family." Tina went silent again.

"Love, I don't know what to say. Just tell me how I can help," Neville said.

"There is nothing you can do Neville. But what if I was wrong also? What if Annie was not my mother either? I know nobody believed me. I am not stupid. Who was I trying to fool? Well, that's it, I'm done. I can't handle any more crap from this world."

She stared out the car window as Neville drove in silence. What have I ever done that was so bad? I can't do this anymore.

***

That weekend, Christine, Linda and Claire were calling to Tina and Neville for a family meal. Tina decided she would tell them about Katie not being her sister. She had prepared a lovely meal and when the girls arrived, they all sat to eat.

"Girls, I have something I need to tell you. It's not

easy for me, so please bear with me," Tina said.

Christine looked at Tina. "Are you OK Mum?"

"I will be, thank you," Tina said. Your father and I were with Katie and James a few days ago. They had something they needed to discuss with me."

"Are they OK, Mum?" Claire asked.

"They're fine but they made a bit of a shock discovery. Katie has discovered she is actually not Annie's daughter. Which means she is not my sister." Tina bowed her head.

"I knew it," Linda said not meaning to speak so loud.

Tina looked at Linda with a scornful expression on her face. "What do you mean? How did you know it?"

"I am sorry, Mum. I just mean I always thought something wasn't right. I know it is a sore subject for you but at least now you know. The truth is always better than a lie. Isn't it?"

Tina thought about that. "Not always Linda." Tina bowed her head again. "For me the truth has always been more painful than the lie."

"I am sorry you're not Katie's sister mum. I know how much it all meant to you." Christine said.

"So what happens now?" asked Claire.

"What do you mean?" Tina asked

"Well, do you think you could have been wrong about Annie as well?"

There was a silence around the table and Tina could sense the girls were all wondering the same thing.

"I don't know the answer to that Claire but I guess I could be wrong. I'm too old to go searching again. I just don't have the strength or energy to put myself through all of that. My secret will be with me when I go to the grave. All the questions I have asked throughout my life have been met with lies and caused me nothing but hurt." Tina bowed her head and sat silently for a few moments.

She raised her head and looked at her three girls. "Luckily, you girls will never know what it feels like to always wonder who you are. You have always known a mother's love. I can't say the same for me. I've had to live my life feeling like someone's dirty little secret and for me that's been the loneliest feeling in the world."

"Ah Mum I hate seeing you like this. You still have us and your grandchildren. To us you are everything. You have to know that," Claire said as she took hold of Tina's hand.

"Thank you love. I know you are right and I will be fine. It is just a bit of a shock, that's all."

***

Tina refused to search anymore. However, she fought her emotions every day. She developed arthritis in her joints and it was believed the stress she was under was the main cause. Soon, every joint in her body was affected and she was in constant pain but this was not the only health problem she would encounter.

She had a cruel and merciless ailment lurking in the shadows that nobody could possibly have seen coming.

Chapter 26

It was the 31stof May 2009, Tina's 70th birthday. She woke that morning after having a restless night. Her arthritis had kept her awake for the most part. She tried to turn in the bed and realised Neville had already got up. He soon arrived in the bedroom with her breakfast. They had been married forty-two years and Neville had made her breakfast in bed every morning. "Happy birthday, love," Neville said, handing her a card.

"Is it my birthday, Neville? Are you sure?"

Neville laughed. "Yes, Tina it's your birthday."

Hmm, that's odd. I was sure that was months away. "What month is it Neville?" she asked.

Neville looked at her a little surprised. "It is the 31st of May love. Your birthday."

"Hmm, so they say," replied Tina.

She ate her breakfast and made her way to the kitchen where Neville had a nice cup of tea ready for her. "You sit in your armchair and I will bring your tea in to you. Remember you have a doctor appointment at ten O'clock."

Tina had forgotten about this. "I don't need the doctor, Neville. What's wrong with me?" she asked.

"You're having a checkup love."

"OK, if you say so," she said as she made her way in to the sitting room to sit in her armchair.

***

They arrived at the doctor's surgery and were soon called in to the doctor's office. The doctor was talking to Tina about treatment for her arthritis. She had been in a lot of pain and her mobility was severely affected. Tina agreed the treatment and then she and Neville left. When they got home Tina went into the sitting room and sat on her armchair whilst Neville went out to the kitchen.

Tina was sitting back in her chair staring at the window. Suddenly, she felt like the room was closing in around her. She sat forward and looked around the room. She could not make sense of her surroundings. As her eyes glanced at the window she saw her doctor looking in at her. *What is my doctor doing here?* Something felt wrong but she did not know what exactly. She could hear her name being called. As the room appeared to return to normal, Neville was standing beside her calling her.

"Penny for your thoughts Tina. You looked like you were a million miles away." He placed a cup of tea and a saucer with some biscuits on it on her chair side table. "Right Love I am off out to the garden."

Tina was still staring at the window. "Neville, before

you go can you see if anyone is at the front door, please? I'm sure I saw the doctor at the window."

Neville looked a little baffled. "OK love, I'll take a look." He walked over to the window and looked out into the front garden. "No, nobody's there. You must be imagining things."

"Yes, I must be. You go out and do what you are going to do."

Neville left the room and Tina sat back in her chair. She was convinced her doctor had been looking at her through the window.

This was not the first time she had experienced this kind of thing. In fact, it seemed to be happening more and more often. I will ring Linda. She'll help me. She picked up her phone and called Linda's mobile.

"Hi Linda, it's Mum. How are you love? Are you alright?"

"Hi Mum, I'm fine. Happy birthday by the way. Are you enjoying your day?"

"Yes, I am, although I am having a bit of a

problem."

"What's wrong Mum?" Linda asked.

"It's my doctor. I think she's following me. I don't know why but she was looking at me through the window just now." As Tina spoke, she knew it all sounded wrong but she was convinced her doctor was watching her.

"Mum, I'm sure she is not. You must have been dreaming or imagining things."

"Yes, I suppose you could be right. Your dad said the same."

The call ended but Tina called Linda another three times that day with the same concerns. She even called Claire and Christine to tell them she was being watched.

There were many instances like this and each time seemed scarier to Tina than the last. It took the girls three years to get Tina to agree to see a doctor as they were concerned about her deteriorating memory.

***

On the 22nd of November 2014, Tina rang her daughter Linda and told her she was tired and in pain but insisted it was her arthritis.

"Mum, if you have pain, you should see a doctor."

"Oh it's most likely my arthritis. There's nothing my doctor can do about it. I'm just feeling so tired, Linda."

"Well, if you are tired then go for a sleep Mum. You must need rest but please promise me you will see a doctor if the pain gets worse."

"I will Linda but what if the doctor sends me to hospital? I don't want to go to the hospital it scares me. If I go to the hospital I may never come home again," Tina could not let go of this fear.

"Mum, you're over thinking things. Please try not to worry so much. You will be fine, I promise."

Linda's daughter, Katlyn, could be heard crying in the background. "Do you have a child with you, Linda?" Tina asked.

"Yes, Mum it's Katlyn. She's hungry again!"

Tina was confused. "Katlyn?"

"Yes   Mum.   Katlyn,   my   daughter.   Your grandaughter?"

"Oh yes, yes of course." Tina tried to sound like she knew who Katlyn was although it took her a while to remember that Linda had a daughter at all.

***

The next morning, Tina woke up with severe pain in her hips and lower back. Neville came in to the bedroom with her breakfast. Tina could barely raise her head. "I'm not hungry Neville."

Neville placed the food on her bedside locker. "Please try to eat love. I'm worried about you." He helped Tina to sit up in her bed and opened the curtains to let some daylight in the room.

"You don't have to worry about me Neville. I'll be OK."

"OK, but if you don't feel any better soon I'm calling the doctor. You need to let me do that at least." Neville left Tina to rest and went back to the kitchen.

Tina looked around her room. On her bedside

locker she saw an old wedding photo in a frame. Memories came flooding back of her magic day. *That was one of the best days of my life.* She reached over and picked up the frame. As she gently wiped the glass with her hand she smiled. Then she saw her mother in the background of the picture and her smile disappeared. She placed the picture back on her locker and lay back on her pillows. The faces of her old friends flashed across her mind.

Her old childhood friend Alice Brown suddenly came into her head. *I wonder how Alice is today. I hope she found her baby boy. I hope her baby boy got his answers and had the support I never had.* Then she thought about Jenny the girl she had met in the hospital when she had Christine. Her baby boy would be the same age as Christine. *I wonder did she have any more children. She could be a grandmother now. I hope life was kind to her.* Tina could feel herself drifting off to sleep and was too weak to fight it, so she allowed herself to rest.

***

When she opened her eyes, Neville was sitting on a chair beside her. Hello love would you like a cup of tea?" Neville asked. Tina looked at the clock and realised she had been asleep for four hours. "Yes, please, and then stay with me for a while."

When Neville returned he placed her cup on the locker beside her. "Love, I wish you would let me call the doctor for you. You're not getting better and I don't know how to help you."

"No Neville. There's nothing the doctor can do for me." She pulled herself up in the bed. "I'm scared. If you call the doctor, she'll send me to the hospital. I just know in my heart that if I go to hospital I won't be coming home."

Neville leaned in close and held his wife's hand. "Tina, I won't let anything happen to you. If you are not any better soon I will call the doctor. OK?"

"OK Neville if you insist."

Neville took her empty cup and told her he would leave her to sleep. That night she woke up to find

Neville standing over her.

"Tina, you're calling out in your sleep. Are you OK?"

She tried to answer Neville but she struggled to get the words out.

"You're not making any sense. I'm calling an ambulance love." He reached out his hand to pick up Tina's phone from the bedside locker. As he spoke to the ambulance control, Tina was crying and insisting she did not want a doctor.

***

The next morning, Tina opened her eyes and looked around the room. She did not know where she was but felt comforted when she saw Neville sitting on a chair beside her bed. He was asleep and Tina was too weak to call his name so she just lay there looking at him. She saw a drip attached to her arm and could hear the gentle beeping of machines around her head.

Neville woke and as he rubbed his eyes, he seemed pleased to see that Tina was awake. "Good morning love." He sat upright in his chair. "I'm afraid I can't make you breakfast in bed today but I'll make it up to you when you get home."

Tina smiled and reached out her hand for Neville to hold. "Neville, I need to talk to you. This is bad. I'm not well at all."

Neville moved his chair closer to Tina. "You'll be fine love. You just need rest that's all. I've called the girls and they're on their way. That will cheer you up."

Tina squeezed his hand to get his attention. "No Neville, I'm not going to be OK. I want you to know I love you. I know I have not made life easy sometimes." She stopped talking as she saw tears in Neville's eyes. She had never seen him cry before. "Neville, nobody ever loved me or supported me like you have. It was always you and me against the world. With you by my side I have been able to get through anything. But I'm tired now. I'm in so much pain and I can't fight it anymore. Please let me go."

Neville rubbed his eyes. "Oh, my love, I know, I

know. I don't want to see you in pain any more. I understand but it is just so hard."

Tina smiled and could feel herself becoming weaker and weaker. "Neville, this is one fight I can't win. Tell the girls I love them. I never did find my birth family. I was fooling myself over Annie." Tina paused as she tried to catch her breath. "You and the girls were all the family I needed. We did a good job with our girls Neville didn't we?"

Tina could feel her thoughts becoming cloudy. She knew Neville was talking but she felt like he was drifting further and further away from her. Then she could feel Neville pulling her arm and just before everything went quiet, she heard the words "I love you, Tina." She opened her eyes one last time and smiled at Neville as her eyes slowly closed for the last time.

***

Tina had drifted into unconsciousness and was placed on life support. The girls reached the hospital and one by one they said their own personal goodbyes to her in their own ways. The life support was turned off and Tina slipped away with the only family she ever really knew by her side.

Chapter 27

That night the girls stayed with Neville. They were reminiscing about their fond memories of Tina.

Claire giggled.

"What are you laughing at?" Christine asked.

Claire sat up in her chair. "Well, in mums last moments you asked if we should say a prayer. I said no because Mum was not religious. But she died at six O'clock when the Angelus was ringing out across Ireland. As if to prove me wrong." Claire wiped a tear from her eye.

"She always did like the last laugh. Didn't she," Claire remarked and they all had a good giggle at this

***

The following few days after Tina's Death Neville was lost. He had never spent a night away from Tina and now he faced the rest of his life without her. He was heartbroken. Neville was not a man who ever complained about his health. However, in the days following Tina's death he had been experiencing minor chest pains. He didn't say anything to the girls. They were dealing with enough after losing their mother and Linda was heavily pregnant with her second child so he didn't want to worry them.

Three days before Tina's funeral Christine brought Neville shopping to buy a new suit for Tina's service. As Neville walked around the shopping centre, he felt a familiar tightening in his chest but tried to ignore it. Eventually he could not hide it any more as he became distressed and unable to breathe.

"Dad, are you OK?" Christine asked as she placed her hand on his shoulder. "Please help me. Help my dad," Neville could hear her calling out for help. A security guard quickly came to their aid and an ambulance was called.

Neville was seen by doctors and admitted to the hospital. Christine, Linda, and Claire arrived and Neville told them not to worry. He told them he was fine. However, the doctors soon gathered around his bed and asked to speak to him. "Neville, we are concerned that you may have a heart condition. Your blood results are a little unclear and we need to carry out further tests. I am afraid you will be in the hospital for at least a week, maybe longer," the doctor said.

Neville shook his head. "No, I have my wife's funeral. I won't miss that. You can't force me to stay here."

The doctor tried to offer reassurance. "We'll see how you are and may agree that you can leave for the funeral but it's important you return that afternoon. We don't want to take any risks."Neville relaxed a little once he knew he could attend the funeral.

Neville was diagnosed with end stage heart failure, which devastated the girls. It was decided that Neville would stay with Claire until he was strong enough to move home again.

During his time with Claire he regularly took bad turns where he couldn't breathe and sadly hospital visits became a common occurrence.

In March 2015, just 13 weeks after Tina died Linda gave birth to her second child. A beautiful baby boy, Jake. Jake breathed new life into their family and gave Neville a reason to be happy. When he called to visit Linda and see his new grandson, he took hold of Jake's little hand and smiled. "Your mother would be so happy for you Linda. She was so happy when you had Katlyn and although she wasn't well when you became pregnant with this little man, I know she was happy for you."

Linda smiled at Neville. "Thank you Dad. I know

she would love Jake every bit as much as she loved all her grandchildren. I am sad she never got to meet him but I will always keep her alive in every story I tell my children."

***

On Sunday the 21st June 2015, Linda and her husband held Jakes christening. It was a special day as it was Father's Day and Neville was looking forward to spending time with the family. After the church there was food laid on in the local pub. Linda wanted a picture of Neville with all his grandchildren around him as it was rare that they were all together in one room. Neville sat in a chair and held Jake in his arms as the remaining twelve grandchildren gathered around him.

"Right, smile everyone," Linda said as she took the picture with her phone.

Neville went back to his seat and Linda showed him the picture. He sat holding the phone and a smile stretched across his face. *Oh, Tina, look at this. Our family doesn't look the same without you here by my side.* Neville often had little chats like this with Tina in his head.

"Are you OK Dad?" Linda asked.

"I'm fine love. I just wish your mother was here to see this. She was so hung up on never having found her birth family. But look at this. For a woman who never knew her parents, who never had siblings of her own, she did well," Neville said handing the phone back to Linda. "Despite all of that, she ended up with three beautiful daughters and thirteen grandchildren. So she didn't do so bad did she?"

***

By April 2016, Neville's health had deteriorated greatly. He had insisted on moving home to his own house but the girls called every day to make sure he was alright. Because of his heart condition he had also developed vascular dementia. He struggled but he never complained.

On the 24th of April, he had arranged to bring the

girls out for a meal to celebrate Linda's birthday. They arrived at the restaurant and the girls and Neville ordered their food from the menu. Neville bought a round of drinks. "Well, happy birthday Linda," he said whilst raising his glass to toast the birthday girl. He had suffered from a heart attack a number of years ago and ever since then Tina had not allowed him to eat Chinese food as she was told that some ingredients may have been the culprit. However, that night he had ordered a chicken curry.

Linda laughed as the waitress placed the meal in front of Neville. "Oh Dad, what would Mum say if she knew you were eating curry!"

Neville placed his finger to his lips. "Well, if you don't tell her she'll never know." Neville smiled and devoured the entire dish. He then followed that with a generous helping of Bailey's cheesecake which he loved.

"OK girls how do you all feel about going on a trip with me this summer? I was hoping we could all go to Blackpool. I've never been, and it was the one place your mother always wanted to go to aswell. So, what do you think?" Neville said before asking the waitress for a round of drinks to be brought to the table.

The girls looked at each other and agreed that they would love to go. It was a lovely evening, full of plan making and laughter. When it was time to go, Claire linked arms with Neville as they all made their way out to the car. Christine and Linda both sat in the back and Claire helped Neville to sit in the front passenger seat. No sooner had Claire sat in the driver's seat when Neville began coughing and struggling to catch his breath.

"Are you OK Dad?" Claire asked.

Neville's could feel his face straining as he struggled to answer but he raised his hand as if to acknowledge that he had heard her. "I am OK," he managed to say but he was really struggling.

"HOSPITAL," he heard Christine and Linda shouting from the back of the car.

"I'm going to bring you to the hospital Dad," Claire

said as she pulled out of the parking space and drove towards the exit of the car park.

"Are you OK Dad?" Linda asked. Neville nodded his head but his surroundings blurred. The car had stopped at this point and he could hear the girls' voices calling him but he could not answer them. He felt like his world was moving in slow motion.

Then, suddenly, a strange calmness filled his body. As the voices of his daughters faded and silence ensued a familiar voice could be heard loud and clear.

"I got you Neville. Time to go now my love." It was Tina and in his mind's eye he could see her with the biggest smile on her face. He knew it was his time and as his eyes closed, he bowed his head and silently slipped away.

***

The girls were devastated. They had now lost both parents and for Linda her birthdays would never be the same again.

Chapter 28

The morning after her dad had died Linda woke up early Jake was fast asleep in his cot. She crept out of the bedroom trying not to wake him or her husband. As she walked onto the landing, she noticed her daughter's bedroom door was open. Katlyn was fast asleep. She loved her Grandpa Neville but at three years of age how would she understand what had happened? Linda closed over Katlyn's bedroom door and crept downstairs to the kitchen.

She made herself a cup of tea and sat herself on the sofa in her sitting room. As she looked directly in front of her on the fireplace mantle stood all her birthday cards in a row. Right in the middle was a card with the words *'To a special daughter on her birthday'* printed across the front. She stood up took the card in her hands and as she read its words. Her eyes filled with tears as the reality set in that she would never see her dad again. It seemed so wrong that less than twenty-four hours ago she and her sisters had been sitting enjoying a meal with their dad who was full of chat and laughter. In a blink of an eye, he was gone and there was nothing she or her sisters could've done to save him.

The sound of her husband Danny coming down the stairs soon interrupted her thoughts. He opened his arms and gave her a warm hug. He knew what she was going through because he had also lost both of his parents. Soon, both children were awake and had come downstairs. Jake was still a baby, he was just thirteen months old, so he would not understand or comprehend what was happening but Katlyn was three years old and she loved going to see her Grandpa Neville.

After Katlyn had her breakfast, Linda sat her on her knee. She told Katlyn that Grandpa Neville got sick and the doctors could not make him better so the angels had to come and bring him to heaven. Katlyn looked puzzled. "But Mammy I need to see my grandpa. Will he be long?"

Linda smiled and gave her a great big cuddle. "No baby, Grandpa can't come home. He has to stay there. But the angels will give him magic glasses so he can watch over us all."

With that, Katlyn jumped off Linda's knee and ran to her toy box. She grabbed her pink sunglasses and put them on her face. "Are these magic, Mammy?" she asked before running off to play with her toys.

Linda sat on the sofa watching as her children happily played with their toys. It was in that moment that she realised her children would now grow up never knowing their grandparents.

How do I navigate the world without Mum and Dad to guide me? she thought whilst wiping a tear from her eye.

***

Christine, Linda and Claire had arranged to meet at their parent's house to discuss what was going to happen next. Linda arrived first. The house was eerily silent. Usually, she would walk in and hear the radio on and the sound of her dad pottering around the kitchen but this day there was only silence. After a short wait, Christine and Claire arrived still reeling from the night before. They all gave each other a comforting hug and sat in the kitchen at the table.

They soon spun into action calling family and friends telling them the devastating news. It was their parents' wishes to be cremated and then, when they had both died, they wanted their ashes to be buried in a grave together so that is what the girls planned.

They gave Neville a lovely sendoff there was a church service and then they went to the crematorium. The church was full of friends and family and the girls were overwhelmed with the support they received. Claire read a reading and Linda read a poem she had written.

As Christine, Linda and Claire walked out of the church behind their dad's coffin they spotted two small snow-white feathers floating in the air – both gently landed on the coffin. A tingle ran down Linda's spine. She believed the feathers were sent from her parents. It was their way of letting their girls know they were together and at peace. It was a beautiful sight and one that they would never forget.

With the funeral over the girls needed to plan the next stage of their parent's wishes. Tina and Neville wanted their ashes to be buried together in a grave so the plot was bought and a date was set for the burial. However, Claire had been in contact with Neville's cousins from the Curragh in County Kildare. These were the cousins who were responsible for Tina and Neville getting together all those years ago so it felt perfect when they suggested the girls took a trip to the Curragh with their parent's ashes. They decided they would scatter some of the ashes in places Neville and Tina frequented all those years ago. The Curragh was such a beautiful place and held so many happy memories. The girls loved when Tina would tell them about how she met Neville and all the happy times they spent together on the Curragh. It was a romantic story the start of a wonderful romance between their parents and they could not think of a perfect place to remember their parents.

The three girls had booked into a hotel and make a night of it. They checked into their rooms and then headed to the bar where they were meeting their dad's cousins. When they met, they instantly connected with each other and it was not long before they were all deep in conversation. The girls sat listening to their father's cousins as they retold stories about their parents and all the mischief they got up to together. It was a lovely afternoon and for the first time in a long time the girls were able to talk about their parents with only tears of laughter in their eyes. The girls were then brought to the old church on the Curragh.

Whenever Tina was visiting her friend Margaret, she always loved to sing in the church choir. Philip, their cousin, showed the girls the exact pew that Tina sat in whenever she visited.

"Your mother loved to sing. She had a beautiful voice. We could often hear her singing above everyone else," Phillip said.

The girls sat in the same spot their mother had sat all those years ago.

"I can hear her now." Linda whispered as she leaned in close to Christine and Claire

Linda closed her eyes and remembered her mother singing Christmas carols to her as a child. She smiled as the memories flooded her mind. They were happy times.

Their parents had a favourite tree that they used to sit under in a wooded area on the Curragh, so the girls scatted some of their ashes around that tree before they went back to the hotel.

Claire laughed. "Imagine Mum and Dad sitting here all those years ago hand in hand, laughing and giggling."

Linda blushed. "I bet they never thought back then that their three children would one day be standing in their courting spot!"

***

The next day, the girls went home and prepared for the final burial of their parents' ashes. The burial took place, and the headstone was erected as planned. At last, the girls now had somewhere they could sit and talk to their parents. This was their final resting place.

Chapter 29

Linda bought a lovely angel figurine and potted flowers for her parents' grave. As she stood at the graveyard gate she could clearly see her parent's headstone, which seemed to stand out amongst all the rest. It was black marble with beautiful gold lettering. There was a black marble curbing enclosing the grave and the inner space was filled with silver/grey and white granite gravel. Linda made her way to the grave and her thoughts strayed back to her mother's cremation. She remembered thinking that her memories were all she needed. However, whilst standing at the graveside she was grateful to have this little space to come and sit with her parents. The headstone was brand new and shiny but her mother's name did not look right, something seemed out of place.

***

Memories of a conversation she once had with her mother came to her mind. She had asked her mother why she was so bothered by not knowing her birth name or where she came from. Her mother sat silently and listened to Linda's questions.

"OK Linda, so if someone asked you who you inherited your lovely brown eyes from what would you tell them?"

Linda had thought that was easy. "I'd tell them I take after you, Mum."

"OK so if you were asked where you were born what would you say?"

"I'd tell them I was born in England Mum, on a

Monday at half-past twelve," Linda had replied looking a little baffled by her mother's questions.

Nodding her head her mother continued. "Ok and what if you were asked why you were called Linda. What would you tell them?"

Linda struggled to understand why she was being asked such things but answered anyway."I'd say I was named after your good friend who was killed in a motorbike accident. But what has any of this got to do with your name or identity?"

Her mother smiled. "Well Linda, imagine not knowing the answers to any of those questions. Imagine not knowing the very basics of your life. Who you look like, where you were born. Not even knowing where your name came from. How do you think you'd feel?"

Linda had thought for a few minutes."OK, I get it. That would be so strange Mum. I don't remember a time when I didn't know any of that stuff. I suppose some people just take those things for granted."

Tina nodded in agreement with Linda. "Exactly. I couldn't answer any of those questions. My curiosity is not just curiosity. It's always been a deep need to know. It never leaves me. The not knowing who I am is the most difficult feeling in the world."

***

The memory of that conversation reminded Linda of just how important her mother's name was to her. She felt so guilty because when her mother thought she had found her birth family, she and her sisters had their doubts but did nothing about it. They saw their mother happy for the first time in their lives and not one of them could bring themselves to shatter her world so they left it alone.

Soon that day whilst standing at her parent's graveside, Linda made a promise to her mother. She promised she would continue her search for her. She was determined to find the truth for her mother. She left the graveyard and on the drive home, she wondered how she would start her search.

Linda arrived home, she immediately picked up her phone to call her sisters and tell them what she was going to do. Christine and Claire were fully supportive and behind her every step of the way, but reminded her it may not be so easy. They told her to be prepared for a difficult search because their mother had been adopted such a long time ago that she may never find what she was looking for. She knew they were looking out for her but she also knew she had to try. They shared their memories of their mother and the various conversations they had with Tina and Linda made notes. The call ended and now Linda needed a plan. She needed to work out her next move.

Linda was living in Ireland. There had been a lot of controversy and scandal surrounding the Irish mother and baby homes. The stories were heartbreaking to read. She wondered if life was any different in England where her mother was born and adopted. Survivors of the mother and baby homes from as far back as the mid-1900sin Ireland were still fighting to gain access to their records. So she knew it would not be easy but she had her mother's determination and was not going to give up no matter what obstacles she came across.

Before she was to begin any kind of search, Linda had to confirm if she and her sisters were correct in their doubts about Annie being their mother's birth mother. She called the adoption authorities in Ireland and spoke to a lovely lady who took all of her mother's details. She also made note of the details from the birth certificate that had led Linda's mother to believe Annie was her biological mother. Within a week, Linda received the confirmation that she and her sisters were correct. The letter clearly stated:

'I am sorry to have to confirm that based on the details you gave this office, there is no possible way your mother could have been the child mentioned on the birth certificate'.

Although Linda had verified her doubts, she did not take any pleasure in being right. All this verification actually achieved was to prove her mother died at the age of seventy-five still a secret, still an unknown and that was so wrong. This discovery made Linda more determined than ever to keep her promise to her mother.

***

After lunch, she opened a box of personal documents that had belonged to her mother and emptied them onto the kitchen table. As she looked through all the papers, she found what she believed was her mother's birth certificate. She sat down to read the certificate and could clearly see where her mother had tried to change her name from Christine to Christina. She smiled to herself as she imagined her mother at fourteen years old making the bold decision to change her name. Seeing this reminded her of when she got married and needed her mother's birth certificate. Her mother told her she was too embarrassed to show it to anyone. She told Linda she felt like a fraud every time she had to use the certificate as a means of identification because nothing on it felt real. Of course, Linda told her mother that to her it made no difference because she was always Mum to her and she always would be.

It quickly became clear to Linda that the birth certificate her mother had used throughout her life was not actually a birth certificate, because her mother's adoptive parent's names were recorded on it as being her parents. She leafed through the remaining documents on the table but could not find anything resembling an adoption certificate. *Surely my mother's birth was recorded somewhere?*

So, with all this in mind Linda made a phone call to the General Registrars' office in the UK because that was where her mother was adopted. She wanted to enquire about locating an adoption certificate and a birth certificate for her mother. The person she spoke to told her they could order the adoption certificate for her. However, she could not order her mother's original birth certificate because she did not know her mother's birth name.

Instead, to gain access to her mother's birth certificate Linda would have to call Kent social services for advice on this matter. So she ordered the adoption certificate and once she had that she would look into acquiring the original birth certificate.

***

Ten days after that phone call her mother's adoption certificate arrived in the post. Linda opened the envelope and her eyes eagerly scanned the contents. A few things did not make sense to Linda. For instance, her mother was born in 1939 but was not legally adopted until 1942. Linda wondered where her mother would have been cared for before her adoption. She also noticed her mother's date of birth was recorded as a given date of birth. This felt like a small thing but surely this information should've been known not given?

She rang the Kent social services to enquire about getting her mother's original birth certificate. They told her she would need to request the help of the Adoption Authority of Ireland and request for them to liaise with the UK authorities on her behalf. She did as advised and the Adoption Authority of Ireland agreed to assign a social worker to her case. The irony of this was not lost on Linda. Her mother used to work as a social worker in the UK and had tried so hard to get help from social workers at that time but none of them could or would help her. They even told her she could face prison or lose her job if she did not stop with her persistent questioning. Yet, it was a social worker that was going to help Linda in her search.

***

Two weeks later Linda received an email from a social worker who introduced herself as Mandy. They both agreed on a date and time to meet up for a further chat. The morning of the meeting came around quickly. She was meeting Mandy in a hotel so she sat in the foyer nervously waiting for her to arrive. It was not long before she saw a tall woman walk through the hotel entrance holding an official-looking folder. The woman walked closer to Linda. She held out her hand.

"Hi, I'm Mandy. You must be Linda." they shook hands and sat down. They both ordered some tea and biscuits from the reception staff. Mandy placed her bag on the floor beside her chair. "Lovely to meet you," she said as she relaxed in her chair. "I was hoping you could tell me about your mother and her story."

Linda told Mandy all about her mother's life. It was a story she had told many times before so she began from the beginning and before she knew it, an hour had passed by.

Mandy sat listening intently to every word. "Wow, what an amazing woman your mother was. It must have been so difficult for her. But can I ask what do you expect to get from this for yourself?"

This question took Linda by surprise. "You know, I've never thought about that before. I've always said I was doing this for my mother. To find out her truth, her identity, which was something she believed had been stolen from her." Linda thought for a moment, trying to find the words to answer Mandy's question. "I suppose I want to discover my mother's story. She was forced to keep everything a secret. It was a secret that almost destroyed her and I want to put that right." Linda took a sip of tea from her cup. "Plus, now I think about it, it would be nice to find living family members. It would be like having a piece of my mother still here still in my life. I miss her so much."

Mandy placed her cup on the table in front of her. "Well, I can certainly understand that." Taking a folder out of her bag, Mandy explained what would happen next.

"I have talked to my counterparts in the UK and they have advised me how we need to proceed. So first, I need your identification papers. Then I need to make a formal request for any files relating to your mother's birth and adoption." She took all the relevant documents from Linda and placed them in the folder which she tucked back into her bag. "Please remember I cannot guarantee anything. Your mother was born such a long time ago and we need to be mindful of the fact that in those days there were no electronic records. Everything was hand written which means handwriting needs to be interpreted. Ink can fade and poor spelling along with human error makes this so much harder. There was also a war going on that saw many records offices bombed and records were destroyed"

Linda Nodded. "I understand that and I also understand I may not find out much but I really appreciate your help. For so long I have felt like I was getting nowhere, but now with your help I really feel like have a real chance of finding some answers."

With that, they said their goodbyes and Mandy promised to call Linda as soon as she had news for her.

Chapter 30

Eventually, after a long six weeks the phone rang. It was Mandy.

"Hi Linda, I have news for you. Kent social services have carried out extensive searches of all available records. They have found very limited information regarding your mother. However, I have your mother's birth name and date of birth. Are you ready to hear it Linda?"

Linda was nervous. She sat down. "Yes, I'm ready

Mandy."

Mandy cleared her throat. "Your mother's birth name was Christine E Barnes and her date of birth was the 31st of May, 1939."

Linda's heart beat faster and faster with every word she heard Mandy speak. It was hard to take it all in. Barnes was a new name, and she was surprised to know her mother's name was actually Christine, after all. She also felt a sense of sadness because her mother was not around to experience this. Her thoughts then turned to her mother's birth parents. "What were my mother's birth parents' names?" she asked.

Mandy hesitated. "Oh I don't have that information. The email I received from Kent lists them as unknown."

This felt wrong to Linda. "But how can my mother's parents be listed as unknown?" she asked. "Surely, they would at least have her mother's surname? After all she was present at the time of the birth and should be recorded somewhere." None of this made any sense to her. "If my mother's parents are unknown then where did the surname of Barnes come from?"

Linda could hear Mandy shuffling papers as if she was looking through documents.

"The information I have given you is all I seem to have been sent. I understand your confusion and you're right, it doesn't make sense. I'll ask my contact in the UK about all of your concerns and see what she says. It could take a week or two but I'll call you as soon as I have an update."

Linda thanked Mandy and the call ended.

***

Linda hated loose ends and although she was glad to have some information, she seemed to be left with more questions than answers. She was an impatient person and two weeks felt like a long time to have to wait for answers so she went online and carry out some research of her own. She found an adoption page on social media and asked if people could help her understand why her mother's birth parents would've been listed as unknown on her mother's birth certificate. Her questions returned many replies and suggestions. One stood out in particular. Someone asked if her mother could have been a foundling baby. She had never heard of this before, so she asked what the term meant. It was explained to her the term foundling baby was used to describe a baby that had been abandoned leaving no trace of who their parents were. Apparently, abandonment was common especially in war times. It was so common that hospitals and special orphanages were set up to care specifically for foundling babies. Linda thought this could be a possibility. It certainly would explain why her mother's parents were listed as unknown.

There were a number of interesting websites dedicated to foundling hospitals. During the 1800s and early 1900's poverty was rampant in the UK. Times were different and life was hard. The lack of contraception and sex education meant that once married, a woman could find herself in a constant state of pregnancy throughout her entire childbearing years. During the period, leading up to war times and times of food rationing, couples would receive more food and dairy rations if they had children or if the wife was pregnant. It is thought many women became pregnant deliberately in a ploy to get more food but because of poverty these women could not keep their babies. Many were married and married couples could not face being shamed for bringing their baby to an orphanage so they would simply abandon them on church steps or in hospitals and tell family their baby had died.

***

Linda logged onto the online birth death and marriage database for the UK and searched using the name and date of birth that Mandy had given her for her mother. There was one birth entry listed in Medway (Kent) under the name of Christine. E. Barnes and the mother was listed as unknown. She believed this had to be her mother's record. It would have been one massive coincidence if it were not.

She called the general registrar's office and spoke to a man in the adoption records section. She explained her mother's story and asked why any parent would be listed as unknown on their database. She also asked if her theory of her mother being a foundling baby would explain this. The man she spoke to was helpful. He searched for records relating to the listing Linda had found. He then placed the call on hold as he said he needed to check something out.

Minutes later the man took the call off hold."Linda, unfortunately I can't discuss individual birth records over the phone. However, I can confirm that your foundling theory is highly possible. If you wish you can order the birth certificate from me today over the phone. You never know you may even discover more information on that certificate." He said this as if he was prompting her to order the certificate. Of course, Linda did exactly that – she ordered the certificate. The man also advised her to contact a foundling foundation in London. The foundation used to run the largest foundling hospitals in the UK at the time of her mother's birth. He advised that the hospitals were now closed but all records were still available and any baby cared for in one of their hospitals would have been recorded in the foundation database.

***

After speaking to the man from the records office, Linda immediately sent an email to the foundling foundation explaining her mother's story. She asked if they could search their records and advise her if any child of her mother's name and date of birth had been cared for in any of their hospitals. Four days after sending the email, she had a reply from a woman who worked for the foundling foundation. She told Linda she had read her mother's story and conducted a thorough search of their entire record database. Strangely, she requested Linda's contact number and asked if she could call her.

Within half an hour of giving her number Linda's

phone rang.

"Hello Linda, my name is Grace and I work for the foundling foundation. Are you available for a chat?"

Linda felt strangely positive about this call. "Yes Grace, I am, and thank you for calling me."

Grace's voice was calm and soothing. "I have read your mother's story and I am so sorry I couldn't find anything helpful for you in our records. If your mother was indeed a foundling baby then I am all too familiar with the emotional rollercoaster that can bring into a person's life."

There was a pause and Linda thought that was it. Grace had simply called to tell her in person that she could not help her. Then, Grace spoke again. "I wanted to help in any way I could so I looked on a few other databases for you. As part of my work I have access to newspaper archives and I know abandoned babies were written about in the local and national newspapers."Linda's excitement grew again."Newspapers were the only way that the police could make appeals to the public in those days. There was no social media back then so I knew there would have to have been a news article relating to your mother," Grace said. "I searched using the name you gave to me and have found two articles that may be of interest to you. The location and name of the baby mentioned in them match the details you have been given. Would you like me to send them both to you?"

Linda felt something she had not felt since she had begun her search – a sense of hope. She was so grateful."Oh Grace, thank you so much. Yes, please, I would love you to send them to me."

"It's my pleasure I'm glad I could help and best of luck with your search."

The call ended, and Linda waited patiently for the email from Grace. As soon as she heard the email notification, she checked her inbox. There was one new email from Grace with two attachments. She read and reread both articles two or three times and felt a wave of emotion rush through her as she read about a blue-eyed, blonde-haired baby girl that had been abandoned at a few days old on the 2nd June 1939. This was the breakthrough she had been praying for but it was also much more than that. Linda knew these articles may be the only remaining evidence of her mothers abandonment, so she felt blessed to have them.

BABY GIRL ABANDONED IN A GARDEN

3rd June 1939

An abandoned baby girl was found late last night wrapped in a blanket in a garden in Gillingahm, Kent. The baby girl was fully clothed, with blonde hair and blue eyes. She was found to be well nourished and wrapped in a blanket. The discovery of the child followed a telephone call to the R.N Maternity hospital, where a man spoke in a 'gruff' voice advising a baby had been abandoned and asked if they could possibly help the infant. The man gave the address of where the baby was left, but before the nurse could take the man's name, he had hung up and police have been unable to trace the whereabouts of this man. The baby was cared for at a nursing home Saturday night but transferred to the county hospital the next day where she is being cared for and progressing well, weighing approx. 6 and half lbs.

Could this really be Mum? Linda asked herself. Gillingham is a town in Kent so it was possible. The baby was said to be just days old when found on the 2nd of June 1939and her mother's given date of birth was the 31st of May 1939 so it all seemed to point to her mother. Linda read the second article.

UNKNOWN CHILD NAMED

3RD November 1939

Several months ago, we reported that an unknown baby girl had been found abandoned in a garden in Gillingham. The infant was admitted and cared for in the county hospital. The Medway guardian committee recommended to the county public assistance committee that the county council adopt the child. The committee also recommended that the baby be given the name of 'CHRISTINE E BARNES' and the date of birth was given as the 31st May 1939. All presented agreed that these recommendations be enacted and the baby should be adopted in pursuant to the poor law act 1930.

Linda could not believe what she was reading. She felt like she was somehow intruding on a part of her mother's life that even she knew nothing about.

A week later, she received her mother's original birth certificate in the post. With all the excitement of the last few weeks, Linda had almost forgotten that she had ordered it. She thought nothing could top the latest revelation.

However, she was about to discover more than she ever thought possible.

Chapter 31

When Linda opened her mother's original birth certificate, she was pleasantly surprised to discover more unexpected details. Her mother's name and date of birth were no surprise. However, there was a little note scribbled in the margin saying 'foundling baby... SENT FOR ADOPTION'. Also, whilst looking at the section that should state a person's place of birth, someone had written an address and noted it as being the 'Address where baby was found'. This address matched the one mentioned in the newspaper articles that Grace had sent to her. Beside the address under 'Name of the father' was a man's name noted as the 'man who found baby.' Shivers ran through Linda's body as she read this new information, and she could not help but wonder if this man could have been involved in her mother's abandonment.

Whilst looking at the birth certificate her phone rang snapping her out of her thoughts. It was Mandy, the Irish social worker.

"Hi Linda, I have heard from the social services in the UK. Unfortunately, they could not shed any light on why your mother's birth parents were recorded as unknown. All they said was that it could have been an administrative error. However, the passage of time has been so great it would be impossible to know for sure." Mandy hesitated as if expecting Linda to be upset by her news. "It's hard to know when to stop searching but it has to happen sometime."

Linda was unsure how she could explain everything

she had discovered since they last spoke.

"Thank you for calling me back Mandy. I have a bit of news for you. This may take a while, but I am sure you will want to know what I have."

Mandy was shocked by the amount of new information Linda had discovered. "Wow, Linda, that is amazing. You didn't need me at all. So you know the truth now. How do you feel and what's next?"

Linda felt a little emotional as she contemplated the answer to this question. "I feel like I've unearthed a dark secret. Like I have somehow intruded into a deeply personal part of my mother's life. It's hard to find the words to describe just how hard it is for me to think of my mother as an abandoned baby. It's just so very sad." Linda stopped talking to take in a breath. "However, I have no regrets at all. The next thing I need to do is find relatives. I need to find a bit of her still alive and well. I want any of her living biological family to know she existed. She was kept a secret for far too long."

Mandy took a deep breath. "Well, I wish you all the very best of luck Linda. However, please tread carefully. I have worked on cases where birth families have not taken kindly to such news. If you find family, they may be shocked to discover that someone in their family who they loved could have abandoned a baby. If you need any further support or advice, please don't hesitate to contact me."

***

Linda knew she should be proud of everything she had done already, but she also believed there had to be more to this story. The only name she had for her mother was her 'given name'. This was no use to her because her mother's given name was not a blood link to anyone. She wondered if there were any living relatives of the man who had found her mother. She thought this must have been big news in his family at the time and maybe it was a story that had been handed down through the generations.

She opened the online census records for the UK and typed in the name and address of the man who found her mother and found one matching record. This record was linked to someone's family tree. When Linda clicked into the tree details she discovered an email address for Sarah the owner of the family tree. She emailed asking if Sarah could help her locate the family of the man in question. Sarah replied a few days later saying she was the man's grandaughter. Linda replied explaining that the man noted on her mother's birth certificate was the man who had found her mother as a newborn. She asked if Sarah was aware of any stories she may have told family about finding a baby all those years ago. She attached some photographs of her mother to her reply because she knew her mother grew up in the same area as Sarah and thought they may jog her memory. The next day she received a reply from Sarah who was intrigued by the story. She said she was very young when her grandfather died so she could not be much help.

However, she recognised Linda's mother from her pictures as being one of her old school classmates. Linda was amazed. All those years ago, her mother sat in the same classroom as the granddaughter of the man who found her and neither of them were aware of their connection.

She was so close to giving up and admitting defeat and wondered if she would ever find her mother's family. She was tired of the constant searching and had become obsessed with her quest to finish what her mother had tried so hard to achieve.

***

Struggling to work out her next move Linda went to visit her parent's grave. The graveyard was a peaceful place where she could just sit and think things through.

Her parents were big tea drinkers. Many world problems were put right over a cup of tea in their house so she would always have a take away cup of tea with her when visiting the grave. She sat on the side of the grave thinking about how hard she had tried to keep her promise to her mother. She leaned her head back, closed her eyes and breathed in the stillness of the air that surrounded her. In her head, she asked her mother to guide her on her search.

As she opened her eyes and straightened herself, she caught sight of a beautiful white feather on her parent's headstone. Her mother loved white feathers and always believed they were signs from deceased loved ones watching over them. Linda felt comforted by this white feather and saw it as a sign from her mother to keep going. She could even hear her mothers' voice in her head. Keep going baby, it is just around the corner. She left the graveyard with renewed energy and gave her search one last push. She had no idea what her plan was but giving up would mean her work so far would have been for nothing so that was not an option.

Later that evening, Linda met her sisters for a meal and a catch up. She wanted to update them both on everything she had discovered so far. She was also interested to hear if they could help her work out what to do next. The table was booked for 8 p.m.

They arrived at the restaurant and took their seat at the table. The waitress brought their menus over to them and they ordered their food. Linda updated Christine and Claire about everything she had discovered so far. Claire and Christine were amazed and told her she had done far better than they could have ever thought possible. Once their food arrived, they began eating and Claire said she had been doing some research and discovered an online DNA testing company. She told Christine and Linda that she was thinking of taking a test in the hopes that she may find a match from their mothers' side of the family.

This sparked Linda's interest. "How does it all work?"

Claire wiped her mouth with a napkin. "It's simple. I just order a test kit, take the test, and post it back to the laboratory." Christine and Linda both listened intently. "When my results are processed, they notify me by email. I'll then be able to view my DNA test results on my private online page. If anyone else on the database matches my DNA then that means we're related in some way. Of course, I would have to work out if they are on Mum or Dad's side of the family which might be tricky but it is worth a try."Claire looked at Linda and Christine to take in their reactions.

Christine placed her knife and fork on her plate. "Why don't we all do a test? Surely that will give us more results?"

Claire nodded in agreement. "There are actually three major companies that are very popular. We could choose a company each|?"

Linda smiled. "That sounds like a plan. Let's do it."

So, all three girls decided who would test with which company and got on with enjoying their evening.

***

Just one week later, all three girls had ordered their tests kits. The results could take up to eight weeks. Linda used the time to learn as much as she could about DNA testing and how to decipher the results.

They decided Linda would have access to all three girls' results when they came through as she was the one conducting the search.

Claire's results came through first. Linda excitedly logged in and looked through Claire's DNA results. It soon became clear that this was not going to be as easy as she first thought. Claire had thousands of DNA matches from all over the world. All matches had been categorised into predicted relationships to Claire. So, based on the DNA, Claire had thousands of predicted third and fourth cousins. In order to work out which side of the family they belonged to; Linda needed to know family names from both sides of her family. This was difficult because she did not know any of her mother's birth family names.

Next, Christine's result came through and they were much the same as Claire's results, with nothing new to report. Linda was disappointed.

About a week after Christine's results came through Linda received an email notification from the DNA company, she had tested with but for once, she could not get excited. She did not expect to find anything new so she closed the notification.

Later that night when her children were in bed, she opened her DNA test results to see what they could tell her. As soon as she opened the page, she noticed she had a top match with a surname she did not recognise. This caught her attention because the match was listed as a predicted first cousin.If this was correct and if this person were connected on her father's side of the family, then surely a first cousin was close enough to recognise the surname.

A familiar wave of excitement washed over her and she ran out to the kitchen to tell her husband about her new find. He told her to try to calm down and look into it a bit more before she made contact with anyone. Of course, Linda messaged her sisters and told them the news. They were both very excited by this latest discovery.

Chapter 32

Linda spent a few days looking at her DNA results specifically her top match, a man called Mark. He had linked a family tree to his account, which meant she could view it and clearly see both sets of his grandparents as well as basic information about them such as their date and place of birth etc. She made a note of his paternal grandparent's details and searched the 1939 UK census records only to discover that when her mother was found they had been living on the road behind the garden where her mother had been abandoned. This felt like more than a coincidence. Finally, all of her frustrations and fears disappeared because she knew her efforts had not been for nothing. She procrastinated for some time with the decision to contact Mark. She had read so many stories where birth/biological families had rejected the people who reached out to them. Linda was worried that this would be the case for her and she was not sure how she would cope with that. She wondered if

Mark had also seen her match and if he was in any way curious about her. Eventually she decided she had to make contact. She knew she had to do it some time. So she typed out her first message to him via the DNA website.

Hi Mark,

I have received my DNA results and notice you are my top match. I'm fascinated by all this and would love to work out how we may be connected? I would love to chat some more

if you are interested. - Linda

Linda also gave Mark her personal email address as an alternative method of communicating. She did not want to jump straight in and tell him she thought his grandparents were the ones who abandoned her mother as a baby. Her mother's story might cause discomfort to any close biological family. She also did not want to come across as someone who was laying blame or judgement at anyone's door.

A few days went by and Linda had no reply from Mark. This was making her very nervous. She wondered if he was simply not interested. However, she also thought maybe he had not seen her message yet. She had a think and decided to look for him on social media. She knew Mark's surname – which was not a common name – and location so she thought it shouldn't be too hard to find him. There seemed to be just one active profile listed under his name and location so she sent a message through that page.

Hello, this is going to sound strange but are you the same person who did a DNA test on the same site as me? If so, then I see we are a DNA match and in some way related! I have sent you a message via the DNA site. If you are not the same person then I apologise for this message.

The next day, Linda received a reply from Mark. He told her he was happy to work out their connection to each other. She was so relieved and was glad he had acknowledged her even if he was not aware at that stage of her mother's story. She knew she would have to be honest with him soon and if her mother's story had taught her anything, it was that secrets and lies caused nothing but harm. She sent Mark another email. In this email, she told him her mother was adopted and had sadly passed away but maybe their DNA connection was from her mother's side. She suggested a phone call and sent Mark her phone number. Luckily, he agreed and they both arranged a time to talk properly.

When the time came, Linda picked up her phone and called Mark.

"Hi Mark, Linda here. How are you?"

"Hi Linda I'm good thanks. So, we may share grandparents. What are your thoughts?"

"Well, yes, I think there is a strong possibility that we do," Linda said.

She told him all about her mother's abandonment and left nothing out. When she was finished there was silence and then Mark spoke. "It is a shock to hear all of this, but honestly, I am not totally surprised either. There were many things about my grandparents that made little sense. But actually, after hearing about your mother's story I think I can understand them a little more."

"Like what?" Linda asked.

"Well, they split up in the 1950s. Their marriage was rocky. Also, now that I think about it my dad had mentioned there were two babies that were stillborn between the years 1936 and 1944."

Linda thought whatever split them up must have been bad, because generally, the 1950s housewife did not leave her husband.

"Well, my mother's year of birth was 1939so it fits into that timeline. Plus, I looked at the 1939 census register for your grandparents and they lived on the road that backed on to the one where my mother was found. That alone would be a huge coincidence, don't you think?"

"Yes, yes, I suppose it would be," Mark said.

"Mark, I want you to know that my sisters and I hold no judgement or animosity towards your grandparents. They had their reasons for what they did and we respect that. I am just so glad to finally have found you. My mother had spent her entire life searching. She died still not knowing who she was." It was important to Linda that she said this as she knew from all her research that people in those days made heart breaking decisions against the backdrop of a world that was merciless and cruel. She was sure that her mother's birth parents only had her best interests at heart.

***

Over the course of the next few weeks, Linda and Mark kept in touch. They exchanged pictures of family members and stories about their parents. Mark also shared information about his grandparents that he felt would be relevant to her search and answer any questions she had. Linda could not ignore the obvious similarities between her mother and Mark's grandparents in the photos they had exchanged with each other. Linda had written tonnes of notes over the course of her search. She even made notes of everything Mark had told her. On one afternoon, it was raining outside and her children were playing in their bedrooms. Her husband was watching football on the television. Linda sat in the kitchen with a mug of tea and took out all her notes. She leafed through the pages and came across the notes relating to her phone call with Mark. At the top of one page in particular were the words:

'Grandparents split up in the early 50's'

Linda thought back to her mother as a fourteen-year-old child and the unknown woman she had met in the church hall. It was that woman who had told her mother she was adopted. *I wonder if that woman could have been her birth mother. That would have been the early 50s. Maybe she had been following Mum. I cannot imagine how heart breaking that must have been for her birth mother. Having to watch her daughter from afar, knowing that she could never hold her or tell her who she was. Maybe her husband discovered she was watching Mum. Maybe that's what caused their marriage to break down. Maybe her mother wanted to get Mum back. Oh, it is just so sad.*

Linda continued to read the words on the next page.

Mark's grandparents had TWO stillborn babies between 1936 and 1944.

I wonder if Mum was one of those babies. It makes sense if her mother was pregnant, she would have had to say something to people to explain why she didn't have the baby she had been pregnant with. However, if this is true then that must mean they were going to keep Mum or they would have hidden the pregnancy altogether. But what about the second baby?

Linda suddenly remembered the mysterious phone call she had received as a young girl from a lady claiming to be her mother's sister. The woman's name was Orla as far as she could remember. *Maybe Orla was the other baby. I wish I had asked Mum more about her. I wish I had helped Mum more when she was alive to find her answers. How could I possibly find Orla now after all these years? Would she even be alive today? I have no idea where she is now. I left it too long.*

***

Even though Linda had discovered so much from Mark, she still needed to look at the DNA and try to see if she could link any more DNA matches to her mother. So she started her family tree and placed Mark's grandparents as her mother's parents. She had to build her mother's family tree back six generations because she knew this would give her the best chance of identifying shared DNA matches by comparing family trees and trying to identify common ancestors between her and Mark. This meant tracing records back to the 1700s, and at times, she felt like she was intruding into people's private lives. When looking at the 1800s, she found records of a man imprisoned for stealing broccoli. He was most likely just trying to feed himself and his family. She came across slave papers where those with money had to register themselves as owners of slaves. It was heart breaking to see people described like the property of the wealthiest in society.

One particular record really stuck out to Linda. A young woman living in the UK had sent a letter to her brother-in-law who lived in America. In this letter, she practically begged him to pay for her, her husband and her children to immigrate to America where he was living. The lady described the country she lived in as slave driven and a poverty hell. In her letter, she said her husband was in poor health and worked night and day for just five shillings, which had to support them and their five children. The woman's pleas were obviously made in vain. Linda found a death record for the lady's husband who had died two years after her letter was sent.

He died in England with his cause of death noted as exhaustion. They obviously never got their chance of a 'better life' in America.

Once Linda had verified every person on her newly built family tree, she was excited to discover that she could identify DNA connections from her DNA results and her sister's DNA results to both of Mark's paternal grandparents and their ancestors. This meant it was highly likely she had found both of her mother's birth parents. She could not explain why, but she always thought she would only find her mother's birth mother. She never dreamt that she would find both.

Mark informed Linda that she had three more cousins. He said he had told them all about her and her mother's story so she decided to contact them and introduce herself. They were all so welcoming. In fact, another of her new cousins decided to do a DNA test. This would simply add more confirmation of their connection with each other.

When her results came in she notified Linda via email. Linda was on a walk when she received the email and could not get home quick enough to take a look. When she arrived home, she immediately logged on to the DNA website and there it was, her other new suspected first cousin was now confirmed. Linda flopped onto the sofa and closed her eyes. She could feel a wave of emotion flood through her body. As she sat forward and opened her eyes a picture of her mother caught her attention. It showed her mother holding an eagle on her outstretched arm. She had a huge smile on her face. At that moment Linda felt a tear falling from her eye.

I did it Mum, I found them for you.

Chapter 33

Linda's search was finally over. It felt only right to visit her parent's grave to tell them her discoveries as that was where she made her initial promise to begin her search. She stood by the headstone feeing proud of everything she had done for her mother. She had set out to find the truth, and the hard truth was her mother was an abandoned baby. She was a foundling. A blue-eyed, blonde-haired baby girl that was found wrapped in a blanket in a garden on a summer's evening in 1939. Linda knew from conversations with Mark that her mother's birth parents had little money. She could only assume they made the impossible decision to give her mother away in the desperate hopes that someone would take care of her and give her the life that they could not. She was not going to judge them because she did not live in those times so she had to respect their decision.

During her search, people had told Linda that Mother Thames took many a baby to their watery graves in times of war. If she could have met her grandparents in her lifetime, she would have hugged them tight and thanked them both for bringing her beautiful mother into the world. For that alone she would be eternally grateful. She stood at the graveside thinking about her mother and the circumstances of her birth. One thing was obvious – there were no winners in her mothers' story. Now her search was complete she felt like she had come full circle.

Whilst looking at the name on her parents'

headstone she realised her mother's birth mother never named her before the courts took her into care. Therefore, it seemed only right to leave the name on her mother's headstone as it was. She was always known and loved as Tina and that name seemed more appropriate than ever.

Linda wondered what she would do with her time now that her search was over. She had accomplished so much yet she still felt like there was more to do. She wanted to highlight the plight of the foundling children. She wanted to use her mother's story to give hope to other people in their own search for truth and answers. She wanted people to know that nothing was impossible. So many times she had nearly given up and walked away. Her mother had walked through her life looking for answers but the truth was she had the key to finding her family inside of her all along. Her birth parents gave her a special gift. It was a gift that nobody could ever take from her— their DNA. Tina had unknowingly passed the same gift to her three daughters.

So in the end all Linda and her sisters had to do was arm themselves with nothing more than a bit of spit in a tube and in a world of billions they found them. They found her mother's family. Linda's only regret was not realising all of this sooner. If she had known about the DNA sites when her mother was alive then maybe her mother could have met her family.

Linda pondered her next steps. She had another plan and left the graveyard feeling ready for her next challenge. When she got home she made herself a big pot of tea and powered up her laptop. She decided the best way to tell her mother's story was to write a book. Being mildly dyslexic had always made writing a challenge for Linda. She had never done anything like this before but she was determined to get her mother's story out there. She opened a blank documentation her laptop firmly believing there was no time like the present.

She wanted it to be a book about her mother and

her quest for answers. Writing her mother's story was easy. It had been there all of her life and she was ready to tell the world. She pondered over the name for the book and nothing seemed appropriate. As a child, Linda's mother had been forced to keep her adoption a secret. She remembered her mother telling her that for her the loneliest feeling in the world was being forced to live her life like someone's little secret. It was that memory which prompted Linda to think of the perfect name for her book.

The words just flowed from her as if her mother were sitting beside her telling her what to write and before she knew it the story was written for all to see. With this book Linda knew her mothers' story would be *A Secret No More*.

Note from the Author

Tina was my mother and this book was inspired by the true-life events that took place in her life. When I began my search to discover her birth story, I had no idea of the journey I would be undertaking. Because of everything I have learned along my way about my mother and her life I have become so very grateful to my parents. They gave me life they gave me their love and they kept me safe in this world. My mother, despite never having any real maternal role model in her life was the most loving woman I have ever known and I am so proud to have had her as my mother.

Thankfully, adoptions today are handled with far more sensitivity than in my mothers' day and not every adoption is a sad one. However, the one thing that does not seem to have changed across the years is an adoptee's need to know who they are and where they came from. Deep down my mother grieved after the loss of her identity that she believed had been cruelly stolen from her. This was the foundation of so much pain in her life. I never understood it but now I do.

I nearly gave up on my search many times but I kept asking myself, *how could anyone be born into this world without a trace. The answer is they cannot.* As long as you carry DNA in your body then the answers are inside you. It is not always easy but they are there waiting to be uncovered.

I hope you feel like you have got to know my mother a little and to those on their own search I wish you the very best of luck. Please do not give up.

As my mother always used to say, "It is just around the corner, so keep going"

Acknowledgements

In Loving Memory of my beautiful mother and father.

Tina Vousden-McClaughry- 31/05/1939 26/11/2014

Neville McClaughry 20/08/1939 – 24/04/2016

Also, thank you to my husband Danny for his unwavering support and understanding during my search. To my children for being the point of everything in my life. I love you all beyond words.

Also, a thank you to my sisters, Claire and Christine, thank you for helping me gather all our memories that contributed to this book. I would be lost without you both and love you lots!

To William, Lora, Lisa and Mike, Thank you with all my heart.

Printed in Great Britain
by Amazon

12095072R00254